# AN
# HONORABLE
# ASSASSIN

# BOOKS BY STEVE HAMILTON

# AN HONORABLE ASSASSIN

A NICK MASON NOVEL

## STEVE HAMILTON

NEW YORK TIMES BESTSELLING AUTHOR

BLACK
STONE
PUBLISHING

Printed in the United States of America

First edition: 2024
ISBN 978-1-9826-2749-2
Fiction / Thrillers / Crime

Version 1

Blackstone Publishing
31 Mistletoe Rd.
Ashland, OR 97520

www.BlackstonePublishing.com

*To anyone brave enough to tell the truth*

# 1

Nick Mason stepped off the airplane in Jakarta and into his third life.

Soekarno-Hatta International was one of the busiest airports in Asia, in the second-biggest city in the world. Mason walked down the long hallway, unfamiliar faces all around him, hearing conversations in a language he'd never heard spoken before. Left behind him was a first life that ended in federal prison, then a second life that ended when he killed the man who had freed him.

Left behind was the city of Chicago, the only home he'd ever known. Everything he had, everything in his life, was gone now except for the contents of the leather bag slung across his shoulder.

Mason flashed back to a day when he woke up in an eight-by-ten cell in USP Terre Haute, the same day he ended up standing in a luxury townhouse looking out at Lake Michigan. He compared that day of sudden transition to today, once again leaving one world and entering another. Impossible to say which was the biggest change, not that it mattered one goddamned bit. He was on the other side of the world now. Different language. Different time zone. Hell, it was Tuesday here, and back in Chicago it was still Monday.

When Mason reached customs, he pulled his new passport from his jacket pocket. It carried a strange name and an address in a city in California he wouldn't be able to locate on a map if you put a gun barrel against his temple. At the window, a man wearing a short-sleeved blue shirt with epaulets on the shoulders asked for Mason's documents. Mason took out the battered picture of his wife and daughter before handing them over. An army soldier stood a few feet away in high paratrooper's boots, a gray uniform, and a dark-green beret. He watched Mason impassively, holding his Indonesian-made Pindad assault rifle at port arms.

As Mason pushed aside the jet lag and focused, he felt something familiar: a moment of pure anticipation, the automatic reaction as all of his instincts came alive and a working plan quickly assembled itself in his mind. *If things go sideways, disable the soldier first. Take his weapon. There's another soldier thirty feet away. How quickly will he react?*

Within two seconds, Mason had picked out his escape route, past the baggage claim area, using the sudden panic that would spread through the crowd as a tactical advantage. *Shoot out the window instead of trying to go out the doorway.*

"English?" the man said.

Mason nodded.

"Reason for your visit."

Mason hesitated for a beat, remembering the laminated ID card that had come in the same envelope as his passport. *Pacific Logistics International.* Whatever the hell that even meant.

"Consultant," Mason said. "Attending meetings."

The man paged through a stack of papers on his stand. Mason worked through the answers to whatever this man was about to ask him next. What he'd be doing for this company, what subject he'd be consulting on, how long he'd be staying in the country.

*They should have given me a full backstory. I'm about to be fucked before I even get out of the airport.*

But the man simply looked at the passport one more time and then stamped it with a visa mark and handed it back to Mason. "Enjoy your visit," he said, and Mason was free to go.

When he reached the end of the secure area, Mason could sense he was passing from the sterile environment of the airport into the true heart of the city. *Jakarta. Indonesia.* More words just as strange as the

name on his passport. Hundreds of people were milling in the baggage
claim area, walking back and forth through the open doors to the heat
and light of the outdoor world. Family members were waiting at the last
checkpoint as two more soldiers stood by with their berets and Pindad
rifles. Mason scanned the faces. He was about to walk past all of them
when he saw a man holding a sign with the name from his passport.

This man was white but built short and thin like many of the native
Jakartans who surrounded him. As if he were scaled intentionally to
blend in. A few years older than Mason, dressed in a dark suit with a
Euro cut. Dark sunglasses. A tight-set mouth. Wavy hair and sideburns
that belonged in another era.

He had already clocked Mason and gave him a nod toward the
doors, and Mason met him there.

"I am Torino," the man said. He didn't extend his hand for Mason
to shake. He didn't take off his sunglasses. Mason studied him, trying
to place the accent. Probably Italian, but not quite like any of the families who owned the restaurants in Canaryville.

"The car is waiting."

Aside from the accent, there was something else about the man's
voice. Something clear and unmistakable: He spoke like a man who
believed he was smarter and more refined than you. And everyone else
in the room.

Mason stored that away, already building a file on this man as he
adjusted the bag's strap on his shoulder and followed him outside. The
tropical air wrapped itself around him like a hot bath towel. A thousand
more locals were waiting for taxis or buses or other vehicles on the curb.
A riot of heat and noise until a black Mercedes G-Class SUV pulled up
to the curb, standing out from the boxy little Toyotas and Mitsubishis
that were lined up and down the loading lane.

Torino held the back door open until Mason climbed inside. Then
he got in next to him. In the front seat sat the driver, a young Indonesian
man with jet-black hair. It was disorienting to Mason, seeing the steering
wheel on the right side and the Mercedes pulling out into the left lane.

Torino took a cigarette from a blue pack marked *Gitanes* and held it between his lips as he lit it with a silver lighter. He snapped the lighter shut, took in a long drag of smoke, and blew it out. "That photograph you had in your passport," he said. "Five minutes in the country and you almost fucked yourself."

Mason let that sink in for a few seconds before he responded. "You own the agent. That's why I didn't need a backstory."

"You could get away with a mistake like that in Chicago," Torino said. "It won't play here in Jakarta."

Mason studied the man's face as he blew out another stream of smoke. It stung Mason's eyes, but he didn't look away.

"You're a private security consultant from Los Angeles," Torino said. "Never married, no children."

Mason kept his eyes on him and didn't say a word.

"You understand," Torino said, "that you don't work for Darius Cole anymore. You work for us now."

"Who's *us*?"

Torino shook his head slowly. "One thing is the same," he said. "I'll say it now, and then I trust I won't have to repeat it. If you fail us, your family will pay for it first."

Mason felt his body tensing up, his hands clenching into fists. Even ten thousand miles away, he could still see the image of Gina and Adriana on that screen in Cole's office, the man's voice describing how they would be taken away and blindfolded, each left alone on a concrete floor for hours. And how that would be only the first step.

Mason forced the memory out of his mind, unclenched his hands, and made himself take a breath.

"I don't *have* a family," Mason said, nodding to his passport. "Remember?"

As they approached the center of the city, he saw vendors waiting patiently on the side of the street, selling fruit, vegetables, grilled meats, cold drinks. The street was filled with bicycles, small cars, small trucks, and a million motorcycles, most looking worn out and underpowered. On the sidewalks, men and women walked quickly in every direction, or they just sat motionless on the steps of every building.

The advertisements were written mostly in Indonesian, with occasional flashes of English. Coke. Nike. Marlboro.

"We're going to the Sultan Hotel," Torino said. "The target is on his way."

*From the airport right to the first job.*

"We just received this information," Torino said as if reading his mind. "It's not optimal, but we need to take this window. We don't know when we'll get another."

Torino opened a folder and took out a five-by-seven photograph.

"His name is Hashim Baya."

Mason took the photograph. A dignified, humorless man with a thin, neatly trimmed beard, dressed in a black suit, at some sort of social function, other well-dressed attendees behind him. He glared back at the camera as if irritated by the intrusion.

Mason studied the man's face, then noticed the symbol on the bottom edge of the photograph's white border. A map of the world with a sword and the scales of justice behind it. He peered closer to read the lettering.

*Interpol.*

"How did you get this?" Mason asked.

"Did you ask your last employer so many questions?"

Mason gave him back the photograph.

"He'll be arriving on a helicopter," Torino said. "He won't stay more than one hour."

"I need to know who'll be with him in the helicopter," Mason said. "And if they'll be armed."

"Your support is already on-site. You'll get the information you need."

"Who's my *support*?"

"You'll be wearing an earpiece," Torino said. "If there are any problems, it's your job to deal with them."

"You think it's that simple?"

"You did it in Chicago, Mr. Mason. Now you do it in Jakarta. The only difference is the time zone."

The vehicle slowed down as it hit the even heavier traffic of down-town. Torino filled the air with his smoke, and the driver stayed silent. Finally, Torino took out another folder and handed it to Mason.

"Baya comes from the island of Sumatra," Torino said, "where they have saltwater crocodiles over twenty feet long. They call Baya 'the Croc-odile' because the Indonesian word for crocodile is *buaya*. But the name would work even without the wordplay."

Mason opened the folder and flipped through several more photo-graphs, each one a snapshot of hell on earth. The first, a bombed-out building. The second, the torn ruins of what was once a human body, lying in the street.

"The Bali bombing of 2002," Torino said. "Over two hundred people killed. Just as many injured."

Mason looked at the next photograph. The body of another man. Then the next. A woman.

"Why are you showing me these?" he asked.

"The group who did this calls itself Jemaah Islamiyah. Three of its leaders were executed by firing squad. Another was gunned down by the police in the street. Your American FBI told the Indonesian govern-ment that al-Qaeda had given Jemaah Islamiyah the money to finance the operation. But they were wrong. It was Baya."

Mason closed the folder and gave it back to Torino. He did a quick rundown in his head of every single target he'd ever been given. Dirty cops, drug dealers—none of them truly innocent men, but the motiva-tion behind killing them was never innocent, either.

"You think it makes it easier if I know I'm taking out a monster?"

"I don't care how easy it is," Torino said, taking one more drag off his cigarette. "But if knowing the target's background gives you a clearer head for the job, so be it."

"If that was an Interpol photo, why aren't they taking care of this?"

"We don't wait for other people to solve our problems, Mr. Mason. And Baya is a unique problem. With so many nations becoming more active in the terror sector, he's one of the last remaining individual spon-sors. Which makes him especially dangerous because one man is always more unpredictable than one nation. And harder to bargain with. And he's just as bad for our business as for everyone else's."

"Did you say the *terror sector*? You make it sound like a commodity."

"That's exactly what it is," Torino said. "It's an energy source that creates change. Sometimes drastic change. Just look at your country after 9/11."

Mason shook his head. He could waste his time trying to understand what shade of gray he'd be operating in today, but in the end it wouldn't matter. The car kept moving slowly through the heavy traffic. Torino checked his watch.

Finally, they came to the entrance of the Sultan Hotel. There was a guard shack and two armed soldiers wearing the same uniforms as at the airport. Behind them rose the hotel itself, thirty stories high, with three separate wings joining in the middle, and beyond that two identical towers rising twice as high. The whole complex looked as if it had been airlifted in directly from Palm Springs.

The driver lowered his window and presented his ID card to the soldier. The young man peered inside the vehicle, nodded to Torino and Mason in the back seat, gave the card back to the driver, and waved him through.

Mason hardly noticed the fountains and manicured lawns as they approached the hotel. Whoever the target, whatever the country, whatever the reason, the process was the same. He was in *mission mode* now. His senses were heightened. Everything started to move in slow motion. His conscience, his humanity—it was all put into a black box and locked up tight.

"Take the bag from the trunk," Torino said as the Mercedes pulled up to the front doors. "Everything you need is inside."

Mason got out, pulled the black suit bag from the trunk, and went through the revolving glass doors into the sudden air-conditioned chill of the hotel. The lobby was busy, with several placards standing on easels. The few words in English made it clear there was some sort of private equity conference going on, which helped explain how everyone was dressed—the men all in serious suits with equally serious looks on their faces. Only a handful of women wearing colorful Western-style dresses, standing out like exotic birds.

Mason could feel the tension in the room. As if everyone was holding their breath, waiting for something big to happen.

He clocked one surveillance camera over the reception desk, another on the opposite wall. There were probably more he couldn't see. Then he spotted the first bodyguard. Standing by a roped-off area of the reception desk while a man in an Armani suit waited for the woman typing rapidly on her keyboard.

The second bodyguard was holding the door for yet another VIP in a suit as he strode into the lobby. The third was standing by the door to the men's room.

Mason waited for the VIP to come out of the bathroom. Yet another Armani. Somewhere, somebody was making a lot of money importing suits from Italy. Mason gave the man and his bodyguard a few seconds to walk past, then went inside. After the bustle of the lobby, the bathroom was an oasis of silence, everything done in marble and polished brass. Mason went right into a stall, hung the bag on the door hook, and unzipped it.

He pulled out the suit and slipped it on. A black Zegna, exactly his size. He fitted the leather holster under his left shoulder for a right-hand draw, checked the magazine and slide action on the Glock 30S, then holstered it and slipped on the jacket. A perfect concealed carry. The last two accessories were a pair of dark sunglasses and a Bluetooth earpiece.

"Primary, can you hear me?" The voice was too loud. He took a moment to adjust his earpiece before responding.

"Yes."

"Support, are you there?"

The other voice came through. "The target arrives in twenty-five minutes."

*A woman's voice.*

"Go to the helipad," Torino said. "East wing."

Mason left the suit bag hanging in the stall and went back out to the lobby. Nobody looked at him. Instead of being one of the few tall white men in a conference full of Asians, the suit and sunglasses had turned him into just another bodyguard. He was essentially invisible.

Except, of course, to the surveillance cameras.

"What are we doing about the video?" Mason said into his microphone.

"Not an issue, Primary." Torino's voice. "Disabled."

"The target took care of that himself." The woman's voice again. As with Torino, Mason struggled to place the accent. French, but not exactly.

"He's bought everyone in this hotel," she said. "Start moving."

Mason found the east wing's elevator, boarded with several men, and hit the button for the top floor. He checked his watch. Twenty-one minutes. The elevator stopped and two men got off. Another stop and the last man walked out, not so much as glancing in Mason's direction. Mason rode alone for the next few seconds, until he arrived at the top floor.

"Location of the helipad," he said into the microphone.

"I believe it's on the roof," the woman said.

Torino broke in. "Support, that's enough."

"Where's the access door?" Mason asked.

"Left from the elevator," the woman said. "Left again at the end of the hall."

Mason moved in that direction, took the turn, then saw the door at the far end of the next hallway with a large *H* in a circle. But as Mason approached the door, something didn't feel right to him.

*A heavyweight's about to land on this roof, come through this door.*
*And this hallway is empty.*

"Support," Torino said, "where are you?"

There was no answer. Mason took the Glock out of his shoulder holster and put his left hand on the door.

"Support," Torino said again. "Say something."

Mason pushed the door open. He felt the rush of warm air against his skin and heard the distant beating of a helicopter's rotors. He didn't see anyone on the helipad.

Until . . . *there*, a movement. In the small glass enclosure on the other side of the roof, where there was room for half a dozen people to safely wait for a helicopter to land.

Mason moved sideways, holding the Glock with both hands.

"It's me." The woman's voice. Not in his earpiece this time, but a live voice as she left the glass structure and came to him across the helipad.

She was five eight, maybe five nine. Built like a dancer, with lean muscles and strong legs. She was dressed in black pants and a simple white shirt—the perfect way for a woman to blend into a hotel's wallpaper. The uniform of a waitress, a housekeeper, any other anonymous female worker who kept a place like this running.

She came closer to Mason. Her hair was a black mass of curls she'd made no attempt to tame. Her eyes were green, flecked with gold. The eyes of a sea-born predator. This close, she didn't blend into anything anymore, but Mason was unmoved. He had left all of his physical desires on the other side of the world—one piece with Gina, another piece buried in the ground with Diana.

"Support, answer me!" Torino's voice breaking through.

"I'm here," she said, the voice doubled in Mason's earpiece. "I was occupied."

Mason looked past her and saw the form of a man lying on the floor of the glass structure.

"They'll be expecting one man on the helipad," she said to him. "Can you handle this?"

She didn't wait for an answer. She walked past him, went to the door, and opened it.

"I'll be inside if you need me," she said as she turned back to him. "My name is Luna." Then she closed the door behind her.

Mason saw the helicopter maybe a half mile away in the eastern sky. It was moving slowly as it approached the pad. This gave Mason one single minute to catch his breath, to look out over the edge of the roof at the city sprawled out beneath him. A layer of gray and brown haze hung over everything, then higher above that a layer of cloud. To the west, a bank of tall buildings pierced through the first layer and touched the second.

*Jakarta*, he said to himself. *From Canaryville to fucking Jakarta fucking Indonesia.*

He brought himself back into the immediate present, practiced the exact sequence of events that would happen in the next minute, one after another.

*Shoot the target as soon as he steps off the helicopter. Two in the chest, one in the head.*

*If anyone else on the helicopter is armed or attempts to stop you in any way, shoot them too.*

*Then turn and leave.*

Mason lined himself up with the empty helipad, the four lights blinking at each point of the compass, trying to anticipate the landing orientation so he could put himself at the best angle.

The helicopter lowered slowly.

It paused, hovering in the air for several seconds. Then it rotated slowly, letting Mason see into every window. Pilot, bodyguard, body-guard, bodyguard.

And with each bodyguard, the barrel of a Pindad assault rifle.

Baya was in the middle of the back seat. As soon as those doors opened, Mason would get one shot off, maybe two, before the body-guards cut him in half.

The helicopter hung in the air for five more long seconds. Then it quickly lifted back up into the sky, tilted forward, and flew away.

# 2

*Where are the Owls?*

Martin Sauvage repeated the question to himself as he inched his way through the heavy Jakarta traffic. It was one of the Owls who had called him with a hurried tip: *Sultan Hotel. Now.* Which was slipping away, but it was useless to honk his horn, useless to look for shortcuts through the solid wall of metal surrounding him on the streets.

Sauvage had been living in Jakarta for almost three months now, the second-biggest city in the world but with no mass transit. He still wasn't acclimated to the traffic this caused, any more than to the hot climate, the language, the culture, driving on the left side of the road, or, God help him, the *cuisine*. He was an *inspecteur* on loan to Interpol from the Police Nationale's main office in Paris—a three-year assignment as a criminal intelligence agent in the counterterrorism program. This made Sauvage a "secondment," a detached police officer who gave up any actual police power the moment he left France. For as long as he was here in Indonesia, he could help send out Interpol "Red Notices"—essentially international arrest warrants—coordinate the local cops, advise them, drink with them after hours, and even sleep with them if he wanted to. But the gold Interpol badge he carried—the distinctive blue-gray map of the world with a sword and the scales of justice behind it—gave him no more official arrest-or-detain power than the tin badges worn by the teenage security guards at Mall Ciputra.

No gun, no handcuffs. Just a little office in the National Central Bureau at Jalan Trunojoyo Number 3, a pale-yellow Honda Brio Satya with an air conditioner that worked maybe half the time, flashing lights, a radio . . .

And memories. The memories that had driven him here to the other side of the world. The two faces that stayed with him every waking moment of every day, and every night. His wife, Mireille, Mimi to him and no one else, and his Jean-Luc, side by side forevermore in the garden cemetery at Père Lachaise, in a lonely corner far from the tourists who came to visit the graves of Oscar Wilde and Jim Morrison.

He had a photograph of them in his wallet. The two faces pressed together. He'd found the picture accidentally folded, two days after that day in November, and still hadn't unfolded it.

Now as the endless line of cars in front of him brought his vehicle to a full stop, he felt that same feeling coming back. The sense memories washing over him: driving through Paris, trying to make his way north. He'd already tried to call his wife as soon as he heard about the explosions in the stadium. Off duty that day, a reservation at the restaurant on Rue de la Fontaine-au-Roi, seven o'clock in the evening, *dix-neuf heures*, with Sauvage running late as always. Calling on his cell phone, over and over again, stuck in the sudden swell of panicked drivers until he finally pulled his car over a mile from the restaurant and ran there, his dress shoes shredding his feet with every step.

Four years later, seven thousand miles away, Sauvage was sweating and his heart was pounding again. From somewhere overhead, he heard the sounds of helicopters, and he had that same impulse to abandon the car, to get out and run.

Hashim Baya may not have been directly responsible for the Paris bombings, may not have activated any of the fuses himself, but he was still a *fils de pute*, a son of a whore, who came from the same place as those ISIL animals who killed a hundred and thirty people that day and seriously injured a hundred more. Including the only two people in the world Sauvage really cared about.

That was why there was a Red Notice hanging over Baya's head.

And that was why Sauvage wanted to find him before anyone else did.

———

*What in actual goddamned hell?*

Mason watched as the helicopter rose high above the hotel. It built up speed, and for a moment it looked as if it would fly away and disappear over the horizon. But then the chopper slowed and started to descend again.

It was landing on the other wing of the hotel.

Mason keyed his microphone. "You've got me on the wrong fucking roof. He's landing on the other pad."

"What did you do?" Torino said. "Why did the helicopter change course?"

"I stood here and waited for it to land." Mason had been in this city three hours and already everything was going sideways on him. "What the fuck else was I supposed to do?"

"Go to the other wing," Torino said. "Get moving."

"You need to pull the plug on this," Mason said. "This mission is blown. Maybe next time, you'll—"

"Shut up and listen," Torino said. "You don't know how rare this chance is. We might not get another one for months."

*So you fucking wait*, Mason thought, but he didn't bother saying it. He was already in motion, crossing the helipad and opening the door to the hallway. Luna was gone.

"Support," Torino said, "where are you?"

"I'm on my way to the North Tower," she said, breathing hard like a woman running at full speed.

Mason got on the elevator and descended to the ground floor. He took one step into the lobby and could already sense that something was different. An electricity in the air, everyone moving with deliberate care, bowing their heads together in groups of three and four, speaking in careful, hushed tones.

The Crocodile had arrived at the party, and everyone knew it.

Mason moved through the crowd. He found the North Tower elevators and saw ten men in black suits waiting there, half of them wearing their obvious wealth and importance as easily and naturally as the other half wore their shoulder holsters. The bodyguards all eyed Mason at the same time, measuring him carefully, instinctively moving their bodies to shield their employers. Mason kept walking, turning the corner and waiting for them to board the elevator.

"Support," Torino said again. "Where the hell are you?"

Luna's voice finally came into Mason's earpiece. "Target's on thirty. The floor is secured. You need a special key for the elevator. And every stairwell is guarded."

"Mason," Torino said, "you need to get to that floor."

"If you got any ideas, I'm all ears."

"It's your job to figure that out."

"No," Mason said. "Right now it's yours."

*Say what you want about my old friend Quintero*, Mason thought, *but he would have had this shit figured out. Even if plan A was fucked, he'd have plans B through Z ready to go.*

"The original plan is compromised," Torino said. "Now you need to improvise. Show us why they sent you here."

*Fuck that*, Mason thought. But already his mind was shifting into another gear. Once again, like that first shift into mission mode as soon as he got off the plane, this was yet another shift that happened outside of Mason's will. From one moment to the next, it was *there*.

He saw another man in an expensive suit, along with his bodyguard, approaching the elevator. Mason quickly scanned the lobby, waiting until the elevator door opened. Then another half beat. Then he moved. He stuck his hand in the door just as it was closing, pushed his way into the car, even as the bodyguard said something to him. Mason didn't understand the words, but the context was clear: *Get the fuck out.*

Mason gave him a fake smile, shaking his head like a dumb American. *No compendre, partner.* The guard was tall and well built. No surprise, it was part of the job description. As he reached past Mason with a large hand to stop the elevator door from closing, he made himself vulnerable. Mason took the man's wrist and bent it painfully backward, driving him into the elevator's wall as he drew his Glock from his jacket. He put the barrel to the guard's head as the boss tried to step around them. One look from Mason, and he backed into the corner. The door closed.

Mason examined the elevator panel. Thirty floors, a special keyhole by the top button, just as Luna had said. "You speak English?" he said to the boss. The man was twenty years older, fifty pounds lighter. Short and compact, Asian mixed with something European.

"Yes." His voice was calm. A man who had already regained complete control of himself.

"Hit twenty-nine," Mason said.

The man obeyed. The elevator started to rise. The movement made the bodyguard flinch, as if he suddenly thought: *Time to earn my money and fight off this intruder.* Mason was ready. He took the gun from the man's temple and drove the man's head into the side of the elevator. The whole car rocked as Mason did it again. Then again.

It's not easy to make a man lose consciousness. Especially a big man. Not unless you have the chance to choke him out by restricting the blood flow in his carotid artery, and Mason wasn't even going to try that. He rammed the man's head against the wall a third and a fourth time, finally had to turn him and finish the job with his right fist. When the man was finally out, Mason stood shaking his hand.

"Why are you doing this?" the man asked.

The elevator stopped at the twenty-ninth floor. The door opened. Mason stuck his head out and looked up and down the empty hallway. He dragged the bodyguard out, reached into his jacket, and took out the man's semiautomatic. A compact Beretta. He slipped this into his waistband. Mason left the bodyguard lying unconscious on the floor—no time to hide him—and stepped back into the elevator.

"Use your key," Mason said. "Top floor."

"My employee had the key. Bad luck for you, friend."

"I don't think so," Mason said. "But if that's true, it's bad luck for *you*." Mason leveled the gun at the man's head.

The man shook his head once. Then he put his hand into his jacket pocket.

"Easy," Mason said.

The man pulled out the key slowly, put it into the keyhole, then pressed the button for floor thirty.

"I think you need a new bodyguard now," Mason said. "Don't worry, I work cheap."

"Do you have any idea who's up there right now?"

"Some guy they call the Crocodile."

The man smiled, shook his head again. "You have no idea, friend."

"If you fuck this up," Mason said, "my first shot goes in through the back of your head and out one of your eyes. You look like a smart man, so I'm sure that won't happen."

Luna's voice broke into his earpiece. "Who are you talking to?"

"Mason, where are you?" Torino's voice. "What's happening?"

"One question at a time," Mason said. "I'm on my way to see the Crocodile."

The elevator continued moving upward. It stopped at the top floor. Mason slipped his gun back into his jacket. Took one last moment to catch his breath.

The door opened.

Two men were standing there. Two men who looked a breed apart from every other man Mason had seen in the hotel. With wide, scarred faces, and long hair tied in a ponytail. They wore loose-hanging *baju koko* shirts, emerald green, with a white filigree pattern around the high collar.

Mason stepped out right behind the boss. The two men in the green shirts stopped him and said something in Indonesian. One of them held out a hand, and Mason understood exactly what he wanted. He reached into his jacket, took out his Glock, and handed it over. He still had the Beretta tucked into his waistband.

*If they search me*, he said to himself, *I'm fucked*. But the two men stepped back and let Mason and the boss proceed down the hallway.

"Where is he?" Mason said, his voice low.

"In the banquet room at the end of the hallway," the boss said. "You'll never get out alive."

"You have to think positive. We're in this together, remember?"

The double doors to the banquet room opened. The group of heavy hitters Mason saw waiting for the first elevator stepped out of the room. They'd just closed a deal with the Crocodile, paid their yearly tribute, or whatever the hell else they were doing. Mason didn't care, was more worried about the bodyguards than about who came out after them. These were the same men who had looked Mason up and down in the lobby, and now here they were, recognizing him again. He nodded to them. *Ten seconds until this all goes sideways.* But he knew these men had to give up their guns at the elevator, so he had one advantage left. At least for the moment.

He felt the weight of the Beretta in his waistband. If Baya was in that room, he'd have armed guards watching him. Two, maybe more. Which meant Mason had to get through the door first, use the surprise to take out the guards first, worry about everything else later.

The door opened again. Mason scanned the interior of the room. A long table. One man sitting at the far end. Mason recognized him from the photograph. *Baya.* With another green-shirted guard on either side of him, as Mason had guessed. A third green shirt stood holding open the door.

It was time to move.

Mason pushed past the man holding the door, drawing the Beretta from his waistband. It was a big banquet room, food and beverages spread out all over the table. Baya sitting seventy or eighty feet away. Too far for one dead shot from a gun he'd never fired before.

"Mason," Torino said in his earpiece, his voice urgent, "we're about to lose the building."

"What the hell are you talking about?"

"They're taking the tower from both ends."

"Who is?"

From somewhere in the distance, outside the walls of the hotel, Mason heard helicopter rotors cutting through the air. Baya looked up in the same moment, heard the same sound, and locked eyes on Mason. One frozen instant, the two men regarding each other from across the room. Baya said something, and the two green shirts near him both drew their weapons. Mason had no shot now. He backed out of the room, even as the green shirts were yelling after him.

"Detachment Eighty-Eight," Torino said in his earpiece. "They're moving on Baya."

"We're *fucked*." Luna's voice.

*Detachment Eighty-Eight.* The words meant nothing to Mason. But now his immediate problem was the green shirts coming after him.

"Just tell me how to get out of here," Mason said.

Silence in his earpiece. The last thing he wanted to hear.

"Respond! Get me out of here!"

Nothing.

He was alone. Ten thousand miles from home.

And he was about to die.

———

Sauvage pulled over a half mile from the Sultan Hotel, the white towers rising high above the grounds. He started running. Within a hundred yards, he could feel the sweat dripping down his back.

A great armored vehicle rumbled by, leaving the road and driving down the sidewalk, tearing up fences, vendors' stands, the signs for a dozen different businesses. He watched the vehicle turn through the front gates of the hotel, clipping the corner of the little security shack and sending the two guards running away. In the sky, three helicopters hovered above the North Tower.

Sauvage made the same turn a half minute later. The same guards who'd jumped out of the way like scared rabbits had recovered their composure and were overcompensating by pointing their Pindad rifles at everyone who dared to enter. Sauvage showed them his Interpol badge, trying to communicate in his passable Indonesian who he was, why he had to be allowed in.

Hashim Baya was in the hotel. *The Crocodile*. And Detachment 88 was about to take him down.

The two security guards looked at each other. Sauvage knew that Baya's presence here probably wasn't a surprise to them—he wouldn't take a chance on landing here if most of the security staff weren't paid off in advance. But Detachment 88's arrival changed everything. This was the one group of heavily armed *peler ngaceng*—literal translation: hard dicks—you do not fuck around with, no matter who's paying you, or how much.

The security guards stepped aside and Sauvage kept running. From somewhere inside the hotel, he heard a burst of gunfire. And suddenly, he was once again back on the streets of Paris, a block away from the restaurant where his family was meeting him. Running, his raw feet screaming at him, his heart pounding. He stopped at the police barricade set up across the street, showed his badge, pushed through the riot police with their FAMAS assault rifles and the clear face shields on their helmets, the *médecins urgentistes* swarming between the ambulances and the buildings. Finally slammed through the front door of the restaurant . . .

Shattered glass. Broken chairs. Tables turned over on their sides like something out of an old American Western movie.

Then he saw it. The blood on the floor.

He was still seeing it, no matter how much time had passed. In the heat and the pain of running and the sound of gunfire, he was seeing the blood once more.

He kept running.

———

Mason heard loud voices behind him. Shouted commands. Footsteps.

He could practically feel the crosshairs on his back.

A door flew open. The sudden, staccato rhythm of shots being fired from a Pindad rifle. Mason heard screams, more shouting, a new set of voices. As he rounded a corner, he glanced back for a fraction of a second and saw one of the commandos behind him. Black tactical vest, a helmet with a clear face shield. An insignia on the man's arm. Mason took a photograph in his mind, didn't process the image until he was already running down the next hallway.

*An owl.*

Mason had no time to figure out who these men were. They were obviously official: police, military, paramilitary—it didn't matter. They were invading the floor and shooting everyone who didn't immediately lie down and spread their arms, and even then Mason wouldn't have bet his life on it.

He burst through another set of double doors, knocking down a man dressed in white. It was an auxiliary kitchen—a half dozen staff preparing the food for the banquet room. Another way to keep the floor secure, with none of the men moving back and forth between the banquet room and the main kitchen.

Mason went to the service elevator and hit the button. The men in white were all yelling at him, but nobody made a move to stop him. The elevator didn't respond—another security measure—and Mason was just processing this when the doors swung open and two of the commandos with the owl insignia burst into the room. Mason went down as the commandos yelled at the staff and started firing a half second later.

Mason fired back, knowing he was hitting the commandos in their technical vests or bouncing rounds off their helmets and shields. But he was pinned down in the corner now and trying to buy himself enough time to figure out where the hell he could go next.

He kept firing, keeping the commandos on the other side of the room. He didn't know how many shots he had left.

*Not enough*, he said to himself. *Unless . . .*

There was a window, just on the other side of the rack of pots and pans. A one-in-a-thousand chance, maybe one in a million, but it was all he had left.

He rolled and fired at the window, shattering it, then kept rolling and came up to one knee, firing two more shots before he heard the click of an empty chamber. He dropped the Glock, grabbed a cooking pan and held it in front of him—a move of futile desperation that was confirmed as soon as the first shot blew through the metal and nearly took his head off. But by that time he was already at the window, jumping

through and reaching with his other hand to grab at the sill, the frame—
*anything* that would keep him from falling.

He saw the parking lot thirty stories below him and struggled to find
a footing on the ledge just beneath the window. It was maybe eighteen
inches wide—not enough room to move quickly, but he didn't have any
choice. He steadied himself and started shuffling sideways, grabbing on
to every window frame as he edged past it.

Mason heard the voices behind him but didn't bother turning to
see who was leaning out the window. He just hoped they weren't crazy
enough to follow him. He rounded a corner, moving as fast as he could
make himself go, bumping into a window frame and catching himself
just as he was about to go backward into the abyss.

Finally, he reached a terrace on the far end of the ledge, grabbed the
railing, and pulled himself over. He took two deep breaths, knowing he
didn't have time for anything more.

Mason heard voices on the terrace level directly below him. He
couldn't go back inside, so he went to the other edge of the terrace and
looked down. The same thirty-story drop, with nothing to climb down on.

*"Jangan bergerak!"*

The words came from behind him. Mason didn't know what they
meant, but he recognized the tone of voice. He turned around to face
the speaker. It was one of the commandos, the barrel of his Pindad assault rifle leveled directly at Mason's chest.

Mason took one more look behind him, made the only choice he
could make, and raised his hands.

The commando was soon joined by half a dozen more, all bursting
through the door at once, and they descended on Mason, knocking him
to the floor, bending his arms behind his back and cuffing him. They
kept speaking to him in Indonesian until finally one man stood him up
straight. "Who are you?" he asked.

Mason stayed silent.

The man yelled something to the other commandos, and they
grabbed Mason by each arm and took him into the building. They all
barely fit into the elevator, each commando taking his turn staring up

at Mason's face. He kept his eyes straight ahead, staying cool and calm.

When the elevator doors opened again, there was bedlam in the lobby, with men shouting and hugging each other, some of them openly weeping. The whole scene was amped up another notch as Mason was led right through it. He felt hands reaching toward him, the commandos pushing the crowd back as they slowly made their way to the exit.

Mason was pushed and pulled through the door, toward a large armored van waiting with its back doors open. A dozen other prisoners were already sitting on the benches that ran on each side of the van. They were all wearing the distinctive green shirts, except for one man. *Baya.*

Mason sat down at the end, his hands still cuffed behind him. The doors were slammed shut. Baya stood up and motioned for the men to rearrange themselves so he could sit directly across from Mason. The men moved immediately to obey this order.

When Baya was settled, he looked Mason in the eye. His face was dead calm. He had the air of a man who had just been seated in the back of his own personal limousine after a routine business meeting, not a man who'd been captured by a whole squad of elite commandos.

Now that he was close, Baya looked a few years older than Mason had imagined. Sixty, maybe sixty-five, his gray hair a little thinner than in the photograph.

Baya said something to Mason. Mason didn't understand.

"Who are you?" Baya said, switching to English. "Are you an American?"

Mason didn't respond.

"Who sent you here?"

Mason kept staring at Baya. He didn't speak. He didn't move.

Baya smiled, then looked to the other men in the van. He said something to them, and everyone laughed.

The van lurched forward and started moving down the driveway, back to the main street. Mason could only guess where they were going. A local police station? No, someplace even more secure. A military installation, or Indonesia's version of a black site. When they arrived at their destination, Mason would be separated from these other men . . .

Or else he wouldn't. And that would be much, much worse. He pictured himself sitting in a common holding cell, surrounded by these men. The guards leaving them alone. For a minute, or for an hour.

Or for the entire night.

What would happen next? A dozen men left alone with the man who had tried to kill their beloved leader this very day?

Mason shifted his body to keep his balance as the van made a tight turn. Baya kept speaking to his men. The cryptic words carried the air of reassurance. Of encouragement. Even without understanding the language, it was easy to see that Baya was a natural-born leader.

The van kept turning, rocking. How it made it through the clogged streets of Jakarta, Mason couldn't even imagine. There were no windows to see out the back of the van. Finally, the van slowed down and came to a stop. Mason heard the driver honking his horn.

Baya said something to his men. Everyone slid down the bench, pressing Mason against the back door.

One beat. Then two.

Then the whole world blew apart.

The blast erupted in Mason's ears, making everything go silent. He was thrown from his seat, scrambled together with the rest of the men in a tangle of arms and legs as the van tipped sideways, landing hard on its side.

Then gunfire. Automatic weapons pounding.

Voices on the other side of the back door. Every man in the van now shifting toward the front. Mason slid with them. Another blast blew the door open.

Faces on the other side, looking in. Strong hands pulling Mason down as the men climbed over him to escape. Baya was one of the last men out, his men forming a living shield all around him.

Mason was forgotten, left behind in the heat and chaos.

He crawled out of the van, still mostly deaf, the sounds slowly coming back to him. He saw dead men on the street, their bodies riddled with bullets. Green shirts. No sign of Baya.

Police sirens. Thick black smoke rising from the front of the van. Blood and blown-off limbs. The commandos firing their Pindads. Other men answering with their own weapons, hiding behind vehicles. Mason couldn't tell where the battle lines had been drawn. They were useless to him, anyway, since neither side was safe for him. He was caught in the middle of a firefight on the streets of a city he did not know.

"Mason!"

A voice from somewhere far away.

"Mason!"

Louder, his ears clearing. He looked and saw Luna, still wearing the clothes of a hotel worker. Yelling out the back window of the black Mercedes as it approached on a busy side street, scattering the pedestrians, who were now running in the opposite direction. The driver stopped the car and threw open the door. Torino came out the other side. Both men were carrying weapons. MAC-10s, an absolute beast of a machine pistol—straight blowback action, 1,250 9mm rounds per minute, long banned in the States. But this was a hell of a long way from the States, and each man opened up in the same instant, providing cover fire as Luna gestured wildly at Mason to move his ass.

The slugs were raking across every vehicle and every building, coming from every direction. Mason made his way across the street, keeping his head down, his hands still cuffed behind him. One of the green shirts appeared on the sidewalk, blocking Mason's path. He raised his gun, was about to fire.

Luna stepped out just behind him, lined him up, and put a round through his neck. The man went down, blood flowing, as Mason finally reached the open door of the car and Torino threw him into the back seat.

Luna got in next to him. Torino was in the front passenger seat, the driver behind the wheel. He threw the vehicle into reverse, turned to check behind him, and pressed the gas.

Then the windshield shattered and the driver's head exploded.

———

Sauvage was following the armored van. He didn't want to lose Baya. Bad enough that he had no official arrest powers, no authority to influence Baya's destination or even to find out where the hell they were taking him. There were a hundred different places the van could go, and once it was gone, Sauvage might never see Baya again.

It wouldn't matter how many contacts he had—inside POLRI, the Kepolisian Negara Republik Indonesia; inside TNI, the Tentara Nasional Indonesia; even inside Detachment 88, the Owls themselves. Sauvage would never be granted access to question Baya. No chance to finally look the man in the face, no intelligence gathered, nothing to be shared with other Interpol offices around the world. Just the most wanted man in the world, now hidden away somewhere in this huge, beautiful, ugly, fucked-up city.

Then the bomb went off, right there in the middle of the street, and Sauvage was once again thrown back to Paris. Not just the sound of the explosion taking him back, but the very *feel* of it, the way a bomb compressed the air like nothing else and sent needles of pain into your eardrums.

It took him a long moment to regain his senses, unlock his own muscles, and finally open the car door. The gunfire started then, and Sauvage ducked down behind his door.

He saw the black Mercedes approach on the side street as everyone else was frantically trying to drive or run away. Saw the woman and the two men shooting. Saw one more man in a black suit, hands cuffed behind his back, making his way to the car.

The man turned once, and Sauvage saw his face. Every other man in that police van had been Indonesian. But this one, the last man out, was Caucasian.

*Who the hell are you?*

Sauvage memorized the man's face. Then the man was gone, pushed into the black Mercedes, and now it was racing down the street in reverse. Until a great hole was blown in its windshield.

Sauvage got back behind the wheel of his car and followed.

———

Mason was thrown against the back seat, the cold metal of the cuffs biting into his wrists. He had no way to protect himself as his head whipped forward, his face bouncing off the seat back, rocking him as hard as any punch he'd ever taken. When the fog cleared, Torino had already thrown open his door, come around to the driver's side, opened that door, and pulled the driver's body from behind the wheel. He let the man fall to the street, got behind the wheel himself, and hit the accelerator. It all happened within a matter of seconds.

Torino backed out onto another main street, sideswiping a car and sending it onto the sidewalk. He accelerated directly toward the intersection, jam-packed with cars waiting for the light. A barrier ran down the middle of the street, separating the two lanes. Torino pulled up the emergency brake and went into a sliding J-turn, bouncing lightly off the car at the back of the line waiting for the light, then released the brake and sped down the opposite side of the street, the warm air rushing in through the blown-out windshield.

In the back seat, Mason shook his head clear and tried to keep the pressure off his wrists. Sirens wailed in the distance, seemingly coming from every corner of the city. Two police cars were behind them. Torino took one turn, then another. Until there was only one police car. Then none.

A little beat-up Honda, pale yellow, stayed on their tail for another few blocks. Torino watched the car carefully, nodding as if approving of the driver's skills. Until he took another series of turns on the narrow streets and lost him.

"Mr. Mason," Torino finally said, his voice calm again and his eyes on the road ahead. "Welcome to Jakarta."

# 3

When Martin Sauvage tried to gain entrance to the Sultan Hotel, he saw that it had been transformed from the most luxurious resort in all of Jakarta into a military zone. The attendees of the private equity conference, or whatever was supposedly going on here, were now all rushing around in their expensive suits, one man after another trying to leave the building, while a fresh troop of Detachment 88 commandos tried to maintain order without having to shoot anyone. The black-suited bodyguards milled around behind their bosses, trying to appear as if they were somehow still essential as the chaos boiled all around them.

Sauvage approached the two commandos standing outside the front door. They looked anxious and trigger-happy, having no doubt heard the reports about the attack on the armored vehicle and the escape of Hashim Baya. Even the most hardened and well-trained soldier got disoriented at a time like this, when the world came off its moorings and suddenly *anything* seemed possible. A new wave of attacks? More bombings, maybe right here in the hotel?

No place felt safe right now. No atrocity seemed too far-fetched.

Sauvage knew the feeling.

He showed his Interpol badge to one commando, then another, until finally he found a third who recognized the damned thing. The local police forces were just appearing on the scene by then, members of the POLRI in their familiar beige tactical vests and black berets, and Sauvage knew this would escalate the tension even higher. The police and the military had been separated for twenty years in this country, just long enough to fundamentally distrust each other.

When Sauvage made it through the doors, he pushed his way past the businessmen until he finally found the manager of the hotel—a frantic hummingbird of a man, about five feet high, dressed in a white linen suit.

"Where is your head of security?" Sauvage asked him.

"He has disappeared," the manager said, looking very much as though he wanted to do the same. "I call him and call him and he does not answer his phone."

"Take me to the security room," Sauvage said. "I want to see the surveillance videos."

The manager led him behind the reception desk, into a back room. The noise from the lobby finally receded as the manager closed the door. For the first time, he seemed to catch his breath.

"It is all here," the manager said, gesturing to a bank of thirty screens. Each showed a different view of the hotel. Lobby, restaurants, elevator bays. Exterior shots of every door.

"You have everything recorded," Sauvage said.

"Of course. Pick a camera."

"That one," Sauvage said, nodding to the video feed from the front door. "Can you go back three hours?"

The manager hit a button on the console. Then another.

"*Bajingan.*"

Then another.

"*Bedebah.*"

Until the manager had gone through every Indonesian obscenity Sauvage knew, plus a few he'd never heard before.

"They've all been erased."

———

Torino kept driving hard through the city of Jakarta, running red lights, jumping sidewalks to make tight right turns. In the distance, from every corner of the city, the sirens kept blaring.

Mason's arms were still cuffed behind him, the metal biting into his wrists. He could feel the blood from the driver's head splattered across his face. He could taste its metallic tang on his lips. He knew that now would be a good time to shut the hell up. "So what the fuck was that?" he said.

Torino didn't answer.

"You didn't even know which helipad he was landing on," Mason said. "What kind of amateur-hour bullshit—"

"They diverted," Torino said, keeping his eyes on the road. "I don't know why."

"That's why you have a backup plan." Mason rattled the cuffs, feeling like a tied-up animal. "That's why you put some fucking thought into this."

"The backup plan was you do your job," Torino said, still keeping his voice even. "Things change, you adapt to it."

Mason took a breath, found the right words: "I'm not arguing this. You left me to die up there."

Torino reached out with one hand and punched at the shattered windshield, sending a rain of glass pebbles onto the dashboard. A fresh wave of hot air blew into the car's interior. Mason watched him as he drove, noted his dead calm just minutes after he'd pulled out the dead body of his driver and left it on the pavement.

*Someday he may do the same to me*, Mason thought. *And forget about me just as quickly.*

"We got you out," Luna said, finally breaking her silence.

"The hell you did. If Baya's men don't blow up that vehicle, they're all taking turns on me right now."

"You need to be quiet," Luna said, turning to face him. There was blood from the driver on her face too. She hadn't bothered wiping it off.

Mason had a half dozen more things to say, but he stayed quiet.

Torino kept driving. They left downtown, crossing a narrow river. An immediate passage from one world into another. Mason saw a crude shelter made from wooden pallets and sheets of metal. Then another and another, until the vehicle turned down a long dusty road and Mason saw a huge pile of garbage and then a line of more scrap-metal roofs reaching as far as the horizon, with the tall buildings looming in the near distance making the scene even more inhumane. An acrid smell of smoke hung in the air, invading the car through the open windshield, and small fires dotted the road ahead on either side.

Men started to emerge from the dwellings, one after another. They stood watching the vehicle carefully as it rolled by.

"Who are these people?" Mason said.

"They come here from all over the country," Torino said, still with no more emotion in his voice than if he were describing an infestation of moths. "They look for work in the city."

Torino brought the vehicle to a stop. The dust hung in the air as he opened his door and got out. He opened the back door. Mason worked his way across the seat, twisted himself to grab the strap to his leather carry-on bag with one hand.

When he stood up, he saw at least two dozen men staring at him. They were all wearing ragged pants, tank tops or faded T-shirts, cheap sandals or flip-flops. Everyone seemed fixed to their spots on the dusty ground until a small child ran by. A woman corralled him, picked him up and took him away, glancing back at Mason with alarm written on her face. He could only imagine what he looked like, this tall American in a suit, in handcuffs, his face and chest spattered in blood.

Torino said something loudly in Indonesian. A half dozen men scurried to find something, then one man apparently won the race when he came back holding a hacksaw.

"Turn around," Torino said.

Mason eyed the man in the ragged clothes, then reluctantly turned around and waited for him to work away at the chain holding the cuffs together. The hacksaw blade was dull, and it took a full minute until the chain finally snapped. Mason worked the kinks out of his shoulders and moved the cuffs enough to stop them from rubbing his raw skin. The man seemed to be waiting to work on the cuffs themselves next.

"No, thanks," he said, picturing the rusty blade cutting through his skin. "I'll get these myself."

Torino gave the man a single bill of currency and he backed away. Then Torino said a few more loud words and tossed the keys to the Mercedes into the air. He turned away while the keys were still aloft, and didn't look back at the scramble going on behind him as he started walking away. "Let's go," he said to Mason.

Mason followed him, down the dusty road that ran along the river, as Torino pulled out his cell phone. A few minutes later, so quickly that it must have been circling nearby, a gray BMW 7 Series came over the bridge.

The car pulled to a stop. A man got out. Large by Indonesian standards. A shaved head, large nose, deep-set eyes. A suit that didn't fit him right.

"This is Farhan," Torino said. "Our new driver."

There was something else that Mason saw in the man, within those three seconds. Something he recognized from pure gut instinct. He'd seen it on the streets of Chicago, had seen it in the cell blocks of Terre Haute. Here, on the other side of the world, where everything else was different, the light shining in this one man's eyes was exactly the same:

It was *hunger.*

He could have come from this very slum, a man born into nothing, who would do *anything* to get out and find his share in the world.

Out of a thousand men—out of ten thousand, a million—there was a reason this man wore a suit while everyone else was in secondhand T-shirts. This man wasn't the smartest, or strongest, or luckiest. He was the hungriest. The most willing to do what other men wouldn't. Even if it meant taking the place of a man who had just had his head blown off his body. Literally sit in the same man's blood and take the wheel.

Farhan looked Mason up and down, measuring him. "You've had a bit of trouble, sir."

A strange thing to say for a man who must have learned English from a Brit, now saying it with an Indonesian accent to a man spattered with blood.

"This is Mr. Mason," Torino said, nodding toward Nick. "He's from Chicago."

Farhan nodded again. "An American," he said, saying the word like a magical incantation. As if Mason came from a land that, even now, was the best destination for a hungry man willing to do any job.

"Get in the car," Torino said to Mason. "We're taking you home."

———

Martin Sauvage had known Jacques Duval since they served together in the Police Nationale. Sauvage was the tough kid who'd grown up in La Courneuve, one quarter Romani (the polite word for "Gypsy"), who joined the Troupes de Marine the day he turned eighteen. After two years, he was back home in Paris, quickly becoming one of the youngest *inspecteurs* on the force.

Duval, a division commandant, kept an eye on the young Sauvage, recognized the talent, the instincts, the drive. When Duval took a leave to serve on loan to Interpol, he asked Sauvage to come with him. Sauvage turned him down flat, told his old boss that nothing in the world would make him trade in his *inspecteur*'s badge for the tin shield of an Interpol agent.

"Why do they bother calling them agents, anyway? They're nothing but glorified clerks. Sitting in their offices in Lyon, taking phone calls from real policemen doing real police work."

Then came Operation Lionfish.

It was the biggest operation in Interpol's hundred years of existence. A series of perfectly timed raids in thirty-four different countries, conceived by the UN Office of Drugs and Crimes but coordinated at the highest level by Interpol. It blew open a vast worldwide smuggling ring, with drugs being sent in shipping containers from South America to North America and Europe, and cash and weapons being sent back in return.

Duval called Sauvage the day after the story broke on every news station in the world. "Still think we're a bunch of glorified clerks?"

Sauvage turned him down again.

Then came Operation Lionfish II. Thirty-nine countries this time. Even more drugs, even more cash and weapons.

Sauvage turned him down again.

Then came November 2015. The Paris bombings.

This time, Sauvage said yes. Because now he'd seen the horror of international terrorism up close. He buried his wife and son and then flew to Jakarta, listening to his first Indonesian language lesson on the plane.

Sauvage stood waiting for Duval in the lobby of the Sultan Hotel, which had cooled down maybe half a degree but no more. He saw Duval approaching the same commandos at the door, showing them a similar Interpol badge. They let him right through. That was how *everyone* reacted to him. Police Nationale, Interpol—hell, he could flash a fake badge from a toy shop, and you wouldn't even look at it because you'd be too busy being impressed by the man's perfect suit, his perfect hair with just the right flecking of gray at the temples, his supreme air of command.

Sauvage was the quarter-gypsy street cop sweating in his rumpled suit. Duval was the *commandant* and always would be.

"Baya was here," Duval said, surveying the lobby. "How did you know?"

"I have a friend who works for the Owls. He tipped me off."

Duval eyed him warily. "You didn't tell me."

"I tried. Your aide couldn't find you."

"What was he doing here?"

"I think he was fundraising."

"Are you joking?"

"He was getting paid off by all these heavy hitters," Sauvage said, nodding to the men in suits. "They called it a private equity conference, but I think it was just Collection Day."

"Paid off to leave their business interests alone," Duval said, already deep in thought. "How very *Venezuelan.*"

"They blew the armored vehicle," Sauvage said. "He could be on another island by now. But there's one thing that doesn't make sense to me."

"What's that?"

"There was a stranger here. I think he was American. I saw him on the streets."

"How do you know he was American?"

"I didn't, not until I came back here and talked to some people. One of these payoff guys heard him talking into his earpiece on the top floor. Said he sounded American. Baya's guards took a shot at him before everything else went to hell. The Owls actually arrested him and put him in that armored van."

"They didn't get an ID?"

"He wasn't carrying one. They would have processed him if they'd ever made it to their base."

"Wait a minute," Duval said. "Do you think he was trying to take out Baya?"

"I think he might have been."

"Shame he didn't. Would have saved us all some trouble."

Not the official Interpol position, but Sauvage understood what his boss was saying.

"They must have caught this guy on video," Duval said. "All the cameras in this place . . ."

"That's the other thing," Sauvage said. "The director of security made sure everything got wiped. Right before he disappeared."

Duval raised an eyebrow. "Baya had this whole place set up. A total blackout."

Sauvage nodded. "He probably had half the staff in his pocket. But not the manager. I already talked to him. Either he's clean or he's the best actor in the world."

Duval went off to talk to the leader of the commandos, leaving Sauvage behind in the lobby. He wandered among the businessmen, listening to their conversations. Until he came to two men huddled around a cell phone.

Sauvage sneaked a look over their shoulders. One of the men was flipping through photographs he had taken during the raid.

"Excuse me," Sauvage said. "May I see those?"

He showed the man his badge. The man handed him his phone.

Sauvage flipped through the photographs, one by one. They were haphazard shots of the lobby, taken at bad angles. The Owls storming through the doors. Men lying down on the floor, covering their heads.

Then, finally: a fuzzy photograph of a man in a suit, being escorted through the lobby, his hands cuffed behind his back.

It was the American.

Sauvage kept flipping through the photographs but couldn't find another shot. He went back to the first and zoomed in on the American. The resolution wasn't good. He'd have to send it back to the office and see if any of the techs could enhance it. But he doubted it would be clear enough to make an identification. For now, all he could do was stare at the vague features of the American's face.

*Who the hell are you?*

———

Farhan drove through the city. Torino was in front, Luna again sitting next to Mason in the back seat. Silent and still, watching the city go by.

Mason smelled something that brought back a long-ago memory. He had started smelling it as soon as he got back in the car, and now it finally broke through into his consciousness.

*Old Spice.*

Farhan was wearing it. Too much of it. But the unmistakable scent took him right back to the owner of that chop shop on Normal Avenue, the old man with the cigar and the little feather in his hat and the Old Spice he generously splashed on every morning. He gave Mason and Eddie a weekly punch list of cars to bring in and he paid them good money for two consecutive summers, until his heart suddenly decided to stop beating.

"You'll find a cell phone on the counter in your apartment," Torino said. "Make sure you have it with you at all times."

Another reminder of the past for Mason, this time the day he got released from prison. How Quintero had given him a cell phone and delivered the same message, but in his own words.

*You're going to answer this phone when I call you. Day or night. There is no busy. There is no unavailable. There is only you answering this phone. Then doing exactly what I tell you to do.*

Different hemisphere, same story.

The streetlights of Jakarta were on now, the city still pulsing and alive after dark. Farhan negotiated the streets with a sure hand, driving like a lifelong native, until they finally arrived at an apartment building, one high-rise in a whole block of them. When the car pulled up to the curb, Farhan got out quickly and came around to Mason's door. Mason grabbed his leather bag and got out.

"Good night, Mr. Mason," Farhan said, with another bow and final shot of Old Spice. "I'm looking forward to working with you. Perhaps we can talk about America sometime."

Luna opened her door and got out on her own. Torino stayed in the front seat and rolled down the window. "I need to call and report on the failed mission," he said. If he dreaded the call, he was doing a masterful job of hiding it.

"I'll take him upstairs," Luna said.

They looked directly at each other for one second. Mason knew he wasn't imagining it, the sudden pulse of electricity in the air as some unspoken message passed between them. Whatever that message was, Mason couldn't decipher it, but it did tell him this: *This woman is Torino's vulnerability. Someday, that could be useful.*

The doorman was a short Indonesian man in a blue uniform. He nodded to Luna and Mason as he held the door open, took in the blood on their clothes without so much as blinking. They rode up the elevator in silence. Luna took out a key and opened the door. Then she held out the key for Mason.

"Tomorrow morning," she said. "Fifty-second floor of the Gama Tower. Be there at nine a.m."

Mason took the key. "Do I have a vehicle?"

"You'll get one when you need one. For now, you can walk the half mile to the tower. There's no reason for you to go anywhere else."

More of Quintero's words coming back to him: *This isn't freedom. This is mobility. Don't get those two things confused.*

"You haven't said much since the . . . mission," Mason said. "Or whatever the hell that was."

She shot him a look. A beat passed as the elevator kept rising.

"I suppose I need to thank you," Mason said. "You saved my life on the street."

"That's my job."

He nodded, then didn't try to say anything else.

When the door opened, Luna led Mason to his apartment. She waited for him to put the key in the lock and turn it.

"We'll see you at nine," she said.

"You're not going to show me the place?"

She hesitated for one beat—the first time Mason saw her have to think before answering him. "No," she finally said. "Torino is waiting."

He watched her go back to the elevator, then step in without looking back at him. He shook his head and pushed the door open to see his new home.

More strange echoes from another day, in what felt like another lifetime—the day that had started in an eight-by-ten cell at USP Terre Haute and ended in a five-million-dollar town house on the North Side. Now here he was, standing in another new home on an overcrowded island he'd struggle to locate on a map. A high-end place by any standard, but with no restored Mustang 390 GT Fastback in the garage. For the moment, no vehicle at all. And instead of a view of Lake Michigan, it was the city of Jakarta spread out below him as he stepped out to the balcony. The air was still heavy and warm, feeling as though it would never be anything else.

Mason went into the bathroom, turned on the air conditioner, looked at the blood on his face and clothes, took off the jacket, and washed up as well as he could. Then he took a can of club soda from the bar next to the kitchen and emptied it into the sink. He found the sharpest serrated knife in the utensil drawer and went back outside, sat down on one of the two balcony chairs, and started to methodically saw at the metal of the can. When he had a thin strip about three inches long, he started shimming it into the ratchet mechanism in the handcuff on his left wrist.

His mind was slowing down now. He could sit in the warm air and try to process what had happened today. He ran it back through his mind. Every minute. Every move.

*Why am I here?*

He got the shim in the right position against the ratchet, and the handcuff came open. He switched to the other wrist, knowing it might take a little longer using his left hand.

*And how am I not dead right now?*

He worked the ratchet with the shim, waiting to feel it release.

*I should feel something. Right now. I should feel like I walked right into hell today and somehow made it back alive.*

The shim caught and the ratchet opened.

*Why don't I feel anything at all?*

Mason dropped the second handcuff to the floor and rubbed his wrists, looking out over the city, listening to the noises from the street below him. The fatigue he'd been holding back one day, two days, however long it had been since he last slept—it all washed over him at once. His ears started to ring again.

Mason got up and went inside, took the laptop out of his bag, and opened it. He had one more thing to do. One more image to put in his mind, so it would be *that* and not the image from this day that he would see as he fell asleep.

He went to his nine-year-old daughter Adriana's Instagram account and scrolled through the new entries. Adriana had a good eye with the camera and knew how to compose a shot. A photograph of her new house just outside Denver. Her new room. Her new school.

Then a photograph of Adriana herself, showing off a new dress. After flying ten thousand miles to climb up thirty stories on a suicide mission, then looking a terrorist in the eye, then watching a dozen of his men gunned down, commandos blown apart by a bomb. Now, here, in this moment, finally seeing his daughter's face. It felt like the first time all day that Nick Mason's heart started to beat again.

He closed his eyes, said good night to his daughter on the other side of the world, and went to sleep.

# 4

On his first morning in Jakarta, Nick Mason stared into the faces of the men he'd watched die the day before.

He was standing on a busy sidewalk, watching twelve different television screens through the front window of an electronics store, as one body after another, each covered by a white sheet, was wheeled out of the Sultan Hotel. Then followed the long sequence of faces—Detachment 88 commandos, businessmen, bodyguards—who had been killed. They didn't show the faces of any of the anonymous men in the green shirts. But they did show the face of Hashim Baya. The Crocodile.

A hundred other Jakartans passed behind him, but no one else stopped to watch the screens. It was just Mason, standing still, looking into the eyes of nineteen dead men.

When the news program ended, he turned away, shading his face from the morning sun. He was dressed in jeans and a white shirt. It was too hot for a jacket. The sunglasses he'd been wearing yesterday had been taken by the commandos when they captured him. He needed another pair.

Mason passed one vendor after another, lined up in tight rows along every side street in this section of town, selling food and cigarettes. Flags, flowers, toys, hats. Newspapers with front-page coverage of the raid at the Sultan Hotel. Many of the vendors called out to Mason, the tall

American in the immaculate white shirt—obviously a man with some money to spend. He ignored all of them and kept walking.

Mason tried to orient himself. He put the building that was his new home in the center of a compass, walked a half mile north, observing every landmark. More buildings, more vendors, the streets jammed tight with cars and motorcycles. He turned back and covered the south, east, and west. Trying to build a map in his mind.

This wasn't Chicago, which he knew like the contours of his own body. This was the second-biggest megacity in the world after Tokyo, spreading out in every direction. It would take him another lifetime to learn it, to gain any kind of tactical advantage.

Mason stopped suddenly. He checked behind him.

Someone was following him. It was a familiar feeling, after all of the time he had spent with either Quintero or Detective Sandoval, or both, watching his every movement. Chicago. Jakarta. In any city in the world, Mason would know this feeling.

He kept walking until the Gama Tower loomed ahead of him. Sixty-four floors—one solid rectangle reaching higher than any other building in the city, with a great round turret on top. When Mason was a block away from the tower, he saw a young girl with a basket of sunglasses. She couldn't be more than nine years old, wearing the white *kebaya* dress that was so common. Her black hair was tied into a single braid that rested on her shoulder.

She gave Mason a shy smile as he picked up a pair of sunglasses and tried them on. Only then did he really see her for the first time, and it hit him just how much she reminded him of his own daughter. Same age, same reserved smile. Looking up at him with careful, intelligent eyes as Adriana would. Except that his daughter wouldn't be alone, selling sunglasses to strangers in the middle of a city. Gina would have a heart attack followed by a stroke, followed by another heart attack, if Adriana were to walk one block alone in *any* city.

"Where's your mother?" Mason asked.

The words didn't register. The girl didn't speak English.

Mason checked the price. Thirty thousand rupiah, not even three dollars in American money. He took out the currency from his wallet, counted out a hundred thousand, and gave it to her. She tried to give him back his change.

"Keep it," he said. Then, before she could figure out what he was trying to say, a large man appeared behind her. A rough face and hair tied back into a ponytail. He grabbed the money from her. When she stood up to face him, the man raised his other hand as if to slap her. Mason stepped forward and put himself between them, grabbing the man's forearm.

"Mr. Mason," a voice said. "You don't want to do that."

Mason turned to see the replacement driver. Farhan. Wearing the same ill-fitting dark suit despite the moist heat rising from the street.

*The man who was following me . . .*

"He's not going to hit this girl in front of me," Mason said. "I don't care if he's her father."

Farhan said something in Indonesian to the man, and he reluctantly backed away. Then Farhan said a few more words, this time to the girl. She kept her head down, didn't look up at him, then finally gathered up her basket of sunglasses and ran away from them, vanishing into the crowd on the sidewalk. Mason was about to go after her because, by his math, she was down one pair of sunglasses with no money in return, but Farhan grabbed him by the arm.

"That's not her father," he said. "That's her *preman*. He charges rent to the vendors. She must be behind on her payments."

"Behind in her . . . *what*? She can't be more than nine years old. Where are her parents?"

"Look around you," Farhan said. "How many children do you see?"

Mason scanned the streets. There were hundreds of vendors, all of them clamoring for business in the morning rush of traffic and pedestrians. Now that he looked more carefully, he could see at least a dozen unaccompanied children.

"You've been here for one day," Farhan said. "You think this is your concern?"

Mason didn't respond. But Farhan drove the point home anyway:

"First thing you should know, Mr. Mason, if you're going to survive in this country . . . You're a long way from America."

————

The National Central Bureau building was a twenty-story gray monolith in the center of the city, overlooking the Gelora Bung Karno Stadium—the GBK, as the local football fans called it. Martin Sauvage was sitting behind his desk on the seventeenth floor, paging through a long list of names, all on American visas.

There were ten million people living in Jakarta, a city originally designed to hold no more than a million. Another two million came into town on any given workday. So out of twelve million, how many were American males, age thirty to forty?

The Interpol tech worked through the database and printed Sauvage a list of over eight thousand names. Sauvage didn't know if he should be surprised by that. He did know that there were a hell of a lot more Americans in Jakarta back in the nineties, when President Suharto was still running things and Indonesia had just joined the G20.

Then came September 11 and, a year later, the bombing of the resort in Bali by the separatist group called Jemaah Islamiyah. The USA put a travel advisory in place for Indonesia and didn't lift it until 2008.

Then, in 2009, the terror came to Jakarta when two Western hotels were bombed five minutes apart. Jemaah Islamiyah claimed responsibility again.

A decade later, the group had been broken up and scattered to the wind. The American CIA captured Riduan Isamuddin, the so-called Osama bin Laden of Southeast Asia, in Thailand and sent him to Guantanamo Bay. As far as Sauvage or anyone else knew, Isamuddin was still there.

Detachment 88 took care of the other JI leaders who dared to stay in Indonesia. They found Dr. Azahari bin Husin, "the Demolition Man," in his hideout in East Java and put a sniper bullet through his chest just before the rest of his men blew themselves up. They caught up to

Noordin Mohammad Top four years later, surrounded his village, and turned his house into a charred shell with no roof.

The Owls did not fuck around.

Of course, even if Jemaah Islamiyah was decimated, there would always be new terrorist cells to take its place. You couldn't spend a day here without hearing about Jamaah Ansharut Daulah, Darul Islam, or Abu Sayyaf. It was hard to keep up with who was splintering off from whom, or what the new objectives were—Sharia rule, women kept in burkas and out of school, all Westerners driven from the islands—or, more importantly, what targets they were going to hit next.

Maybe Duval was right. If Baya was the new money man and there was an American in town trying to kill him, why should they even bother trying to stop him?

Sauvage thought about it. His old cop instincts were telling him that he had to find this American. That was all he needed to keep going. But at some point, Duval would appear in his doorway and ask him why the hell he was wasting time on this, and Sauvage would need a reason. A set of words that would add up to something more than just a gut feeling.

And then it hit him.

*He was there. In the building. Before me. Before the Owls.*

*He knew how to find Baya, better than anyone else.*

Sauvage picked up the phone and called his tech. "I want you to reprint this list," he said. "But instead of alphabetical, I want it sorted by date of entry. Start with yesterday and go backward."

*If you want to find the crocodile, find the crocodile hunter and let him take you right to him.*

———

As Mason rode up the elevator with Farhan, he once again caught the strong scent of Old Spice. *The guy must bathe in the stuff,* Mason thought, but he didn't say a word about it.

When they arrived on the fifty-second floor, Torino was waiting for them. He was dressed in another impeccable European suit, freshly groomed. He glanced at his watch—an unspoken observation of the fact that nine a.m. had passed a full six minutes ago.

"Thank you," Torino said to Farhan. "You can leave him in my hands now."

Farhan nodded, bowed to both men, and disappeared.

"This is your official place of employment," Torino said, leading Mason through the double glass doors with eye-level letters spelling out *PLI*. They walked past the receptionist, a local Indonesian woman wearing a floral silk blouse. She glanced at Torino once, then at Mason, the whole process happening within a half second. Then she looked away without saying a word.

"This way," Torino said, leading him down a long hallway. Mason peeked into a dozen offices on the way and saw more locals, men and women, all well dressed, all seemingly busy, talking on telephones or staring at computer screens and tapping away on keyboards. Nobody met Mason's eye for more than the same half second.

"You will not be interacting with anyone in this section of the floor," Torino said, continuing down the hallway. At the end was an unmarked door, as nondescript as the door to a mop closet, but it had a combination lock. "I'll give you the code when we're on the other side. Do not write it down. And never let *anyone* else through this door."

Torino hit five numbers quickly, then opened the door to a separate set of offices. Maybe a dozen of them, all windowless, lit only by recessed pot lights in the ceiling. With no visible daylight and no visual contact with the outside world at all, Mason had a sudden claustrophobic feeling as if he were trapped a hundred feet underground.

He once again looked into the offices as he passed them. In each, an Indonesian national sat behind a desk, staring at a computer monitor. Torino paused in each doorway, said the same sentence in Indonesian. Each of Mason's fellow PLI employees scanned his face, as if memorizing it. Then they went to the next door, and the process repeated.

"Who are they?" Mason said. "What do they do here?"

"They do their jobs," Torino said. "That's all you need to know. Just remember their faces in case you see one of them in the field."

Mason tried to do this, but he was more interested in another face:

the man he'd seen on the video screen in Chicago. The man who'd sent him here.

"Is the boss here?"

Torino stopped walking and gave him a look. "Is that a joke?"

"No, it is not a joke. Is he here?"

"This is one regional office out of hundreds around the world."

"So where is the boss's office?"

Torino gave him another look. "On another continent."

So, not in Asia. But Mason was going to need a little bit more information.

"Why are *you* here?" Mason asked. "Of all the places for a slick Italian to end up."

More fishing. Every detail could be important.

"There are a quarter-billion people in Indonesia," Torino said. "On seventeen thousand islands. It's been the center of world trade for fourteen centuries. Gray market, black market—it all still comes through Indonesia."

"Center of the world. I get it. Doesn't answer my question."

"Then maybe you should stop asking them."

"Tell me more about Baya. Why do you need to kill him?"

Torino shook his head in disgust. "*Il proiettile non chiede alla pistola perché è stato sparato.*"

"What does that mean?"

"*The bullet does not ask the gun why it was fired.*"

Before Mason could respond, a figure appeared in the hallway. A woman in a dark-gray business suit. White blouse, black hair tied up with a rogue curl on her forehead. Green eyes. For that one fraction of a second, Mason was back in the town house on the north side of Chicago, morning sun streaming through the windows, Diana coming down the stairs, clean and bright and dressed for a long day at the restaurant. The woman looked back at him, and the spell was broken.

It was Luna.

"He's left the island," she said to Torino, barely glancing at Mason. "I can't locate him yet."

"You'll find him. A crocodile can only stay under the water for so long."

"Do you seriously think we're going to get another shot at this guy?" Mason asked. "He'll be surrounded by an army from now on."

"So was Napoleon," Torino said. "There is always a way."

Before Luna turned away, her eyes finally met Mason's. She nodded and then went back into her office. Torino stood there for a beat too long, staring at the empty space where she'd been standing. The look on his face, as much as he tried to hide it, was another piece of intel for Mason to file away.

*The age-old story, and he's got it bad.*

Torino shook it off and nodded at Mason to keep following him. He stopped at the last door, at the very end of the hallway. Mason stepped past him, into his office. There was a desk, a chair, a phone. Nothing else.

Torino opened one of the desk drawers and took out a box of business cards. "Keep some of these with you at all times."

Mason picked out a card and read it. It was embossed with the same name that appeared on his passport, along with his new title.

"Director of security," Mason said. "In other words, I'm your bodyguard."

Torino shrugged. "It doesn't matter."

"What does *PLI* stand for?"

"Pacific Logistics Incorporated."

"Which means what?"

"Again, doesn't matter."

"If somebody arrests me, I should know what my company does."

"If you're arrested again," Torino said, "you already have bigger problems."

Mason picked up the phone, heard a dull, flat buzzing that sounded nothing like an American dial tone. He put the phone back in its cradle and looked at the blank walls. They were covered with gray fabric, as if to absorb noise.

"At least my prison cell had a window."

Torino ignored that, took a step closer to Mason. "Let me see your wrists."

Mason pulled back his sleeves. Torino frowned when he saw the still-red rings from the handcuffs.

"Keep those hidden," he said. "And give me your passport."

Mason handed it over. Torino took a new passport from his breast pocket and put it down on the desk.

"This one has a new visa stamp. You just landed on American flight one-seventy-two this morning, out of Los Angeles."

*So I couldn't have been at the hotel yesterday,* Mason thought. *I wasn't even in the country yet.*

"This office is completely secure," Torino said, nodding at the fabric-covered walls. "That makes this, your apartment, and the company vehicles the only safe spaces in the city. Never discuss our business anywhere else."

Mason kept looking at the passport, at the strange name below his face.

"We'll locate Baya, I promise you. And then you'll have the chance to redeem yourself."

Mason took a breath, counted to three, then started speaking. "I told this to your partner and I'll tell it to you—"

"She's not my partner. She's another employee of the organization."

*Yeah, sure she is.*

"It doesn't matter," Mason said. "You sent me into a kill box yesterday."

Torino studied him carefully. "What is your point?"

"I'm not going on another assignment for you unless I see the plans first. Blueprints of the building. Method of entry. Primary exit, secondary exit . . ."

Torino listened to him, nodding his head slowly.

"I want it all," Mason said, "laid out on paper, with time to study it. *And approve it.* If there's something I don't like, I'm going to change it. And if the mission can't be done, we're not even going to try it. Do you understand me?"

"I think I do," Torino said, showing no emotion at all. "Come with me."

Mason picked up the passport from the desk, put it in his pocket, and followed. Torino went down the hallway to the room Luna had gone into, and opened the door and held it for Mason. Unlike the other offices, it wasn't just a desk and a chair and a computer screen. The room was twice as big and there were half a dozen screens, and a whiteboard on the wall with dates and times written in blue ink.

Luna turned around to look at the intruders. "I told you I'm working on it."

"Bring up the feed from Denver," Torino said to her.

The word went right through Mason. *Denver.*

"What are you doing?" Mason said.

"He needs to see it," Torino said. "Right now."

Luna eyed Mason for a moment, shook her head, then turned to the screen directly in front of her chair. She opened a window and ran through a long list of menu options, finally selecting one and clicking on it. Another window popped up. It took Mason a moment to figure out what he was seeing.

An empty kitchen. A refrigerator, a stove, a counter, a sink. Nothing unusual. But he knew what it meant.

"They're thirteen hours behind us," Torino said. "It's just after eight p.m."

Mason kept staring at the screen.

"What time does your daughter go to bed, Mr. Mason?"

He turned to him. "I'm going to fucking kill you."

"I don't think you are," Torino said. Then to Luna: "Try the bedroom."

She didn't move.

"The bedroom."

She chose another option from the menu. Another screen popped up. A bed. A single lamp flooding the room with soft light.

Two people.

A woman.

A young girl.

The woman was reading from a book. The girl was listening, the covers tucked up around her neck.

Mason moved closer to the screen, leaning down for a better look. Every detail of the scene. His daughter, Adriana. And Gina. There was no sound, just the silent image from the other side of the world. Mason kept staring at the screen until Luna finally closed it.

"No," he said. "Bring it back."

"I'm sorry," she said.

"I told you when you got off the plane," Torino said. "I didn't think I'd have to remind you again so soon."

Mason turned and put one hand on Torino's chest, drove him back against the wall. The impact of his body made the entire room shake.

One second later, Mason felt something press against the small of his back. In another tenth of a second, he was in a ball on the floor, his entire electromuscular system shut down by fifty thousand volts of direct current.

The current stopped for a moment, long enough for Mason to un-clench his body. When he reached up toward Torino, he felt the current ripping through his body one more time.

"A black van will pull up in front of the house in nine minutes," Torino said as he dialed a number on his phone. "Two men will get out. One will go to the front door. The other will go to the back. They will kill the current husband while your ex-wife and daughter watch. Then they'll both be blindfolded and taken into the van. They'll be driven to the nearby mountains. Once there, they'll be separated for twenty-four hours."

The current stopped again. Torino bent down further, looked Mason in the eye, and said, "The men are already close by. Unless I stop them."

"Stop them," Mason said, struggling to regain his breath.

"Excuse me?" He bent down further.

"I said stop them."

Torino stood up straight, hit one button on his phone. Luna stood watching, holding the stun gun in her right hand.

Mason got to his feet. He kept his eyes closed for a long time, or-ganizing his thoughts and trying to put together his next words. Every cell in his body wanted to destroy this place, burn this entire building to the ground, but not before choking the life out of every person in this office, man or woman.

"Do you have anything else to say?" Torino asked him.

Mason left the room, went through the secret door, through the front section of the office, through the glass doors, to the elevator, down to the ground level, and out onto the hot streets.

He tried to breathe, but the air was too heavy and stale and tasted like diesel fumes. If only he could have one minute of cold Chicago air, standing on the shore of Lake Michigan on an October night . . .

He took out his cell phone and fumbled with the international calling protocol until he finally figured out how to dial Gina's number.

The call didn't go through.

Five seconds later, the phone rang. Mason answered and heard Torino's voice. "Every call to the house is monitored, Mr. Mason. If you attempt to contact your family again, or if you call someone else and have *them* attempt to contact them . . ."

Mason hung up. He was about to throw the phone onto the pavement, but he stopped himself. Even if he could talk to them, what would he say? How could he convince them to leave, and where could they even go that an organization with global reach couldn't find them?

Another thought came to him—a sudden realization that felt like a solid, unavoidable truth.

He was never going to see them again.

Ever.

Mason started walking down the street, with no idea where he was going. That's when he saw the girl again. The girl who had sold him the sunglasses before the man took all of the money. Mason tried to call to her, but she was already in motion, carrying her basket and running away from him.

He followed after her. He didn't want to chase her down the street and turn this into another bad moment in her life. But after everything that had happened since he arrived here, Mason needed to do this. Just give this girl every goddamned rupiah in his wallet.

He caught a glimpse of her as he turned the corner, and he pushed his way through the hundreds of people on the sidewalk—more street vendors, food carts, vegetable stands, all packed closer and closer together as he left the central downtown area behind him. He saw a flash of her again but then had to wait as a train cut across the street, moving slowly, dozens of vendors moving out of its path, waiting and then moving back onto the tracks as soon as the train had passed.

Mason saw her one last time, a hundred yards down the railroad tracks. He walked quickly to close the gap and turned the corner into a long line of metal-and-wood shanties, like the makeshift houses he had seen last night on the other side of the river, where Torino ditched the Mercedes. He walked slowly down the narrow lane between the shanties, dozens of faces peering out at him.

Then Mason stopped dead. He knew he was being followed again. He turned quickly, just in time to spot Farhan behind an abandoned truck. Mason kept moving forward, took a right turn, and made his way down another long, narrow alley. He built a quick map in his head, made another right turn and doubled back, left the shanties, and made his way through the downtown buildings again. He knew without looking that Farhan was thirty to forty yards behind him.

Mason ducked into a doorway, nodded an apology to the old man who was squatting there, and waited until the heard the sound of dress shoes on pavement. Then he stepped out and grabbed Farhan by the jacket.

"I'm just trying to protect you," Farhan said. "There are dangerous parts of this city that you don't know about."

Mason let Farhan go, and the man took a beat to try to smooth out his rumpled jacket.

"You'll never find her," Farhan said.

"I need to give her her money."

"You scared her," Farhan said. "And you scared her *preman*. He won't want the trouble, which means she'll never be allowed to come back to that spot again. She'll have to find a new place to sell her sunglasses. And find a new *preman* who'll probably charge her even more."

"What are you telling me? That I just ruined her life?"

"I'm sorry," Farhan said, shrugging his shoulders. "I told you, you're a long way from America."

It hit Mason like a second gut punch. After seeing his own daughter on that video screen, feeling so powerless . . . Now this.

"Listen," he said. "You have to help me find her."

Farhan gestured to the shanties all around them. "Do you know how many people live here? Just in this *kampung*?"

"She can't be that far away."

"Look around you, Mr. Mason."

Mason scanned the narrow lane. One ramshackle hut, made of scrap metal and plywood and God knew what else. Then another, and another. Stretching out in a long line. One line of hundreds.

Farhan was right. But Mason didn't care. "I'm going to find her."

"All right," Farhan said, "I will help you. But you have to do something for me in return."

Mason looked at him. What possible thing could he do for this man?

"Buy me a drink," Farhan said, "and I will tell you."

# 5

"This is not your city," Farhan said. "You are a visitor. A *bule*, they would call you. And Jakarta is nothing like the cities where you come from."

The two men were sitting at the rail in a place called Jimm's in the Bellagio Boutique Mall. It was a place that tried to look like an American sports bar. Pennants and photographs all over the walls. Televisions hanging over the bar showing ESPN. It wasn't totally convincing and it sure as hell wasn't Mitchell's on Halsted Street, but if nothing else, Mason got to listen to a couple of expats playing pool and speaking perfect American English while he nursed a cold bottle of Budweiser. Not a Goose Island, but it still made him feel maybe 1 percent less far away from home.

"You think you can survive here," Farhan said, "just because you're the big strong American."

Mason took another hit off the beer.

"Don't get me wrong, Mr. Mason. The people who live in this country are the kindest, most gracious people in all the world."

Mason didn't know if that was true. He'd been in the country for maybe thirty hours, and already many of its citizens had tried to kill him. But then, he wasn't exactly the typical tourist.

"When you walked around this city," Farhan said, "did you see it? The way everyone smiles at a stranger?"

Mason thought about it. Farhan was right about the smile. It wasn't a big American toothpaste-commercial smile he'd seen. It was subtler, more understated. An easy and natural openness Mason had seen on almost every face. But then, on some of those faces—not most but some—that smile was followed by something else, as soon as the wearer processed who Mason was and where he obviously came from: *Your American dollars have been turned into rupiah, and now they are burning a hole in your pocket. How can I help you lighten this burden?*

"So why don't you think I can survive here?" Mason asked. "If everybody's so wonderful . . ."

Farhan looked at him sideways. "Do I have to tell you?"

"Go ahead."

"My father was born in Sumatra," Farhan said. "Where all the biggest saltwater crocodiles live. Do you know how they catch them?"

Mason shook his head. *Enough with the goddamned crocodiles already.*

"They'd put a live chicken on a big hook, hang the chain on a tree branch over the river."

"If you're trying to tell me I'm the chicken—"

"No," Farhan said, "you're the foreigner with the gun, who kills the crocodile."

Mason just looked at him.

"The crocodile is revered on Sumatra," Farhan said. "A man who is born on the island is allowed to kill it. But not a man like you. If *you* kill the crocodile, you will never make it off the island alive."

Mason took one more hit off the beer, put the bottle down, and slid it away.

"I will keep you safe," Farhan said. "But you have to promise that you will take me with you when you go back to America."

"You can't keep me safe," Mason said. "Don't even try. And by the way, you're supposed to take a little bit of that Old Spice and slap your cheeks with it, not pour it all over your fucking body."

Mason started to get up. Farhan reached over and grabbed his forearm.

"I want to go to America. I will do anything it takes."

"Find that girl," Mason said. He broke his arm free from Farhan's grip, threw some money on the bar, and walked out.

———

Martin Sauvage stared at the face of the American. It wasn't a photograph. It was a drawing done by one of the local sketch artists, sent over on Sauvage's request from POLRI. The artist had worked patiently while Sauvage played back his memories from the day before. The armored vehicle half-destroyed by the bomb, Baya's men streaming out the back door, followed by the last man: white, fair skin, in the neighborhood of six feet tall, lean but muscular, light-brown hair cut close. Sauvage was almost certain he saw a thin scar running along the man's right eyebrow.

Now that he had the final sketch in front of him, every detail seemed right, and yet the overall effect was too blandly anonymous. It was a white face that could resemble any of a thousand men, especially to an Indonesian's eye. The old racist line that, unfortunately, was grounded in true human anthropology: *They all look alike to me.*

No, he couldn't send this out over the wire in a Red Notice. He knew he needed more. But he also knew this: *If I see him again, I'll know him in a second.*

His phone rang. It was the receptionist he shared with six other officers. The boss wanted to see him right away. Sauvage took the drawing with him and went down the hall to the corner office. Duval sat behind the desk, listening into his phone with a pained expression on his face. He looked briefly at Sauvage and nodded to the guest chair on the other side of the desk.

Sauvage sat down. Duval kept listening, massaging the bridge of his nose with two fingers. Until he finally said, "*Terima kasih,*" and hung up. Indonesian for "Thank you," literally meaning "It is accepted with love," although Duval was clearly not loving anything he'd just heard.

"That was Senior Commander Yuwono," Duval said. "He's going to issue another shoot-to-kill order at noon."

Sauvage nodded. He wasn't surprised. Yuwono had done the same thing the previous summer, although he didn't use the words "shoot to kill" or whatever the Indonesian equivalent might be. It was something vaguer like "The officers have been ordered to respond firmly and quickly to any resistance." Official-sounding words that really meant nothing more than blood in the streets.

"Baya has them running scared," Sauvage said. A statement so obvious, Duval didn't even bother acknowledging it. A man who used black money to finance radical terrorism, who freely landed on the roof of a downtown hotel and then escaped from Detachment 88, the best squad of commandos in the country . . .

*Yeah, he's gotten their attention.* Which meant another month of trigger-happy POLRI, with Interpol agents like Duval and Sauvage standing by with their tin badges, watching it all happen.

These were the words that men like Duval and Sauvage lived by: *Lethal force is permitted only in cases where there is an imminent threat to life.* It was the accepted international law, the standard recognized by Interpol agents all around the world. But here, today, those words meant almost nothing.

"You're leading the IRT," Duval said, meaning the Incident Response Team. "I need you to keep me in the loop at all times. Do not make any moves without talking to me first."

Sauvage nodded. He took out the drawing that the sketch artist had done, and slid it over the desk.

Duval took a moment to process what he was seeing. Then he slid the sketch back to Sauvage. "Stop wasting time on the American," he said. "If he's really going after Baya, then one or both of them will be dead soon. I don't want you to join them."

———

Luna sat at her desk, facing eight computer monitors, watching all of them without limiting her focus to any one screen. She listened to the voices in her earphones. A series of running conversations taking place in seven different countries at once.

More than her ability to fire a gun or disarm a man, it was her facility for languages, along with her talent for filtering important information from random noise, that had brought Luna to the Indonesian office. Here, to this land of a quarter-billion people on seventeen thousand islands, with easy access to the entire South Pacific, China, India, Japan—to more than half the population of the world.

Torino walked into the office and stood behind her. She ignored him, even as she felt a hand on her shoulder.

"Batam, confirm," she said, speaking in English. She listened hard for the response, until a lone voice came to her from the northernmost island in the country. Then she took off the earphones and looked at Torino. "I know where he's going."

Torino nodded. "We should send Mason alone this time."

She kept staring at him.

"He's the assassin," Torino said. "Let him do his job."

"If we don't help him, it's a suicide mission. With a ten percent chance of success. And I'll make sure that's in the report."

Torino took his hand away. "Prepare the mission," he said, and walked out of the room.

————

Sauvage walked down the plaza street, just outside the stadium. It was his habit to leave the office every day at lunchtime. He didn't want to be like the other agents who stayed inside all day, who took private cars back and forth between the office and their high-rise apartments, never setting foot on the foreign soil or interacting with the locals on the streets.

It was a huge and mysterious city, a foreign world of its own, and Sauvage was still trying to understand its rhythm. An armored POLRI vehicle drove by, honking its horn and forcing other vehicles off the street. The "respond firmly and quickly" order had been issued just a few minutes ago, but already Sauvage could see the change in every armed officer on the street. A day like this was a reminder that Suharto, who had once ruled this nation for thirty-one brutal years, still cast his long shadow over the city. The country's freedom was young and fragile. How easy for this capital city to slip right back into a police state.

Sauvage's cell phone rang. He answered it, stopping on the sidewalk to listen carefully.

"Are you absolutely sure about this intel?" he said. "If I were Baya, that's the last place I would go."

———

Mason walked back through the street, passing the vendors selling everything that could be sold and the smoke of a hundred cooking fires. Men and women, young and old, stared up at him as he passed. Children either cowered behind their parents or dared to circle him before running back to safety. The oppressive midday heat beat down on everyone and everything.

Mason was looking for the young girl who had sold him a pair of sunglasses and was still owed her money.

Was that the only reason he wanted to find her? Was it because she reminded him somehow of his own daughter back home? It was more than Mason could explain, even to himself. Maybe this was just the one simple thing he could hold on to, the one thing he could make right, here in this place where everything else was beyond his control.

His phone rang. When he answered it, he heard Luna's voice:

"Wheels up in thirty. We're going to Singapore."

# 6

Nick Mason found himself, once again, in a different world. But this time, he had to travel only fifteen miles to get there.

The team had set out from the Indonesian island of Batam, a strange mix of halfhearted luxury and squalor, partially built hotels next to tiny huts and garbage heaps. The city-state of Singapore was just across the busy strait that separated the Malay Peninsula from Indonesia. The sun had almost set, the last of the burning light reaching across the water from the western horizon. Not even seven o'clock yet, and the night was beginning—a way of life on all of these islands that hugged the equator, with twelve-hour days that started early and ended early. Boat traffic was busy on the strait—speedboats running circles around the slower ferries, luxury yachts taking tourists to the nightclubs and casinos of Singapore, a few smaller boats bringing men to the cheaper prostitutes of Batam.

Mason was onboard a Millennium 140 superyacht. The boat had no name. The sides were an unbroken shade of marine white. Cabin windows shaded, no chrome on the gunwales. Even the hull number was artfully covered by a tarp taken from the lifeboat. With 5,300 horsepower in the water jets and another 4,700 in the booster, this yacht was the fastest in its class, probably anywhere in the South Pacific. But it did everything it could to escape notice.

Only from inside could you appreciate the yacht's luxury. Master's quarters and five staterooms. A meeting room with seating for ten, all doors tightly closed. Mason sat across from Torino, Luna to his right, Farhan on the diagonal. The three crew members were elsewhere on the boat while the captain piloted it across the strait.

Torino pressed a button on the table's electronic console, and a large LED screen lowered from the ceiling. An image appeared. A man's face—the same face Mason had seen in Chicago, on the computer screen in Cole's office. The man who had informed Mason that Mason had been working for him all along. The man who told him he'd be on a plane to Jakarta the next morning.

Mason studied the face carefully. White, mid-fifties. Dark hair cut close, with gray on the sides. Radiating intelligence, self-assurance.

*The boss.*

"You'll be on land within thirty minutes," the man said. "The Singapore team is already in place."

Mason shifted his focus to everything else he could see on the screen. The background behind the man. An office wall, on one side the edge of some piece of artwork, on the other side the corner of a window.

Daylight. Natural sunlight streaming into the room.

Mason did the math in his head. Going on eight p.m. here, probably the middle of the day in this man's location.

Anywhere from four to nine times zones away.

Europe. Africa. The Middle East.

"The Singapore team will locate Baya as soon as he lands," the man said. His English was clean and precise. Too much so. A man who had learned it as a second language. "You'll be notified as soon as we have a window."

Mason had a dozen good reasons to stay quiet, but he spoke anyway. "Are you telling us you don't know when he's going to be there?"

Torino, Luna, and Farhan all looked at him at once, holding their breath. The face on the screen froze.

"Mr. Mason," the boss said after a beat. "Your job right now is to stay silent and listen to the plan."

"This isn't a plan," Mason said. "A plan means a map. Layout of the building. Entry. Exit. A plan means you have some fucking idea what's going to happen and—"

"Mr. Mason," the boss said, his voice sharpening. "You don't a have a need to know those details yet. When the window is open, you'll move in and execute your part of the plan."

"Another suicide mission."

The boss took a breath and let it out. Then he said, "I shouldn't have to explain this to you, but if you insist on wasting our time . . ."

Mason felt Luna's hand close tightly around his wrist. Mason shook it off.

"The Singapore Exchange is down fifteen percent today," the boss went on. "That's over a trillion American dollars in valuation."

Mason watched the man's face on the screen, not even sure how to respond. *We're about to get our asses blown off and he's reading us the fucking* Wall Street Journal!

"That's just one day's worth of damage to our organization, Mr. Mason. A security issue in the Asian region affects all of our interests there. And none of this would be happening if you had succeeded on your last mission."

As Mason looked away, he caught sight of Torino, staring at him with a tight, painful grimace.

"We cannot afford to miss this chance," the boss said. "Baya will land in Singapore within the next three hours. That's as narrow a window as we're going to get."

"We'll wait to hear from the team on land," Torino said, finally finding his voice. "We won't fail."

The man on the screen nodded. He didn't look completely convinced. Then the screen went blank.

Torino drew in his breath, seemed to go through a dozen different things he could say, finally settled on one. "You fucking American fool. Do you have any idea who you were just talking to?"

"No, I don't," Mason said. "What's his name?"

Torino just looked at him.

"Where was he calling from?"

"We don't have time for this," Luna cut in. "We have to get dressed."

"Into what?" Mason said.

"This is the richest city in Singapore," she said. "And we'll be track-ing one of the richest financiers in the world. Wherever he goes, it's not going to be cheap."

Farhan got to his feet, opened one of the doors, and motioned to Mason. "This way. I have your clothes ready."

Mason kept staring down Torino for another beat, then finally got up and followed Farhan.

When Mason was out of the room, Farhan grabbed him by the elbow, glanced back into the room, and leaned in close. "I told you, *saudara*. I will watch out for you."

"Just do your job," Mason said. "And stay out of the way."

———

Martin Sauvage touched down at the Singapore Changi Airport just after five p.m. An Interpol aide was waiting for him and drove him in his car toward the Interpol office in the Tanglin district. Sauvage looked out the window with undisguised wonder. He'd lived in Jakarta long enough to feel like one of ten million people pretending every day that the Third World didn't surround the city, sometimes as close as a jaywalk across the street. But now, after a thirty-five-minute flight, he suddenly found himself in the jewel of the South Pacific, rising high above the water and shining as brightly as the city of Oz.

The Interpol office was a marvel of modern architecture, looking like many layers of metal and glass plates stacked on top of each other. The largest regional office outside Lyon, it had become Interpol's main base of operations for this half of the world—the HQ of Asia, with a staff of eight hundred, about a third of them "secondments" like Sau-vage, officers on loan from a hundred other countries.

And, like Sauvage, effectively stripped of most of their powers.

Sauvage entered the building, passing four armed guards at the door, all holding HK416 assault rifles. The men were members of the Special Operations Force, elite soldiers chosen from the Commandos formation.

Indonesia had Detachment 88, and Singapore had the Special Operations Force, even better-equipped and better-trained. It had taken each of these men four extra years just to earn the right to wear this uniform.

An aide was waiting for him. "Inspector Sauvage," he said in a heavy Scottish brogue. "Welcome." When you were in an Interpol office anywhere in the world, you spoke English, French, Spanish, or Arabic.

Sauvage nodded to the man and shook his hand.

"President Kovalov is waiting for you," the aide said.

Sauvage didn't try to hide his surprise. Duval hadn't said anything about Interpol's president being here.

"He just arrived," the aide said. "He's anxious to speak with you."

The aide led Sauvage up the curving staircase, with large windows overlooking the evening traffic. Sauvage reviewed everything that he knew about Kovalov, which wasn't a hell of a lot. He'd been president for just over a year—a controversial pick given Russia's history of using Interpol as its own private international police force, issuing scores of Red Notices to track down political enemies and dissidents in other countries. Sauvage and his fellow agents were still holding their breath, waiting to see how badly this presidency would damage Interpol—just one hazard of working for an agency that was beholden to no one and everyone.

Kovalov put down his phone when Sauvage was led into the office. He stood up and shook the man's hand firmly. He was shorter than Sauvage expected, less severe-looking, his eyes less cold—in other words, everything he didn't expect from the head of one of Russia's security branches.

"How is your boss?" Kovalov asked in a heavy Russian accent. "Jacques and I have known each other for years."

"He's fine, thank you. I'll give him your regards."

"Forgive me," Kovalov said, "but I want to get right to this matter. You know Hashim Baya as well as anyone in Interpol. The Crocodile, as they call him. Am I correct?"

It was true that Sauvage knew all of the hard intel: where Baya was born, where he went to school, where he had made most of his money in the legitimate world of commercial development before moving into the shadows. The operations he had allegedly financed, a long string of terrorist acts attributed to groups like Jemaah Islamiyah, included the Bali bombing that had killed over two hundred people and severely injured just as many more.

But for all of the facts Sauvage could recite, he still didn't know the man. Not where it really mattered. He didn't know what motivated him, what drove him to suddenly begin using terror as a weapon against the world. Baya didn't strike Sauvage as a wild-eyed fanatic. He wore an Italian tailored suit, not a shalwar kameez.

For Sauvage, Hashim Baya was the ultimate enigma.

"I need you to help me understand something," Kovalov said. "This is the most secure city in the Pacific Rim. Maybe all of Asia. The most advanced technology, video surveillance on every corner. The most well-trained security force. Virtually incorruptible."

Sauvage nodded along with each point. The president was right. Singapore was the last place you'd go to evade notice. Or to buy your way out of it.

"So tell me," Kovalov said. "After barely escaping that raid in Jakarta, why would he come here?"

Sauvage tried to think of an answer. Anything at all he could say. There was nothing. He had no idea why Baya would come to Singapore.

And he was afraid to find out.

———

The sky was fully dark by the time the nameless yacht approached the Marina South Pier. Mason stood against the transom in the stern, watching the city's lights. He was dressed in a black Boglioli suit, perfectly tailored. White shirt and a black bow tie. He looked over at Luna in her black Versace dress—strapless, one thigh-high split. Diamonds hung from both ears, more diamonds around her neck. Torino came up onto the deck, wearing a suit the same color as Mason's.

As they pulled into a private marina just west of the main pier, Farhan deboarded first. He wore a simple suit with a straight black tie and a chauffeur's hat. Mason held out his hand for Luna as she stepped down the ladder. She took it without saying anything, then left him behind and went up the dock.

As they passed through the gate, their passports were handed back to them. The crew had already taken care of all the processing. Mason glanced at the fake name again before putting the passport back in his pocket.

Farhan pulled up to them in a black Mercedes-Maybach. Black was the theme for the evening. The other three team members got in, Torino in the front passenger seat, and they left the marina, joining the line of traffic into the heart of the city.

"You do everything we tell you," Torino said without looking back at him. "No cowboy shit or I'll put a bullet in your head myself."

———

Sauvage waited in the central control room. A half dozen techs operated a bank of video screens, the digital feed provided to Interpol by the Special Operations Force. Kovalov stood next to him. He'd taken control of the operation, and Sauvage could feel the tension in the room. Having the president of Interpol directly leading an operation was not a common occurrence.

"We have the airport covered," Kovalov said. "Every helipad, all of the marinas. Every possible point of entry."

"We don't have intel on how he'll arrive?"

"Singapore has two hundred kilometers of coastline. That's the weakest link."

One of the techs switched to the feed coming from the South Marina. Then another to Keppel Harbour. More than a dozen major ferry lines arrived in Singapore from different points in Indonesia and Malaysia. An arrival every few minutes, bringing more and more people as the city's night life officially began. Tourists, businessmen, sellers and buyers, all drawn to the glittering lights.

Sauvage watched with a growing unease as the overloaded ferries emptied their passengers through the processing gates and into the city. He wanted to stop them, wanted to close every port of entry and seal off the city, but he knew that wouldn't happen. He didn't have the power to do it—not even Kovalov did—and even if the ports were closed, Baya would simply wait until they were open again.

Or else find another way in.

"There," Sauvage said when he spotted a figure on one of the screens. "Zoom in."

The tech put his crosshairs on the figure that Sauvage had indicated, and enlarged the view until it was almost too grainy to make out.

"Is that him?" Kovalov said, leaning in closer.

"No," Sauvage said. "He wouldn't just walk off a ferry. But I think that's one of his men."

It was the green shirt with the white trim along the collar. Sauvage remembered seeing it worn by the scores of men who were taken with Baya in Jakarta.

"There's another one," Kovalov said, pointing to another man in the same shirt. "And another."

Sauvage looked from one screen to another—a different harbor, unloading a different ferry. He saw a green shirt waiting in the processing line, with another just behind him. And then another and another.

*Why the shirts? They must know we'll recognize them.*

It was a mystery he didn't have time to solve. He checked his watch. It was just after eight p.m.

And Singapore was being invaded.

————

As Mason stood in the Gardens by the Bay, the park that stretched along the waterfront, with the futuristic artificial trees rising over the sidewalks, he stared up at the eight-billion-dollar Marina Bay Sands, the most mind-bending landmark in all of Singapore. Maybe all of Asia.

There were three separate bowed towers rising fifty floors above the ground, with a giant boomerang-shaped structure seemingly balanced across the top. An impossible, otherworldly thing to build, unlike anything he'd ever seen in Chicago or anywhere else, and yet here it was in front of him. From the very top of the boomerang, what they called the SkyPark, a hundred distant faces peered down at him.

"Nothing yet." The voice in his ear, Luna's. He was wearing a Bluetooth earpiece again and felt the weight of a new Glock 30S in the holster beneath his jacket. It had been left for him in the trunk of the car, courtesy of the Singapore team.

He considered the people all around him. Some were his allies. But he had no idea how he'd ever know unless somebody started firing and everything went to shit.

"Mason." Torino's voice.

"Nothing," Mason said. Then he spotted the man about fifty yards ahead of him. He was wearing the green shirt with the white trim. Mason tracked him down the sidewalk, keeping his distance as the man waited at a crosswalk.

"I have one of his men," Mason said. That same sensation coming over him now, the automatic shift into mission mode. Everything slowing down and coming into hyperfocus.

"Keep on him," Torino said.

*No shit*, Mason thought. He waited until the pedestrian light turned, and followed the man across the wide street that ran in front of the Sands.

"He's going into the Sands," Mason said. "I'm right behind him."

———

In the control room, Sauvage watched one of the green shirts walking toward the entrance of the Sands.

"Do we have a feed inside?" he asked.

"I can get one," the tech said. A minute later, Sauvage saw the interior of the lobby. A hundred well-dressed patrons milling around, walking in every direction, to the restaurants, to the casino.

*There.*

He saw the man in the green shirt standing in the center of the lobby. Seeming to wait. He was joined by another green shirt. Then another.

"What the hell?" Sauvage said as it all came back to him:

It was his first on-the-ground introduction to Hashim Baya, or at least to his influence. Detachment 88, working on an Interpol tip, found a PF-98 Queen Bee unguided missile—stolen from an Indonesian military installation—pointed directly at the Sands from across the straits.

The missile never fired. It was all tracked back to Jemaah Islamiyah. Who else? But how did they get their hands on such a weapon?

It took money. And influence.

It had to be Hashim Baya.

Now Sauvage was watching Baya's men gathering in the very same building they had once tried to blow up with a missile. One of the biggest and richest casinos in the world. A Louis Vuitton Crystal Pavilion that floated on the water. A nightclub, the Pangaea, that served a cocktail garnished with gold flecks and a one-carat diamond for the smooth price of twenty-six thousand American dollars. The ultimate symbol of Western decadence in Southeast Asia.

Was Baya going to try to destroy it again? Or was he just making a statement? That he wasn't weak, that he hadn't gone into hiding, that even after barely escaping the raid in Jakarta, the capital of his home country, he could still go anywhere in the world he wanted? Walk through Times Square or down the Champs-Élyssés?

No.

Somehow, that didn't feel right to Sauvage.

He didn't need to flex his muscles for anybody. This was something else.

Sauvage kept watching the men on the screen as they finally started moving again. He was about to look away when he caught sight of another man, this one in a black suit.

"That one," Sauvage said, pointing to the figure on the screen. "Let me see him."

The tech zoomed in on the man's face as he paused for just a moment.

*The American.*

"I'll stay in contact," Sauvage said as he brushed past Kovalov. "I'm going to the Sands."

On a quiet and dark section of Singapore's north shore, across the river from Malaysia, a small fishing boat cut its motor and drifted toward a lonely dock.

One of the passengers looked across the river into the Malaysian jungle and remembered a time when he had been there as a boy. His father had taken him on a hunting trip, and when they were deep in the jungle, they had both seen a large bird flying through the trees high above them. The boy's father had put a hand on his shoulder and stopped him abruptly, then had pulled him back into the cover of an areca palm frond.

"What is that bird?" the boy had asked him, in Indonesian.

"That is the Malaysian honey buzzard."

"That is a funny name."

"Listen carefully," the father had said. "Whenever you see that bird, you must make sure to take cover. Never let that bird see you on the ground."

"Why, will it attack us?"

"No, something much worse. Do you see that beehive, in that highest tree?"

The boy strained to look. He could barely see it, a dark mass two hundred feet above the ground.

"That's the giant honeybees' hive," the father said. "If they decide to attack you, they will sting you a thousand times. No man can survive that."

That made the boy afraid. Even now he remembered the feeling.

"If the bird sees you," the father said, "he will fly up and strike at the hive until they come out. Then he'll lead them down to you, and the bees will believe that you are the enemy, not the bird. You will die on the ground as the bird flies back to the hive and enjoys his feast."

Hashim Baya had remembered that lesson, of the bird who was smart enough to create its own fatal diversion before raiding a beehive, for the rest of his life. And he remembered it now as he stepped ashore onto Singaporean soil.

# 7

Nick Mason walked through the most extravagant casino in Asia, wearing a tailored Italian suit that cost more than the down payment on his first house back in Canaryville. *I'm in a fucking James Bond movie,* he thought, even as he realized the hard reality: James Bond acted of his own free will, not with a constant threat to his family hanging over his head.

And 007 was never stupid enough to try to kill someone with a thousand other people in the room.

Mason circled the casino slowly, trying to look like nothing more than another well-dressed foreigner deciding which game to play. The polished, mirrored floors reflected the intricately sculpted gold lattice that stretched high above the entire gaming area. Dealers wearing white shirts and gold vests were busy at every table. There was a buzz in a dozen different languages, the hollow metallic ringing of the electronic slot machines from the next room. A thin haze of cigarette smoke hung in the air.

"What's the play?" Mason said into his Bluetooth. "We won't have a clean shot with all of these people in the room."

"Luna's above you," Torino said from wherever he was in the building. "Locate the target and then get out of the way."

Mason didn't look up immediately. He walked a few more yards and then let his gaze drift upward. Through the sculpted gold lattice, he could barely discern the outline of a walkway circling the entire casino.

Luna's voice materialized in Mason's ear. "I'm in position."

Mason pictured her assembling a sniper rifle. With a decent scope, it wouldn't be a hard shot as long as she had a clear sight line through the lattice.

But even at this distance, a scope needed to be zeroed in—something Eddie the onetime army sniper had told him more than once. He flashed back to the last time Eddie had covered his back. Then he came back into the moment when he saw a man in a green shirt walking into the casino.

It made no sense. This guy wasn't even trying to hide who he worked for. *Might as well wear a fucking sports jersey with Baya's name on the back.*

Mason watched the man circle the room; then he saw two other men in dark suits approach him. Obviously, plainclothes security forces. They stopped the green shirt, whispered into both his ears, then each grabbed an elbow and led him away.

Mason spotted another green shirt. Then another. More security men coming into the room, trying to do this without causing any commotion. Mason kept watching. It was like a video game as more green shirts entered the room and as the dark suits scrambled to quietly intercept them.

Patrons were starting to notice what was going on around them. The buzz got louder. A few people headed for the exits. Everyone else stayed in the room, a distracted and curious mass of gamblers who were temporarily forgetting about their games. The dealers looked up from the tables, confused and agitated.

More green shirts came in, this time in one thick mass. At least twelve of them, walking in tight formation. Mason strained to see the man who walked in the center.

A flash of a white dinner jacket. A neatly trimmed beard. Dark sunglasses.

Hashim Baya.

Mason spoke into his Bluetooth: "Target located."

The Special Operations Force had a security center just outside the hotel. It blended into a line of other nondescript maintenance and storage buildings—part of the 250-acre nature park when it officially opened in 2012, then later upgraded with even better surveillance equipment after the missile scare. Sauvage left his Interpol vehicle parked outside and entered a special code into the digital lock on a side doorway. A uniformed SOF commando opened it.

"I need your commander," Sauvage said, flashing his Interpol badge.

The agent was under no obligation to honor the badge, but he nodded and took Sauvage into the surveillance room on the second floor. There was another bank of video screens—even more than at Interpol. The screens were watched by a mix of dark-suited agents and more uniformed commandos.

Sauvage found the commander, introduced himself, and said, "Bring up the Sands. The casino."

The commander gave an order, and an instant later the large central screen showed the casino floor. Sauvage saw three men in green shirts being escorted to the exit.

"We're intercepting every one of them we can find," the commander said. "If it's wearing a green shirt, we're stopping it."

"Where are you taking them?"

"We have a holding cell on Commerce Street. It's already full."

Sauvage kept peering at the screen. "You have other angles?"

Someone toggled to another view. Another man in a green shirt being calmly removed from the casino. He didn't put up a fight, didn't protest in any way.

"This make any sense to you?" Sauvage didn't expect a real answer.

Another view. This time, a large group of green shirts entered the room. In their midst was a man wearing a white dinner jacket.

Neatly trimmed beard. Dark sunglasses.

*Baya.*

The Sands wasn't much more than a hundred meters away. Sauvage could have covered the distance in a matter of seconds, could have pushed his way through the men surrounding Baya before they even realized what was happening.

He could have gotten close enough to look Baya in the eye.

The commander had a different plan. "How the hell did he get onto this island?" he yelled, seemingly to everyone else in the room. "Seal off that room! Get everyone else out!"

"You're going to tip him off," Sauvage said. "And cause a mass panic."

"Would you rather he blow them all up, Inspector?"

"Nothing will happen as long as he's in the room," Sauvage said. "A man like that pays for suicide bombers. He doesn't become one himself."

Sauvage kept watching as Baya walked among the gaming tables. His men surrounded him and pushed everyone else away as they made their way through the room.

Why did he come here? Gambling was haram, one of the forbidden things in Islam, right up there with eating pork and drinking alcohol.

"Cover every door," the commander ordered a subordinate. "Nobody comes in; nobody wearing a green shirt goes out. Get the undercovers to start clearing the rest of the floor, one table at a time. No panic, no rush. Just make it happen."

Sauvage kept watching the man on the screen. The man who had taken his family from him.

It couldn't be this easy.

———

"Where's the target?" Luna said.

"He entered through the easternmost door. One hundred yards in, now moving north."

"The poker tables?"

"Just beyond. I'll get closer."

Before Mason could take a step, one of the dark-suited agents approached him. "Sir," the agent said, "you need to leave right now."

"I'm just finding my wife," Mason said. "Then we'll go."

The agent hesitated a beat, then finally let Mason walk past him.

"Baccarat tables," Mason said into his Bluetooth as he spotted the phalanx of green shirts. "They're still moving."

"The white suit," Luna said. "I have him."

Two more black-suited agents pushed past Mason, heading toward the group.

"They're closing on him," Mason said. "You don't have much time."

———

Sauvage watched the man in the white suit pause by one of the tables, as if he was considering making a bet.

*What the hell? It's insanity.*

"We're moving in," the commander said. "We have the group surrounded."

A circle of black suits closed in like a great, living net about to capture an entire herd of animals at once.

"We've got him," the commander said. "There's nowhere to go."

Sauvage held his breath and watched, already working it out in his head: Singapore would have official jurisdiction, but in all of Asia this was the one place where Interpol held the most sway. That meant Sauvage might just get a shot at him. He could actually sit in the same room with him, the two men on opposite sides of a table. Face-to-face with the Crocodile.

"Where is he?" the commander said, peering at the screen. "*Where is he?*"

———

"Where is he?" Luna said. "I can't see him through this goddamned lattice."

Torino's voice: "Track him. Wait for him to reappear."

"I know what I'm doing," Luna said. "Just get me a clear shot again."

Mason spotted the long rifle barrel extending from the railing. Then he scanned the room and figured the geometry: Baya needed to move a good ten feet in one direction or the other.

Mason was caught inside the circle of black suits now—ordinarily the last place in the world he wanted to be, completely surrounded not just by cops but by supercops. But in this moment, he was nothing more than an innocent bystander caught in the wrong web. Mason moved forward, tried to push his way past the first green-shirted man.

He needed to make Baya move. Play dumb, make a scene—whatever the hell it took.

Mason tried to push his way past another green shirt. The man turned and yelled foreign words in his face. Another green shirt grabbed at his arm. Then a black suit grabbed that man, and from one second to the next it was suddenly a rugby scrum, every man either pushing or pulling away from the center of the pile.

"I don't see him!" Luna's voice in his ear, cutting through the indistinguishable shouting of the men.

Mason pushed through, searching for the one white jacket. The entire mass was moving now, toward the nearest exit. The green shirts trying to escape, or the black suits trying to remove them—Mason couldn't tell, and it didn't matter anyway.

*Where the fuck is Baya?*

There was a bottleneck at the doorway, everyone pressed closely together. Luna's voice in his ear again. "I don't have a shot!"

The men spilled out into the huge lobby. The uniformed commandos were waiting for them. Mason kept searching for the white jacket even as a commando pulled him aside, demanding to see his passport.

Mason didn't respond. He kept scanning the room all around him.

There was nowhere for Baya to go. Nowhere to escape. But somehow, he had disappeared.

————

Sauvage held his Interpol badge in front of him as he worked through the opposite door of the casino, watching as the men were surrounded and pushed out into the lobby.

Sauvage followed, his badge still held before him. Some of the agents responded and let him through—for others it took precious more seconds to explain himself. When he finally reached the lobby, he saw the uniformed commandos sorting through the green shirts as if panning for that one nugget of gold.

He didn't see the white jacket.

But as he kept searching frantically, he caught sight of something else. There, by the door, a man in a dark suit.

*The American.*

A commando was examining his passport. Sauvage called across the room: "Stop that man!"

He grabbed another commando and tried to explain what he needed, finally gave up, and made his way through the throng, pushing and being stopped again and again, watching helplessly as the American finally went through the exit, out into the night.

When Sauvage finally fought his way to the door, the American was gone.

———

"I see him!" It was Torino's voice in Mason's ear now. "Moving east from the Sands. Into the park."

Mason ran across the street, feeling the weight of the Glock shifting in his shoulder holster. Horns honked at him as he made the other side and entered the great park.

"I need more," Mason said into his Bluetooth. "Give me a landmark."

Not that he knew one thing about this place. If this were any park in Chicago, he'd have the guy.

Another voice came on the Bluetooth, speaking a language Mason didn't recognize. Then another.

"That's the Singapore team," Torino said. "They have containment. He's moving toward the Flower Dome."

"What the hell is that?"

"On the water. The dome on the left."

Mason made his way through the park, passing under the towering artificial trees. All around him were hundreds of people. Thousands. Taking pictures, speaking every language on earth. Black-suited agents were sprinkled liberally through the crowd, many of them eyeing Mason with alarm as he ran.

"I'm moving closer," Torino said. "I may have a shot."

"Don't be a fool," Luna said. "Wait until I'm close enough. I can get up onto the walkway and—"

"We don't have time for that!" Torino said. "If I have a shot, I'm taking it. If I'm caught, you two get back to the boat."

Mason was getting closer to the clear domes, each one impossibly huge and lit up against the night sky.

He spotted the group of green shirts and ran faster.

———

Sauvage ran through the park, breathing hard. He had managed to connect his earpiece and was patched through to an open line, Interpol and SOF working together. A constant stream of orders, punctuated by reports of a sighting just outside the hotel, then in the park, then near the Flower Dome. They were chasing a ghost, everywhere and nowhere. It was all impossible, but Sauvage didn't have time to make sense of it. He just kept running.

This buzz, this madness, this feeling of no breath and bleeding feet. Of being late yet again to where he needed to be.

Again, just like that November day in Paris.

Sauvage saw the crowd of men and drew on a second wind that came from somewhere inside him. More commandos, more green shirts. Rifles waved, handcuffs slapped on wrists. Men spread-eagled on the ground all around him.

Sauvage made himself stop and catch his breath. He scanned the scene carefully. No white suit. No Baya.

But there, on the opposite side of this concrete plaza, in the ambient glow coming from the huge dome behind him, Sauvage saw the American again. And this time, the American stared right back at him.

They didn't nod at each other. Didn't make any formal acknowledgment at all. They didn't need to.

From one moment standing still, to the next: Sauvage was running again, as fast as he could.

———

Mason saw the stranger on the other side of the plaza and flashed back to the street in Jakarta. The explosion, then the doors of the van thrown open. Mason out on the street, gunfire and blood and chaos.

A pale-yellow car stopped on the far side of the street. One second to see the stranger's face and the way he took stock of everything around him. One second for Mason to recognize what he'd know anywhere in the world.

This man was a cop.

The same cop who was moving toward him now. Mason slipped away, along the edge of the dome, back into the darkness.

A voice in his Bluetooth, in another language.

"They have him," Torino said.

More voices, shouting. To Mason it was just noise.

"One person talk," he said. "In English. Tell me where he is."

"They say he's back by the marina," Torino said.

"We're all getting played here," Mason said. "You know that, right?"

More noise in Mason's ear. A dozen voices at once.

"They're building a hotel right across the street from the marina," Torino said. "They say he's inside."

Mason remembered the hotel. He had seen it when they all got off the boat. Two city blocks down the street, already twenty stories high, lit up with the construction lights that hung on the upper, still-open floors.

*Why the fuck would he go there?*

But everyone else was already moving. The green shirts of Baya's men, the black suits of the Special Operations Force, uniforms of the local cops, and whatever the hell his Singapore team members were wearing. Several packs all hunting the same prey, with one wild-card cop directly on Mason's tail.

Mason ran through the forest—a real forest of actual trees this time, not manmade constructions—then around the edge of a small lake and back toward the waterfront. He passed one dead cop on the ground, then a man in a green shirt, then another man dressed like a tourist—either a real tourist or someone trying to look like one. He picked up Torino at the edge of the construction site. Luna was still somewhere behind them.

More bodies lay on the ground, all along the entrance to the site. In the darkness, Mason couldn't tell which side they were on or if they were just innocents caught in the cross fire.

Torino appeared at his side. "Let's go," he said. He pushed a chained gate open, just wide enough to slip through. Mason followed him.

The facade was already roughed in around the ground floor. Here inside the gate, everything was even darker. A pure blackness untouched by the ambient light of the sky or of the city around them.

"No fucking way," Mason said. But Torino had already moved to the nearest door. It was a simple sheet of plywood. He pulled it open and went inside.

Gunshots splintered the wood. Torino dived sideways, and Mason put his back against the door's edge. He looked down and saw Torino holding his arm.

Mason waited a beat, peeked around the edge, drew fire, and spotted the flashes from two guns. Eleven o'clock and two o'clock. He went to one knee as he put himself in the doorway again, heard the slugs passing above his head as he fired two shots at the first target, then two at the second. Two more at each before retreating.

Silence.

Mason stepped inside, ready to fire again. Two men in green shirts were on the ground.

"Torino is hit," Mason said into his Bluetooth.

"I'll live," Torino said. "Find Baya."

As Mason advanced through the ground floor, his eyes adjusted to the darkness. Until he could finally make out the figure against the far wall. He ducked behind a cement mixer.

*If he wanted to shoot me, he already would have.*

"I'm right here," the man said in an impassive voice. "What are you afraid of?"

Mason looked around the cement mixer. The man was standing with his hands out. Mason couldn't see anyone else around him.

Mason stood, pointed his gun at the man's body mass, and took a few steps forward. The man didn't move.

Mason came closer. The man was wearing a white dinner jacket. He had taken off his sunglasses.

Could this really be the Crocodile? The international financier of terror himself, hiding in this dark half-built room?

Mason had seen Baya in the van, and now as he came close enough to put his gun against this man's chest, he learned three important facts:

Number one, this man had the same build and the same neatly trimmed beard, but he was *not* Hashim Baya.

Number two, as Mason reached to open the man's jacket, he saw that it was green on the inside. How many of these men could have posed as Baya, all over the goddamned city, just by turning their jackets inside out?

And, number three, now that the man's jacket was open, Mason saw the explosives on the suicide vest strapped around his waist.

It all happened in an instant. As the man reached down to pull the detonator, Mason dropped his Glock and grabbed the man's hand. As they struggled, Mason realized the man was trying to force himself down to the ground. The explosives must have a secondary mercury detonator—the bomb goes off as soon as your body is no longer vertical.

Mason fought to keep the man standing and to keep his hands away from his chest. Their faces were close enough to see each other clearly. Mason and the man who seemed happy, even wild-eyed *ecstatic*, at this chance to give up his life.

Mason was losing the struggle. He couldn't keep him up for much longer.

Adriana's face flashed in his mind. Then Gina's.

Then a bullet passed cleanly through the man's forehead.

Mason caught him just in time, held him up, and turned to see Luna behind him, holding her Glock.

"Get out of here," Mason said. "Right now."

"I think I can deactivate his vest."

"*Think* is not good enough," Mason said. "Get the fuck out of here."

Luna hesitated, then turned and ran. Mason waited a few beats, his arms starting to quiver under the dead weight. He backed the man against the wall, let him slide downward into a sitting position. He wasn't even sure *that* would work. One slightly wrong move, and it would be over.

A flash of light and . . . He didn't even know if he'd feel it.

When Mason was satisfied that the man might stay in this position, he carefully let go. He backed away a few steps, saw the man start to tilt, and made his decision. He ran.

Just as he cleared the doorway, he felt the heat and the concussive force against his back.

———

Sauvage stopped running when he heard the explosion. It came from the direction of the marina.

"I have an explosion on the waterfront," he said into his earpiece.

He heard the confirmation from the SOF commander. Forces were on the way.

He didn't hear anything from Interpol HQ.

"President Kovalov," he said. "Are you there?"

Nothing.

Then the distinct sound of gunfire on the line.

Sauvage started running again.

———

Back at the Interpol office, the second and larger suicide squad gained entry to the building, shooting their way through the few remaining commandos left on guard. Two of the suicide squad had been killed, as well as all six guards, including the two gunned down at the top of the stairs.

Kovalov was on the phone in his office when he heard the shooting.

He put down the phone, opened the bottom drawer in his deck, and took out his Makarov .380 ACP. A weapon he was forbidden, as an agent of Interpol, to use anywhere outside this building.

He shot the first man who came through the door. He was about the shoot the second when that man opened his vest and detonated the explosives strapped around his chest.

———

When Sauvage arrived three minutes later, he was not allowed into the building. He stood outside and stared up at the windows that had been blown out on the front side of the building.

He had been thinking too small, he realized. He figured all Baya wanted to do was plant his flag in Singapore, make a point to the rest of the world that he could go anywhere he wanted to.

But Sauvage never dreamed he would actually take out the president of Interpol.

———

Luna wrapped up Torino's bloody arm. He'd been hit high in the triceps, close to the shoulder. Mason stood alone against the stern rail of the boat. He stayed there for a long time, looking out at the lights of Singapore as the boat made its way back to Indonesia.

The team had failed. Again.

Mason had no idea what this would mean for him.

Or, ten thousand miles away, for Gina and Adriana.

———

Singapore was a modern citadel surrounded by countries that, in many ways, were still trapped in a distant past. But the explosions on this night broke open a wave of primal, animal panic across the entire city.

Businesses barricaded their doors. The piers were closed. All flights to and from the airport were canceled. Armed commandos patrolled every inch of the Gardens by the Bay. There were flashing lights around the sites of both explosions, the sirens still echoing in every corner of the city. Everyone had to wait through the night for the city to breathe out again.

A single figure stood on the SkyPark, the giant boomerang atop the three pillars of the Marina Bay Sands. From here, this man had the perfect view of the city, looking down at it and watching the events of the night unfold like pieces moving on a great game board.

As the man stepped away from the view, another man handed him a thin file folder. When he opened it, Hashim Baya saw an old mug shot of the man he had met in the armored van in Jakarta, along with the man's name and hometown.

The man who, Baya now knew, had been brought to this side of the world with the singular goal of killing him.

The man who was still out there somewhere, in the chaos of this city or, perhaps by now, on the water that surrounded it.

The American, alive and still hunting.

Nicholas James Mason of Chicago, Illinois.

# 8

Farhan found Mason on the afterdeck. He came to the rail and stood beside him, looking out at the fading lights of Singapore.

"They want you below," Farhan said. He was still wearing his chauffeur's uniform.

Mason didn't move.

"They sent me up here to find you," Farhan said. "They want you right now."

Mason waited another beat, then followed Farhan down the stairs to the main cabin of the yacht. Torino and Luna were in the meeting room where the team had been given their briefing earlier that evening. Torino sat with his shirt off, his left arm heavily wrapped in white bandages. His face was drained of color and there was a raw scrape across his left cheek. Luna sat next to him, her arms folded, staring ahead at nothing. She had put on a white bathrobe over her dress.

"Hit the bone?" Mason asked, nodding at the bandages.

"All muscle," Torino said. "Clean through."

"He's lost blood," Luna said. "Someone should look at it."

"We have someone in Jakarta," Torino said.

"So what happens now?" Mason asked. He took a quick glance around the room. Two doors, but only one leading outside. If Torino said anything to heighten the threat against his family because of this mission's failure, Mason would need to act. The Glock had been taken from him as soon as he stepped onto the boat. But now he noticed the grimace of pain on Torino's face as the man shifted in his chair.

He was weak. Even unarmed, Mason could kill him in five seconds.

Torino pressed the button on the table, and the video screen lowered from the ceiling. It blinked to life, and they all saw the same dead-serious face they had seen on the way to Singapore.

"Before we do anything else," the boss said, "I want your briefing."

Torino nodded once, then began. He detailed the entire mission— every move they had made, from the moment they set foot on Singapore soil. Locating Baya, pursuing him, the trap in the abandoned building. The boss listened to every word carefully, until Torino was done. Only then did he speak.

"Mr. Torino, your job is to plan and coordinate the mission. How do you end up running down the streets like some kind of gunslinger and then getting yourself shot?"

"I didn't have confidence that Mason was—"

The man cut him off. "This is not about Mason!" For one moment, the machinelike facade was broken. "You've had two windows now and you've missed both of them."

The room was silent as the boss took a moment to read something on his desk, probably a written report.

"Mr. Mason, what's your view of this mission's failure?"

The room stayed silent for another beat. Mason considered what he should say, weighing the risks of putting anyone else in this room in a bad light.

*Fuck it.*

"What mission?" Mason said. "We got sent to kill someone who wasn't even there."

The boss nodded in silence, then said, "Bad intel?"

"How many times do I have to say this?" Mason asked. "You don't move until you have a map, a blueprint, a timeline, a way in and a way out. And your target is clearly identified."

"It sounds like you're trying to avoid accountability," the boss said.

"I'm not avoiding anything. You can't blame me for something I had no control over. And if you do anything to my family . . ."

Mason took a beat. *For once in your life*, he told himself, *get a grip and be smart.*

"If you play that card," Mason said, "you lose me as an asset. You know it and I know it."

The boss processed this. Everyone in the room waited silently.

Until finally the boss spoke: "We're going to do things differently. Mr. Mason will take tactical control of the next mission, once the target has been located again. Mr. Torino, you will move back to Support."

Torino stared across the table at Mason.

"Now, get back to Jakarta," the boss said. "And find your target."

———

It was just after four a.m. in Singapore when Martin Sauvage finished his two projects. Once he found the video surveillance from the Marina South Pier, clearly showing the four figures coming ashore from the Millennium yacht, he could establish the beginning of the timeline. Three men in suits, one of whom put on a chauffeur's cap. The fourth, a woman with black curly hair, wearing a skintight cocktail dress.

Sauvage followed all four members of the team from one camera's view to another. It was made more complicated as they split apart, but he patiently worked each thread separately until all four were reunited on the boat approximately two and a quarter hours later.

One of the men was the American, the man Sauvage had tried to chase down himself. The other two men and the woman were unknowns.

The ship itself was also unknown. Sauvage could make out no hull number or other external markings in the surveillance video. And even if he could, it probably wouldn't matter. The ship would be owned by a private individual in a foreign country outside the reach of Interpol. Or else, it would be registered to a shell company that was owned by yet another shell company, in an infinite loop leading nowhere.

All Sauvage had was the silent video, after the sun had gone down and all of the shooting started, and the American and one of his team-mates were converging on the half-built hotel just off the Coastal Expressway. The teammate goes down. The American goes inside. The woman shows up and also goes inside. The woman comes out first, then the American, simultaneous with the flash of light.

Then onto the boat and they are gone.

That was the first of the two projects. The second was much easier to put together—the single video surveillance outside the Interpol office. A dozen commandos leave the building. Ninety-plus minutes pass with nothing remarkable to see on the streets. Then the six men converging, appearing out of nowhere. No vehicles seen. Just an empty street in one moment and then the men coming together in the frame, from six different directions.

They storm through the front doors of the office, assault rifles already blazing and shattering the front windows. Twenty-nine seconds pass, and then another flash of light.

Sauvage sat back in his chair, rubbing his eyes. He was in a guest office at the Special Operations Force headquarters building in Singapore's central district. The sun was just coming up. The city was waking up from a troubled night. A nightmare that was all too real.

Sauvage would take these videos back to Jakarta with him. But before he closed the files, he checked the two timelines once more. He compared those to his own timeline: arriving in the city, going to the Interpol office, then the SOF outpost near the Sands. Then everything that happened afterward. He came to two conclusions:

The American, and the other three with him, had been one step ahead of Sauvage all night long.

And Hashim Baya had been another step ahead of them all. Enough to send everyone else running around in circles while he took out the president of Interpol himself, turning the whole night into the biggest fuck-you of all time.

*How does he know what we're going to do before we even do it?*

Nick Mason walked down the busy street, feeling the morning heat as it wrapped its arms around him. He breathed in the pungent chaos of Jakarta, a dramatic change from the immaculate, almost sterile air of Singapore.

This felt more like home.

The thought surprised him, but it was true. If Singapore was the North Side of this part of the world, with its clean streets, expensive Rush Street restaurants, and the ivied walls of Wrigley Field, then Jakarta was the South Side, with the dumpsters in the alleys, Harold's Fried Chicken, and the gaudy exploding scoreboard of old Comiskey Park.

Mason walked by the electronics store where he had seen the news reports of the raid on the Sultan Hotel. Today, the screens all showed the wreckage of the Interpol office in Singapore, and the dozens of carefully roped-off crime scenes all across the rest of the city. As Mason kept walking, he scanned the street carefully, pausing on every young face.

He was looking for the girl.

He did not see her at her usual spot just outside the Gama Tower. She had been replaced by a young boy selling knock-off DVDs of American movies. Mason stopped and asked the boy in English if he knew where the girl was. He looked back up at Mason, not understanding a word. Mason gave him a fifty-thousand-rupiah note, worth less than five dollars American. The boy held it with wide eyes, said a few words to him in Indonesian, and shouted them again even as Mason turned and went inside the building.

Mason found Luna in the control room. The six different computer screens showed a mixture of videos and rolling streams of text and numbers. Raw information that Mason would never be able to decipher. Luna sat in the chair, staring straight ahead. She was wearing a simple outfit of slacks and a white blouse. No makeup. The way she had looked last night, in Singapore—that was mission mode only.

She glanced up when she noticed Mason, as if breaking from a reverie. She went back to typing on her keyboard without saying a word.

"Where's Torino?"

She just shook her head.

"You know why he went into that building ahead of you . . ."

She stopped typing and turned her chair. "He put his emotions before the mission's objective," she said. "Even with an American on the team, he's the one who turned into the cowboy."

Mason nodded. "Show me the house."

She didn't move.

"I want to see it," he said. "Bring it up."

She typed on her keyboard for a few seconds. Then the image appeared on one of the screens. The house in Denver. As Mason stared at it, he saw his ex-wife, Gina, sitting at the kitchen table. She was going through a pile of bills—just another everyday chore.

"She's remarried?" Luna asked.

Mason nodded.

"If they end up fucking on the kitchen table, you're going to regret this."

Mason looked at her.

"Your family is not in danger right now," she said. "Like you said last night, you're still a valuable asset. But that could change in a minute."

"I know."

He put the phone in his pocket and turned to leave.

"Mason," she said.

He stopped.

"Next time you find a suicide bomber, don't send me out of the room like you're a fucking superhero."

"You're welcome," he said, and then he walked out.

Torino was approaching the same doorway. His left arm was in a sling. He eyed Mason for a beat without saying a word. Mason kept walking down the hall.

He went into his own empty office, sat down at the desk, wondering what the hell he was supposed to do there. But then another figure appeared in his doorway. It was Farhan.

"I found the girl from the street," he said. "Come with me."

———

"Why did you leave the office?"

Martin Sauvage was back in Jakarta, sitting across from Jacques Duval in the boss's office. He'd known this man for over a decade, going back to their days in Paris. They had worked the streets together, solved cases, broken up riots. Duval had attended the christening of his son. Duval had even flown all the way back to Paris to attend the funeral of that same son and the woman who bore him. In all that time, Sauvage had never heard him ask a question like this.

"I should have stayed," Sauvage said. "Borrowed a pistol and died alongside President Kovalov."

"You're not answering my question. Why did you leave?"

Sauvage waited a beat. There was no other way to say it.

"I saw the American."

Duval let out a breath and looked out the window, shaking his head slowly.

"He was ahead of us here in Jakarta. I knew he'd be ahead of us in Singapore. Find the American and you find—"

"So did he? Did he lead you right to Baya?"

Sauvage waited a beat. "You know he didn't."

"I'm not saying you could have stopped six men in a suicide squad," Duval said. "But I've seen you on the streets. I think there's a chance you would have found a way to make it turn out different."

"The president of Interpol is dead and it happened on our case. I get that. But—"

"Do you know how many countries were against his appointment? Now Kovalov dies a goddamned hero and Russia wants their director of foreign intelligence to take over. Who's going to say no to them right now?"

"I can't help you with any of that," Sauvage said. "All I can do is find Baya."

"This is personal for you," Duval said. "I know that. But maybe that was a mistake."

"What are you saying?"

"I never should have asked you to hunt the man you believe responsible for the death of your wife and son."

"Jacques, whatever you're about to do . . ."

"I can't sit by and watch this thing destroy you," Duval said. "You've had enough."

———

As Farhan led Mason through the streets of Jakarta, it felt as if the city were swallowing Mason whole. Every street was choked with cars—honking and coughing exhaust and never moving any faster than Mason could walk—with motorcycles streaming past them and sometimes onto the sidewalks. As Farhan took one turn and then another, the streets confounded any attempt by Mason to visualize where he was or which direction he was walking in, or how he could ever retrace his steps.

"Where the hell are you taking me?" Mason asked.

"To see the *preman*."

Mason grabbed Farhan by the shoulder and stopped him. "I thought you said you found her."

"I found the man who can tell us where she is. That is just as good."

Mason remembered the face of the man who had taken away the money that Mason tried to give her. Who had raised his hand as if to slap her across the face.

*Yeah, maybe it would be good to see him again.*

Farhan took Mason down one more crowded street until they came to a bar surrounded on three sides by wooden fences painted neon yellow. It was a world away from the touristy American sports bar they had drunk in before. This one was strictly for the locals, dimly lit and half-full of morning drinkers. The long, rough wooden bar was held up by several shipping crates turned on their sides. A bald man who weighed well over three hundred pounds—an anomaly in a city of bantamweights and welterweights—stood in the aquamarine glow of a hundred backlit liquor bottles. Farhan exchanged a few words with him. As the man listened, he kept eying Mason suspiciously. A well-dressed American had no business here.

Finally, the man threw the dirty towel he'd been holding into a sink and led Farhan into an office behind the bar. He glared at Mason as he stepped back from the door. He said a few words that Mason didn't understand—probably not his own personal best wishes.

The office was so small, there was barely enough room for a desk and chair. But Mason recognized the man sitting there, talking on a cell phone. He was wearing a long white shirt, which made him look like a barber away from his chair. He put the phone down, stood up, and said something to Farhan. Then to Mason: "I speak fine English."

"Where's the girl?" Mason said. "The one who tried to sell me the sunglasses?"

"Is there a problem?"

"You took the money I gave her," Mason said. "I want her to have it."

The *preman* looked to Farhan, confused, as though he wanted Farhan to explain to this American how things worked. "She was overdue on her *sewa*. She is not a good seller."

"How old is she?"

"I do not know. Nine?"

"Where does she live?"

The *preman* shrugged. "She lives in the *kampung*."

"Where exactly? I want to give her the money I owe her."

"I told you, sir. That was—"

"Yeah, that was the vig you take off nine-year-old girls working in the street. Just tell me where she lives."

The man smiled as he looked to Farhan again. *This ridiculous American asking these ridiculous questions.* "You go to the *kampung* and you start asking for Belani. In a few days, maybe you find her."

"Belani," Mason said. "That's her name?"

"Yes, it means 'little bird.'"

"I'm going to ask you one last time," Mason said. "How do I find her?"

This time, the *preman* said something in Indonesian.

"I'm standing right here," Mason said. "Say it in English."

"You are making him uncomfortable," Farhan said to Mason. "He would like us to leave."

"Just give us an address," Mason said. "Or a landmark, or directions, or whatever we need to find her. Then we'll leave."

Farhan said something else to the man, then to Mason: "Perhaps if you offered him a fee for his time and consideration."

"For fuck's sake," Mason said, taking out his wallet.

"I think five hundred thousand rupiah might do it," Farhan said.

Mason did the quick math in his head. Not quite forty dollars American. He counted out the bills and put them on the desk. The man collected the money, wrote several sentences on a piece of paper, then gave it to Farhan.

As they left, Mason turned to the man and said: "I don't know how to say this in Indonesian, but in English you're just a fucking pimp."

———

Farhan walked beside Nick Mason in the heat and chaos of the *kampung*. This one was even larger than the slum Mason had seen on his first day in the city, where Torino had gotten rid of the Mercedes with all of the bloodstains and stray brain matter from the first driver. Now that driver's replacement was leading him down a long line of shacks made from the wooden slats of soda crates, sheets of corrugated metal, sometimes cardboard boxes. Then into alleys between old concrete buildings, then outside again to another row of freestanding shacks. A thousand small cooking fires sent plumes of oily smoke into the air. Laundry hung from every available hook, nail, and peg, drying in the midday sun. A thin river of raw sewage ran down one side of the street.

Mason could not conceive of living in a place like this, but it was home to countless thousands of people. Along with the other slums in this country, many millions. A city of its own, in the shadows of the tall buildings of Jakarta's downtown.

"You do not understand," Farhan said as he surveyed the shacks, looking for the right one.

"I know," Mason said. "This isn't America. Just save it, all right?"

The two men walked down the line. A man came out of one shack to stare at them. Another sat on a wooden box by a fire and yelled something that Mason could not understand. Farhan consulted the directions the *preman* had given him, until finally he found the one shack in the middle of the row, with only a single yellow sheet of plastic on the front to make it stand out from all of the others.

There was no door to knock on. Just the hanging yellow sheet. Farhan knocked on the door frame and called in a greeting. The sheet was pushed aside, and a woman peered out. She was young, in her mid-twenties. Farhan exchanged a few words with her and then he turned to Mason. "This is her mother."

Mason did the math in his head. Pregnant at fifteen, say, then a child at sixteen. He looked into the shack and saw two other children. A boy, maybe two years old. A baby.

"Where is Belani?" Mason said.

The woman perked up at the sound of her first child's name. She had a brief conversation with Farhan.

"She has become a *pembantu*," Farhan said to Mason. "A maidservant. She will send money home every month."

"She's nine years old," Mason said. "How is she going to—"

The woman cut him off, said something loudly with her hands clasped together.

Farhan listened and then translated: "She says it is a blessing. It will help the whole family."

Mason looked into the shack again and fought down an impulse to say something about how great a blessing it would be if this woman stopped having babies. Even if she could somehow understand him, he didn't want to be the foreigner who could so easily say it out loud.

"Where is the house?" Mason said.

Farhan asked the woman. She obviously didn't want to tell them.

Mason took out his wallet, thumbed through the bills and came up with an even million. One million rupiah. Just under seventy bucks American.

"Get the address," Mason said to Farhan. "I still need to give Belani her money."

———

An hour later, Mason stood before a large house in the Central Business District. It was inside what they called the Golden Triangle, the area bounded by three streets that formed one of the most desirable neighborhoods in Jakarta. Every house on this street made a postmodern statement, which meant everything was concrete and glass, and put together as if by a child stacking rectangular blocks.

The door was answered by a local woman wearing a plain blue uniform. She looked more like an attendant in a rest home than a servant. Farhan spoke to her in Indonesian. Mason recognized the name "Belani" and nothing else in the conversation. Until the woman smiled politely and shook her head, and Mason got the general idea: *No, you cannot see our newest young servant.*

"Ask to see the owner of the house," Mason said.

Another few words spoken. Another shake of the head.

"They are not at home," Farhan said. "She would like us to leave now."

Mason looked in over her shoulder and saw an immaculate white carpet with chrome-and-glass furnishings. The woman closed the door firmly.

"What will happen to her?" Mason asked as he stepped off the porch.

Farhan didn't answer. He didn't meet Mason's eyes.

Mason moved closer to him. "Tell me the truth."

Farhan shrugged. "It will be better than for many. That is all I can say."

Farhan tried to step away, but Mason grabbed him by the shirt and held him still.

"Is this legal?" Mason asked.

"There are new laws," Farhan finally said. "They are trying to deal with human trafficking in Indonesia, but . . ."

Farhan looked away.

"But what?"

"They haven't dealt with these labor agencies yet."

"A labor agency? Is that what they call it?"

"She will send money home," Farhan said. "Just like her mother said. But that money will be part payment and part loan. It will create a huge debt. She will have to work her whole life just to repay it."

"She's an indentured servant. A slave."

"When she is . . ." Farhan said, trying to find the polite words, "physically mature, she may stay here, or she may go to another place. For other types of service."

Mason looked back up at the house. Now there was a movement in a second-story window. A young face appeared. It was her.

*Belani.*

Mason raised a hand to wave to her. He noticed that she was wearing the same blue uniform he had seen on the woman answering the door. There was a flash of recognition on the girl's face. She remembered him, remembered the day on the street.

The recognition disappeared as she was startled by something behind her. Now Mason saw a half second of pure animal fear on her face as she was yanked away from the window.

In his gut, Mason knew he had just made her life even worse.

———

At the end of another merciless hot day in Jakarta, Martin Sauvage sat on the back deck of his apartment. It overlooked a small park, where the children of Interpol officers and other expats played on rickety swings and jungle gyms. Sauvage watched them as he sipped from a glass of Bordeaux.

He put the glass down and picked up the photograph. It was the photograph he'd been carrying in his wallet for three years. The photograph he'd found folded together after the Paris bombings and had never unfolded since.

Not for the first time, he wondered if today was the day he would unfold the photograph.

*No, not yet.*

He wiped his face and asked himself a set of questions:

*Why am I here? Why did I put my badge and my gun in a drawer, put my career on hold, along with my whole life—whatever there was left of it—to come to this place on the other side of the world?*

Then he answered himself:

*I came here for one reason. To find one man. No matter what anyone else tells me, whether I'm wearing a badge from the Police Nationale or a badge from Interpol or no badge at all.*

*No one will ever make me stop hunting him.*

———

Across the city, twelve kilometers away, Nick Mason sat on his balcony high above the street, feeling the evening heat rising from the concrete fifteen stories below him. He had his laptop on the table next to his chair. A glass filled with American whiskey on ice. Mason leaned back in his chair, staring at one picture after another on the screen.

A new school year was coming. Always a nervous time for her. Adriana would be in fifth grade. Mason remembered the sleepless nights, wondering about the new teacher, the new routine. What must it be like now? A completely new school with a thousand new faces.

Her Instagram page was filled with a dozen new photos, Adriana in one new school outfit after another. New jeans, new blouses, new shoes. All paid for by Brad. She was smiling for the camera and for her thirty-five followers—most of them probably old friends from Chicago—but Mason could see the fear underneath the smile. He knew that her stomach was already tied up in knots, and school hadn't even started yet.

*I want to be there*, he said to the screen. He reached out and touched the pixelated image of his daughter's face. *I want to be there so bad. Just to tell you that everything's going to be okay.*

He flipped through the rest of the shopping photos until he got to the very last one, a simple image of a Gina giving Adriana the hug that Mason couldn't. He felt everything empty out from inside him. And then one final thought came to him:

If his own little girl was scared to death of going to a new school, how must Belani feel right now?

Mason got up, put the phone in his pocket, and went out into the night to find the one girl in the world he could still help.

# 9

Mason made his way through the dark side streets alone, struggling to locate the bar where Belani's *preman* kept his office. There was still heavy traffic on all of the main streets, and many of the small clubs on the side streets were still open, the patrons taking standing eight counts as they leaned against walls and each other, watching Mason with open curiosity as he walked by. If Vegas was the city that never slept, then Jakarta was the fever dream that never broke.

He was about to give up and call Farhan when he finally stumbled down the right street and recognized the yellow fence. The bar had been half empty and quiet during the day. Now, after midnight, it was full of men drinking, many of them spilling out onto the sidewalk. Loud *dangdut* music blared from the open doors and clashed with the other music from up and down the street. When Mason stepped inside, twenty men turned to stare at him. The same large bald man was working the rail.

Mason pushed his way past the drinkers and went to the office door. He was about to turn the knob when he felt a heavy hand on the back of his neck. Mason grabbed the man's wrist and bent it back. The man let out a cry of pain and Mason pushed him out of the way.

Mason kicked the door open. A local girl, maybe sixteen or seventeen years old, was sitting on the desk. The *preman* tried to get up, but

Mason came around and shoved him back into his chair. The girl slid off the desk and ran out of the room.

"I'm going to buy Belani's freedom," Mason said. "How much will it take?"

The man looked up at him with wide eyes, then said something in Indonesian that Mason didn't understand.

"You were speaking English eight hours ago," Mason said. "Don't tell me you forgot how."

"What are you doing here?"

Mason let go of him and wiped the man's sweat from his hands. "How much for her freedom?"

"It does not work that way," the man said. "She works in a house now."

"I know. I saw the house. Who owns it?"

The man hesitated, glancing at the door for some kind of help that hadn't arrived yet.

"You're going to set up the meeting," Mason said. "Tonight."

"That is impossible. The deal has been made."

Mason grabbed him again, pulled the collar tight around the man's neck. "You're going to unmake it."

"His name is Safiz," the *preman* said, clutching uselessly at Mason's hands. "He is from Brunei. A very rich man. Very stubborn. He will never . . ."

The *preman* stopped talking when the bartender came rushing into the room. It was already crowded enough, and now the huge man was trying to swing a large wooden club at Mason's head. Mason ducked and it glanced off this shoulder. Mason grabbed the club as the bartender was reloading for another swing. He kicked out the man's knee, and he went down in a heap. The *preman* slid open his desk drawer and grabbed for something. Mason hit him in the throat with the club—not with lethal force, just enough to make him forget about the gun or knife or whatever the hell he was reaching for in the drawer.

The bartender was blocking the door as he tried to get back to his feet. Mason hit him in the groin and folded him in half again, stepped over, and finally looked down at the club in his hand. It was a cricket bat, the first one Mason had ever held. It had a good weight to it, but it could never take the place of a Louisville Slugger.

Mason dropped it on the bartender's chest and walked out of the place.

———

On the Interpol floor of the National Central Bureau at Jalan Trunojoyo Number 3, all of the office lights were off. Except one.

Martin Sauvage sat at his desk, watching a video at quadruple speed with bloodshot eyes. He'd been watching it now for over seven hours.

The video had been taken from a surveillance camera mounted high on a wall in the Jakarta airport, just past the customs line. The vast majority of foreign visitors came into the country through this airport, and every one of them walked through this bottleneck, standing in one of six lines to answer questions for a customs agent before receiving a stamped visa in their passport.

Seven days a week, twenty-four hours a day, the camera recorded the traffic coming through these six lines, and now Sauvage was watching the feed.

Because this was all he had left.

If Baya hadn't made the video from the Sultan Hotel conveniently disappear, Sauvage would have had clear footage of the American walking into the front lobby, going to one of the elevators, going up to the floor where Hashim Baya was not-so-secretly receiving his visitors. He would have seen the shooting, the American's arrest, then the American being brought down through the lobby again to be put into the armored van. Sauvage would have had a thousand different shots to choose from—clear shots of the American's face, any one of which he could have blown up and used to make an official identification with Interpol's facial recognition program.

Without that footage, Sauvage had only three things:

A blurry cell phone photograph taken by a bystander in the Sultan lobby. Unable to be enhanced to the point of identification.

A series of video images from the surveillance cameras in Singapore. Again, unable to be enhanced to the point of identification.

And last, a crystal-clear mental image of the American inside Sauvage's own head.

Which was what led him to the customs feed. By the end of the first hour, he had settled into a rhythm. Playing the video at maximum speed, he watched for male visitors coming through the lines. He would slow down if he spotted anyone with the right build and wait until he got a decent look at the man's face. Then he would speed up again to the next candidate.

He had started at a point three days before the raid on the Sultan, figuring that was how long the imported American shooter would need to set up for the hit. He moved forward from there, to the next day, then to the next. He was on the morning of the raid now. It was getting more and more unlikely that the American would come through customs right before going to the Sultan.

Unless that was the point all along. Get the American on the ground, make the hit, get him out to minimize his exposure.

Or else plan on the American not surviving the day at all.

Maybe he had no idea what he was getting himself into.

Sauvage leaned back into his chair, rubbed his eyes. He was going to have to back up three more days, he realized. Then another three days. Then another.

*Or hell, maybe I'm wrong and he's been here for a month. Or even longer.*

Sauvage leaned forward in his chair, checked the time stamp on the video, and was about to hit the stop button. Then he saw a flash.

Two uniformed officers stood guard in the customs area, armed with their Pindad rifles. Most of the time, they were out of the frame. But sometimes Sauvage would see an officer on the edge of the frame for a few seconds. Stepping in at the request of a customs agent to persuade a visitor to show a little more compliance. Or just relieved at the end of his shift by another officer.

But here, Sauvage saw the officer leaning into the frame for a beat. And then he disappeared.

Sauvage backed up the video feed and noted the six visitors at the six stations. The guard appeared, then was gone, and the six visitors were all still in their stations. Except one. Station four was now empty.

He backed it up one more time and watched the time stamps go by—something he never would have noticed had he not been paying close attention:

Exactly one minute and forty-two seconds were missing.

It wasn't that hard to pay one corrupt chief of security to wipe a hotel's surveillance feed, Sauvage said to himself. But this was on another level.

Who the hell was the American working for, anyway?

———

Mason stood watching the house. The stark rectangles and the palm trees surrounding the house were all lit by a thousand small lights carefully mounted around the grounds. The upstairs window where he'd seen Belani looking down at him was dark.

Mason knocked on the door, asked for the man named Safiz, then spent the next few minutes pantomiming his way through a half dozen servants until the man himself appeared. He wore a neat beard and was dressed in a white dinner jacket. And for one half second, Mason was back in Singapore, chasing the phantom Hashim Baya. He shook that off and asked the man if he spoke English.

"It is very late," the man said. "Who are you?"

"Whatever you paid for Belani, I'll double it."

The man cocked his head and gave Mason a vague smile. "You are American."

"Does that matter?"

"The girl works for me now. Please leave."

"She's nine years old," Mason said. He put out his hand to stop the door as the man tried to close it.

"The police are on the way," the man said. "Leave or you will be arrested."

Mason looked toward the end of the street and saw the flashing lights. The police car was momentarily held up by the traffic. He played it out in his head, how this would go, trying to explain to the POLRI that he was trying to buy himself a nine-year-old girl.

"We're not done," Mason said. He went down the front steps, took a turn on the sidewalk and then another, until he had disappeared into the city.

———

Sauvage brought up the visa list on his screen, sorted it by time of entry, and printed out the list of visa stamps made right around the time of the gap in the video feed. He spent the next hour re-creating the sequence, matching the visitors coming through the different stations—two men, then a woman, then three men coming through station one, putting them all together like strands of DNA and paying close attention to station four. When he was done, he had a complete list of every visitor receiving time stamps.

Nobody was missing.

Whoever got through the customs line without being recorded on video had also had the time of his visa stamp removed from the database.

Sauvage thought about what this meant. Somebody had erased any trace of this man's entry into the country.

*No. If you're the American, you need a passport and you need an active visa. A real one. There's no reason to get tripped up just because the wrong official happens to check it.*

He thought about it for three more seconds before the answer came to him: *You make it work for you. You get your visa postdated so it appears you got here* after *the attempted hit on Baya.*

Sauvage shook himself awake, then began advancing the video again, matching the visa stamps to the incoming visitors. It was grueling work that made his already weary eyes hurt like hell. But he kept going. One hour, then two, through the less-busy arrivals from the overnight flights, into the rush of the morning.

He counted the passengers coming through each station, matching the log of the visa stamps. He got lost three times and had to backtrack and pick up the thread. He could barely even see straight anymore.

And then he found the mismatch.

It came exactly twenty-four hours after the gap in the video. He cursed himself for not knowing to start there—it was probably easier simply to change the date and keep the time of the original stamp.

Sauvage double-checked it. In a one-minute period, six different visitors came through the stations. But there were seven different visa stamps made on that minute. Of those seven visas, four went to men. And of those four men, one was clearly too old. That left three. One from China. One from Japan.

And one from America.

Sauvage read the name. It had to be a fake. He ran the passport number through the American database and brought up the file. The Jakarta airport received more than one million passengers in a given week, but Sauvage had just narrowed them down to one man.

The sun was coming up outside his window, but Sauvage didn't care. Because there on his computer screen, staring back at him from a fake passport, was the face of the American.

———

It was just after nine a.m., and the traffic was barely moving on the *Jalur Kendaraan* in South Jakarta. A solitary man hopped a pedestrian barrier and made his way across the lanes of traffic. He stopped near the left rear passenger's door on a white Audi S5 and tried the handle. It was locked. A tenth of a second later, he swung a steel baton and shattered the window. He reached inside and pulled the door lever, then got into the back seat.

The man in the back seat, the Bruneian businessman named Safiz, was already frantically dialing a number on his phone. Mason took the phone from him, then pointed his Glock at the driver as he turned to face him.

"Give me your phone," Mason said.

The driver handed it over. Mason slid both phones into his pocket.

"I know you," Safiz said, studying Mason's face. "From last night."

"Do you?" Mason said. "What's my name? Where do I live?"

The man didn't answer.

"Here's the important thing," Mason said. He leaned forward and lowered his voice. "*I know you.*"

The man looked back and forth between the gun barrel and Mason's face.

"You own a private forex company in Bakrie Tower. Your wife's name is Maryam. You have two children, Akeem and Nayla. Nayla is about Belani's age, isn't she?"

"What do you want?"

"You're going to pack up everything Belani owns in one bag," Mason said. "You're going to take her to the south entrance of Merdeka Square, and you're going to leave her there."

"She works for me. I am paying her family."

"No. She works for me now."

The man stared at him. "You really think you can do this?"

"We'll find out together," Mason said. "But you need to remember something. If anything happens when we come to pick her up . . ."

Mason leaned forward again.

"Of if anything happens to Belani's family, if anybody comes around looking to take her back . . . *Anything*, Safiz. If she falls on the sidewalk and skins her knee, I'm going to assume you were behind it and I'm going to come find you. And your family. Do you understand?"

If there was anything in this world that Nick Mason understood, it was the power of a threat made against a man's family. Here, in this car, it happened to be a lie, because Mason was not the kind of man who would follow through on such a threat. But that didn't matter as long as the threat was understood and believed.

Safiz nodded.

"Noon," Mason said. "Merdeka Square. South entrance."

Mason got out, leaned down, and looked back in through the smashed-out rear window.

"Good luck with the traffic," he said. Then he was gone.

———

Martin Sauvage drank a cup of coffee while he waited for the Interpol facial recognition program to finish its run. There were forty-four thousand faces in its database. All of the worst internationally known criminals in the world. Terrorists and fugitives. Child molesters and human traffickers. Facial recognition was still a processor-intensive task that could take hours to run, even on the fastest machines in the world. And false positives were still a persistent problem.

While the power of the cloud did its work, Sauvage studied the rest of the information he had. Any alien entering this country was asked to state a "reason for visit." Some people would simply say "tourism," but if you were working in Indonesia, you would be expected to state your employer. Here on his visa application, the American had stated he was working in the security field, employed by a company named Pacific Logistics International.

Sauvage had never heard of the company, but that meant nothing. There were thousands—more like tens of thousands—of companies in this city. The question was, would the American give a fake name for his employer? Or a real one?

Sauvage gamed it out, playing both possibilities in his mind. A fake company had its obvious benefits to a man trying to remain hidden, but if he was picked up on the street for something, he'd be taking a risk that they'd do an immediate search. Instead of just letting him go, they'd want to know why his employer didn't exist.

But he already had a fake visa stamp, altered to make it look as if he entered the country a day after the assassination attempt at the Sultan. If he wanted that part of the visa to do its job, why compromise the whole thing with a fake employer?

To Sauvage, the answer was clear: The company was real. His name was fake, and the job he supposedly did there would be fake. But the company would exist, just in case anyone ever checked.

The program was still running, but now Sauvage had another lead. Somewhere in this city, out of the thousands and thousands of office doorways, the lettering on one of them read *Pacific Logistics International*.

———

Mason walked the four sides of Merdeka Square. The Monas, the National Monument, rose four hundred feet over the center, a simple tapered column with an observation platform at the very top, celebrating the country's freedom. It was a sunny afternoon, not as oppressively hot and humid as usual. Thousands of local citizens walked through the park or pedaled colorful rental bicycles.

Mason watched the traffic on each road bounding the park. He timed a walk from the south edge of the park to a narrow side street a half click to the east. Then he planned out an alternate route. And then an alternate to that.

Then he left the park and took a cab to the office. He called Farhan on his cell phone.

"I'll be there in twenty minutes," he said. "The pickup is at noon."

———

Martin Sauvage had not slept in over thirty hours. But he knew he was close, and he had to keep going.

He looked up "Pacific Logistics International" on the Internet, but of course, life was never that easy. He went through the Interpol database, then the POLRI database. At lunchtime, he walked down to the Tax Directorate General's office and talked to a clerk at the collections desk.

*You can hide from everyone else in the world, but you can't hide from the taxman.*

Sauvage knew that every company that did business in Indonesia was subject to a flat 25 percent corporate tax. Again, it was a matter of risk versus reward. If the American officially worked for Pacific Logistics International, why risk the added exposure by not paying your taxes?

The clerk didn't question the Interpol badge. He came back with the tax records for PLI. The company had been in business for just over seven years. And the office was on the fifty-second floor of the Gama Tower.

Sauvage was one step closer.

———

At one minute before noon, a white Audi S5 with one brand-new rear window pulled off the road running just south of Merdeka Square. A man got out of the back seat, followed by a young girl. The girl had a purple bag slung across her back.

The driver of the car waited while the man escorted the girl down the tree-lined walking path. They did not speak to each other. Finally, as they came to the open square itself, the man stopped, said one word to the girl, and then turned around. The girl watched him walk away. She stayed perfectly still.

Mason watched the scene through a pair of Zeiss binoculars. When the man got back into the Audi, he started moving. He approached through the trees on the southern edge of the square, paused one moment, then stepped out into the sunlight. The girl was still standing there.

"*Kamu aman*," he said to her, the words that Farhan had taught him. *You are safe.*

The girl looked up at him, unafraid.

"*Ikutlah bersamaku.*" Come with me.

Mason took the bag from her in case they needed to move fast. Everything she owned in the world weighed barely five pounds.

He took her by the hand and led her directly east. A black sedan was waiting for them on the side street.

Mason and Belani got into the back seat. Farhan put the car in gear.

In the shadow of a national monument that stood for freedom, Mason was taking Belani back to where she had come from.

———

Sauvage stood in the lobby of the Gama Tower, scanning through the business directly. He didn't see Pacific Logistics International, but that was not a surprise.

He went up to the fifty-second floor and saw the PLI logo on the glass door. A well-dressed local woman waited at the reception desk.

Sauvage didn't go through into the office. He hung back and watched as several employees left at the end of the workday. They were all locals. He didn't see the American.

*Come back tomorrow*, he said to himself. Then he went home to finally get some sleep.

———

Mason walked with the girl down the dusty street of the *kampung*. Farhan walked a step behind them. When they got to the shack, he would translate Mason's proposal to Belani's mother: Whatever the rich man was paying her, Mason would double it. Belani would stay home with her, help take care of the other children, and go to school. Mason had every possibility mapped out in his mind.

But when they got to the shack, it was empty.

Belani had been eerily calm every step of this journey, from the square into the car of a man she barely knew, all the way back here to the *kampung*. But now as she saw her home standing empty, she started to cry.

Mason bent down to her, but Belani pushed him away and ran off down the street. Mason ran after her.

"Belani!"

As he called after her, the men on the street started to gather together. Mason finally found Belani at the end of the next street, bent down close to her. "*Kamu aman*," he said, wishing he knew more words to say. "*Kamu aman*." *You are safe.*

A local man approached them, carrying a homemade machete. It looked like a lawn mower blade attached to a wooden axe handle, but it was still dangerous.

"Take it easy," Mason said, but the man came closer.

Finally, Farhan arrived and spoke to the man. The man kept staring at Mason as he stepped away.

"Where's her mother?" Mason said to Farhan.

"The family next door said she left last night. Nobody knows where she went."

Mason let out a breath. What to do now?

"We have to get out of here," Farhan said, eyeing the other locals.

"You need to find her mother," Mason said as he took Belani's hand and led her down the street.

"Someday, you're taking me to America with you," Farhan said. "This is understood?"

*What the hell*, Mason thought. "Fine. Whatever. If I ever go back, you're coming with me."

———

"Do you speak any English?"

Mason looked across the table at the nine-year-old girl, who had just finished her third piece of *ayam goreng*, the spicy fried chicken that Mason had bought from one of the street vendors.

"Small English," Belani said.

Mason nodded. He wasn't sure what to do next.

Then on a whim, he took out his laptop and opened up Adriana's Instagram feed. He paged through all of the pictures: the new house, the new clothes for school, the shots of Adriana with Gina and Brad. Belani stared at the girl who was right around her age but living in a world she could barely imagine.

"*Putri?*" Belani asked.

Mason didn't know the word, but he could guess what she was asking. "This is my daughter," he said. "Adriana."

"Adriana," Belani said, pointing at the screen. Then at Mason: "*Ayah?*"

"Yes," Mason said. "I am her *ayah.*"

———

Sauvage took the rest of the week off from work after telling Duval that if he wasn't on the Baya case anymore, he needed to take some time for himself. He was back at the Gama Tower the next morning, dressed in jeans and a faded T-shirt, with a baseball cap he could pull down to hide most of his face. He waited in the public area just outside the front entrance. There were dozens of street vendors, businesspeople coming in and out of the tower.

He stayed there most of the day, taking breaks only to eat or use a bathroom. But he never saw the American.

He was back the next day. Then the next. He kept moving to a different position every hour, kept watching the people going in and out of the building.

No American.

The fourth day was a Friday. It rained hard during the morning, and Sauvage felt punished for his stupidity. Just because this was the guy's official employer didn't mean he actually came to this office.

Sauvage was thinking about how good dry clothes would feel.

Then he saw him.

It was the American, approaching the building. Sauvage had a clear path to him. He could step out and easily intercept him.

And then what? He had no gun, no handcuffs. No arrest power.

Even if he could get a local officer to detain him, or call Duval and tell him he needed to pull every string he could, there would still be no direct physical evidence to use against the man. No conclusive video putting him at the Sultan or in Singapore. Nothing but the word of an Interpol agent who would swear he saw him at both locations. Where he had tried to kill the financier of terror whom everyone else in the world was already chasing.

*I may not be able to touch you*, Sauvage thought. *And maybe I don't even want to. Not yet. Because you're going to lead me right to Baya.*

———

The rains came harder every day. Mason and Belani settled into a routine, the closest thing to a real life that Mason could imagine here.

He slipped the doorman a few million rupiah to keep an eye out for her. The doorman offered to have his wife come stay with her during the day when Mason was out. She would even try to pick up on wherever the girl had last had her daily lessons.

Eventually, Mason felt comfortable going back to the office every day. He watched Luna and Torino working every angle to find Baya. The crocodile had gone deep underwater somewhere. But the team kept looking.

Sometimes as Mason was walking to or from the Gama Tower, he'd stop and feel eyes on his back again. But whenever he turned to see who was watching him, nobody was there.

Two weeks passed. One evening, as he was eating dinner with Belani and teaching her the English words for the food, Mason got the call.

It was Torino. "Get down here. Right now."

Mason slipped the doorman a few million more rupiah on the way out. When he got back to the office, both Torino and Luna were in the control room. There was a map on the large screen.

An island.

"Where is this?" Mason said.

Nobody answered for a beat.

"It's a nightmare," Luna finally said. "We won't get within a hundred miles."

"Mr. Mason was put in charge of the next operation," Torino said. "I'm sure he'll come up with something brilliant."

"*Where is this?*" Mason repeated, stepping in front of the screen.

"It is called Jolo," Luna said, "and it might be the most dangerous island on earth."

# 10

Nick Mason had grown up stealing cars on the South Side of Chicago. He got his bachelor's degree in taking down drug dealers. He did his postgraduate work in high-end commercial robberies. Along the way, he developed a strict set of rules to keep himself alive and out of prison. Those rules never failed him. It was Mason who had failed his own rules, *one time*, and that was how he ended up spending five years at the United States penitentiary in Terre Haute, Indiana.

Where he immediately made a new set of rules. Stripped down to the basics, pure survival from one day to the next.

Now that he was on the other side of the world, none of his old rules seemed to apply anymore. Even worse, he still couldn't figure out what the new rules should be.

The only rule he had found in this place was that every rule was a lie and every lie would kill you.

He had this thought again as he stared at the satellite image projected onto the large screen. A green figure-eight-shaped island, like two tennis balls in a sock.

"A half million people live there," Torino said. "Including a few hundred members of Abu Sayyaf, the most notorious terrorist group in this hemisphere."

Mason looked over at Torino. *Worse than the guys we've already met?*

"In 2004, Abu Sayyaf put an empty television set filled with explosives on a SuperFerry and detonated it on the open water. Killed over a hundred people. The largest terrorist attack in the history of the Philippines."

"Not a suicide bombing?"

Torino shook his head. "Most of these guys don't care about seventy-two virgins in paradise. They want fear, they want notoriety, and they want money. Which is why they've moved on to kidnapping. It's a lot more profitable."

"Who do they take?"

"Anyone. Journalists, tourists, soldiers. They hold them for ransom, behead the men if they don't get paid. The army has already been fighting them for thirty years, but now everything's been escalated. This whole area is a war zone now."

"Zoom out," Mason said. He stared at the screen as the map was enlarged to show the rest of the Sulu Sea.

"Borneo's right here," Torino said, pointing to the much larger island south of Jolo. "This western side belongs to Malaysia, the eastern side to Indonesia. Both countries have officially joined with the Philippines to fight Abu Sayyaf, but it's not exactly a model of cooperation. The coalition keeps falling apart, until the next big kidnapping."

Mason nodded, still staring at the island in the center.

"The Philippine military keeps invading Jolo. They shoot everything that moves, but by then Abu Sayyaf are already gone. There are a thousand other islands they can move to, and they are welcomed on almost all of them. It's like Somalia combined with Vietnam."

*Pirates and jungle warfare*, Mason thought. *This is not what I fucking signed up for.*

"You can put Baya on the island right now?"

"That's what our intel says."

"And this group is loyal to him?"

"Beyond loyal. They had funding from Libya in the beginning. Cash and Russian arms. When that stopped, they tried to self-fund with the ransom money. But now business is starting to dry up because they're too busy fighting off the Philippines and there's not enough rich European tourists stupid enough to go sailing near those islands anymore."

"So it's all Baya now," Mason said. "He's their money."

"You thought the green shirts were bad," Torino said. "These men are like his own personal army of jungle guerrillas."

"So why is Baya hiding there now?" Mason asked. He stepped closer to the screen, stared closely at the one island in the middle of a thousand others.

"Maybe we finally scared him," Torino said. "We're getting too close."

Mason turned to look at Torino. "You believe that?"

"No," Torino said. "I do not."

"A helicopter would be seen and heard from twenty kilometers away," Luna said, finally speaking up. "A boat, almost as far."

"Unless we went at night," Torino said. "With an electric motor."

"And then what?" Mason asked. "How do we locate him on the island?"

"We have personnel in the Philippines," Torino said, shaking his head. "But they will not go anywhere near this island. For any price."

"Then we'll have to go gather our own intel," Mason said. "When can we leave?"

———

Martin Sauvage sat on a concrete bench one half kilometer away from the Gama Tower. The American was upstairs, presumably in the Pacific Logistics International offices.

Martin had his laptop open, the screen tilted down to keep it out of the bright sunlight. His research had led him to the fact that Pacific Logistics International was owned by another company called Southpoint Holdings, which was owned by the Asia Platinum Group, which was owned by something else and then something else. None of this was a surprise.

Interpol's facial recognition program had come back with four false positives. Again, not a surprise. Whoever had hired this target would make sure not to choose someone with an existing international profile. That left the huge FBI database, assuming the target was American, which would have meant a probable hit within minutes, except for three problems:

Sauvage was Interpol. Strike one. He was operating on his own, without official authorization from the top brass. Strike two.

And strike three, the FBI was filled with flaming American assholes. They had plenty of advice for you on how to do your job, but no interest when it came to actually helping you.

He knew he couldn't just call the international liaison and ask a favor, not without it getting back to Duval within five minutes. Which left that one agent he had met at the cybersecurity conference in London. He could picture the business card the agent had given him over drinks, but couldn't bring up the name. Wayne Something, or Something Wayne?

*You need to be better organized.* Mireille's voice in his head. *You should carry a little case in your suit pocket, for whenever someone gives you a card.*

"*Payung? Payung?*"

Sauvage looked up, squinting in the sun, to see the boy standing in front of him. Maybe twelve years old, his arms full of white umbrellas.

*Who the hell needs an umbrella on a day like this?* he thought until he saw the boy gesturing at his laptop. It was a sun umbrella. And it would give him better cover, too, if he wanted to remain unseen.

Sauvage took out two ten-thousand-rupiah notes and gave them to the boy. He tried to give Sauvage two umbrellas, but Sauvage waved him away and the boy ran back into the middle of the square, shouting "*Terima kasih!*" behind him. *Thank you.*

Sauvage checked the front door of the Gama Tower. Still no sign of the American. Then he noticed a half dozen other young vendors approaching him. A European rich enough to own a laptop, and generous enough to overpay for an umbrella.

He was the target now. If he tried to follow in the car, he got stuck in traffic. If he did it on foot, he turned into the Pied Piper.

It was officially the worst city in the world to tail someone.

The name came to him: *Payne! Not Wayne, Payne! Agent Roger Payne of the F B fucking I.*

He didn't know where the name had come from. Maybe Mireille had sent it to him from wherever she was, looking down at him on this concrete bench in the sweltering heat.

Sauvage blew a kiss skyward and got out his phone to call the FBI general information office.

———

"I still have not found Belani's mother, Mr. Mason. She has disappeared into the air."

Farhan walked with Mason through the hot *kampung*, wiping at his neck and trying to stay a full step ahead as if to prove his initiative. The midday sun assaulted them.

"We're leaving tomorrow," Mason said. "We have to find Belani's mother today."

Farhan threw his hands up. "You ask the impossible."

"I don't speak the language," Mason said, stopping in the middle of the potholed street paved with rubbish. "I can't get the word out. You spread the word about the reward, right?"

Farhan hesitated. "I did, yes. But you have to be careful offering so much money. People will do whatever it takes to claim the reward."

"If it leads me to Belani's mother, I don't care."

Mason checked his watch.

"I have to go get ready. Stay here and don't come back without Belani's mother."

———

Sauvage trailed several meters behind the two men, struggling to keep the American and his Indonesian partner in sight. Sauvage was a European sweating through a dress jacket, in the middle of the *kampung*. There was no place for him to hide.

He watched the American walk down one crowded alleyway after another, while his partner kept knocking on the doors of the shacks, be those doors corrugated metal, wood, cardboard, fabric, or nothing at all. Then they'd continue down the next street.

Finally, the two men stopped and had an animated conversation. The American left the Indonesian man behind, turned, and walked straight back toward Sauvage.

He ducked out of the way and watched the American pass by. He was moving like a man who had someplace to be. But after watching him for hours, a new question burned in Sauvage's mind:

What the hell was the American doing in this kampung?

When he followed the American back to his apartment building, he got what he thought might be an answer, or at least part of it. A young local girl, maybe eight or nine years old, ran toward him on the sidewalk, followed by a middle-aged local woman trying to catch up to her. Sauvage saw a flash of alarm on the American's face, quickly hidden by a fake smile. Then he hustled both the girl and the woman into the building.

"I still don't know who you are," Sauvage said out loud to the American assassin, "but you just got even more interesting."

——

The flight was scheduled to leave first thing the next morning. They would fly out of the smaller Halim Perdanakusuma Airport on a private jet, its actual owner presumedly just as hard to pin down as the owner of the private yacht that had taken them to Singapore. Nick Mason sat with several maps spread across his kitchen table, along with every recent news article about Abu Sayyaf. It was the Islamic State doing much of the bombings in the cities, demanding an autonomous state in the southern islands of the Philippines. Standing out in that effort were Abu Sayyaf, the heavy hitters brought in for the worst of the bombings and, above all, for the high-profile kidnappings and the deadlines-until-beheadings that would dominate the headlines for weeks at a time.

If the Islamic State was an army, then Abu Sayyaf was its special forces. Nick Mason had to find a way to infiltrate it, with exactly three other people helping him.

"*Apa yang kau baca?*" Belani said. She sat on the opposite side of the table, eating a bowl of *soto*, a yellow soup with goat meat that the doorman's wife had made for her.

Mason flipped past the articles with the most violent images. He brought up the translation program on his phone and tried to sound out the words:

"*Apa yang kamu lakukan hari ini?*" What did you do today?

Belani laughed at Mason's pronunciation, then spent the next minute patiently waiting for him to translate her reply:

*We did my lessons, and we took a walk to the park.*

Mason tried not to show his reaction again. He'd already spoken to the doorman's wife, trying hard not to come down too hard on her. But even in such a huge city, he didn't want Belani out in public yet, not if that meant even a small chance she could be spotted by the man he took her from.

Belani pointed at Mason's laptop. He didn't have to translate anything to know what that meant. She wanted to his see his daughter again.

He brought up Adriana's Instagram page. There was a new set of photographs, Adriana with a new friend, the two girls sitting on the couch together, then later on the floor watching a movie and eating popcorn. A sleepover.

Mason stared at the image. This one simple thing that maybe made his daughter a little happier, that maybe made her feel less alone. It was almost scary how badly this choked him up.

Then a shot of Adriana with Gina, and Adriana turned away.

"*Kapan saya akan melihat ibu saya lagi?*" she said.

Mason worked out the words. *When do I get to see my mother again?* Then he worked out his answer:

*Soon. I promise.*

———

Mason left the apartment at 6:15 a.m. Belani stayed upstairs, asleep in the guest room. On his way out the door, Mason spotted the doorman and took him outside for a quick conversation. Farhan was already waiting at the wheel of the black Mercedes.

"If I don't come back," he said, "You take Belani, ask her for everything she knows about her mother. Then you find her. Do you understand?"

The doorman processed everything Mason said, working hard to filter it through his third language. Mason pressed a large wad of rupiah in his hand, and that made the processing go faster.

Mason thanked the doorman and got into the car next to Farhan. At this hour of the morning, Farhan was fresh out of the shower and deep into his bottle of Old Spice. Mason just shook it off as the car pulled into the early morning traffic, followed a few seconds later by a pale-yellow Honda.

———

Sauvage had arrived back at the American's apartment building just in time to see the black Mercedes pull out into the traffic. He settled in behind it, watching the stoplights carefully. He had to blow through a few red lights to keep in touch with the vehicle, all the way through the heart of the city toward East Jakarta. Sauvage yawned, short on sleep. But at least this early hour meant slightly less traffic to fight.

The car eventually turned into the Halim Perdanakusuma Airport. It was the baby brother airport in town, much smaller than Soekarno-Hatta. Sauvage parked a quarter kilometer away and watched the American get out of the vehicle with the same Indonesian man who'd been with him in the *kampung* yesterday. Sauvage trailed behind them as they went into the single terminal. He had to be more careful than he would have been amid the chaos of Soekarno-Hatta.

Mason and the other man were met by two other individuals: a European man in a tailored suit, and a European woman. Now that all four were together, Sauvage remembered seeing this same team coming off the boat on the surveillance footage in Singapore. But this time, Sauvage's eyes paused on the woman for an extra beat. Dark curly hair, dark eyes. Something else, a strong sense that she might share some of his own Romani blood.

A minute later, the foursome was on the move. He stayed behind them in the airport as they proceeded to a special exit door for private flights.

*Now what?*

When Sauvage went to the large window and looked down at the tarmac, he saw the foursome climbing the stairs into a Gulfstream. Ninety seconds later, he was still standing with his hands on his hips as he watched the plane taxi to the runway.

Sauvage started working through a series of airport security officers until he found one who recognized his Interpol badge well enough to entertain a request for information. Nearly an hour had passed when Sauvage finally convinced this officer to share the Gulfstream's flight plan.

"Zamboanga City," the officer said.

"I'm sorry, where is that?"

"Philippines," the officer said. "On the island of Mindanao."

"How do I get there?"

"Best way is to charter a private plane, just as they did."

"What if I can't do that?" he asked. "What's the quickest way to get there right now?"

The officer thought about it. Not a good sign. Like the old American joke, *you can't get there from here.*

"We have a flight going to Cebu," the officer said. "From there, you can catch a local flight to Mindanao. Then get a car or take a cab."

*Which will take all fucking day*, Sauvage said to himself.

He thanked the officer, got out his phone, and stood looking at it, going through all of his options. Finally, he brought up Duval's name and hit the connect button.

"It's Martin," he said as soon as Duval answered. "Please listen carefully. The American and his team are on their way to the Philippines."

"Wait," Duval said. "Stop. Where are you?"

"I'm at Perdanakusuma. They took a private jet from here to Zamboanga City. Which means Baya must be there."

"Zamboanga City, you say?"

"On Mindanao."

He heard Duval taking a deep breath on the other end. Until he finally spoke again.

"Martin, what are you doing? You're not on this job anymore. You're supposed to be—"

"I don't have time to explain this to you," he said. "I followed the team and watched them take off."

"You had specific orders to leave the American alone."

"I know. You can reprimand me the next time you see me. But like I tried to tell you, it's not about the American; it's about where the American is going. And right now he's flying to Zamboanga City. If we notify our agents on the ground, he'll lead them right to Baya."

There was a pause as Duval typed away on his keyboard. "I don't get it," he said. "I'm looking at the map right now and I see no strategic reason for Baya to go there."

As the line went silent for a few seconds, Sauvage glanced up at a large map on the airport wall. The hundreds of named islands that made up these South Pacific nations. The thousands more, all too small to be anything other than dots on this map. He focused on the Philippines and the island of Mindanao. There were larger cities they could have flown to: Pagadian, Koronadal, Cagayan de Oro. Why would Baya go to this minor city on the last western edge of the island?

He kept staring at the map, willing the answer to appear. Then he focused on the expanse of blue next to the island. The Sulu Sea. And the string of islands they call the Sulu Archipelago.

The buzzing in his ear resolved into words. "Martin, are you still there?"

"Yes," he said. "I know why they flew there. It's on the edge of the Sulu Sea."

A silence on the other end as Duval put it together. "Abu Sayyaf," he finally said. "Baya may be funding them now."

"Of course he is," Sauvage said. "It's a perfect match."

"I'll call Manila." Duval left the thought hanging because they both knew that the effectiveness of any given country's Interpol office began with its relationship with the standing police force. And the Philippine National Police had a certain reputation that stood out even in this part of the world, where corruption hummed like a constant background noise. The last time Sauvage saw the "Corruption Perceptions Index," he noticed that while Indonesia was ranked an unimpressive 96th out of 180 countries, the Philippines was even further down the list at 117th, tied with Egypt.

Meaning that a man like Hashim Baya might not have much problem buying influence, protection, or pretty much anything else he wanted.

And then there was the matter of the ongoing war. "I know the military has been conducting operations in that area for years," Sauvage said. "Especially Jolo."

"Exactly," Duval said. "If they're already at war with Abu Sayyaf, what are they going to tell me if I ask them to go down there and look for Baya for us?"

"It's not just for us. It's for them as much as anyone."

"I know," Duval said. "I can already hear myself saying that. A rousing speech about how we're all on the same team. But how do you think that's going to go over right now?"

Sauvage kept staring at the map. "He's *right there*, Jacques. I can feel it."

"I'll do my best. But you need to promise me something right now."

"What's that?"

"Promise me you're not going there."

Sauvage didn't respond.

"Martin, did you hear me?"

"I'll talk to you later, Jacques."

Sauvage hung up the phone and went to the ticket counter.

# 11

Mason and the rest of the team touched down in Zamboanga City just after eleven a.m. As they made their way through the single large terminal, Torino caught up to Mason and walked beside him. "The Japanese made POWs build many of these airfields during the war," Torino said. "Americans, Brits, Australians. When they were done, they were all marched through the jungle until they died."

Mason didn't know why he was getting this history lesson right now. Or what the secret message behind it might be. Or why Torino was going out of his way to deliver it. But he did know one thing:

He would need to kill this man, Mason realized without surprise or remorse. And probably soon.

A black van was waiting for them outside the airport. The driver gave them a nod as they got in, and never said a word as he drove them through the heart of the city. It was cleaner than most of Jakarta, with less noise and chaos, but when they got to the port, everything started to look a lot grimmer and closer to the bone. There were few women or children in this part of town, just stone-faced men going about their serious business.

Mason pictured the map in his mind. They were on the western edge of the big island called Mindanao. The watery horizon they were seeing now as they stepped out of the car was the Sulu Sea, with the islands of the Sulu Archipelago strung out in a line to the southwest. From where they stood, they were about fifty kilometers away from Jolo.

Mason was acutely aware of being watched as he walked along the busy dock. He clocked every man's eyes scanning him, measuring him, then looking away quickly. And then invariably pausing when they saw Luna.

Four Filipino men were waiting for them on the dock. They had prepared two boats: one twenty-one-foot streamlined cigarette boat and a smaller sixteen-foot hybrid—not as fast but capable of switching to quiet electric power when needed. They had also brought two metal boxes containing three Czech CZ Scorpion submachine guns, one German HK G3 sniper rifle with scope, and four Glock 17s—undersized but indestructible as carry weapons.

In the distance, a sound like thunder rolled across the open water of the Sulu Sea. Luna stopped to listen first, then every man, one by one.

It wasn't thunder.

One of the Filipinos stepped away to make a call on his cell phone. "The military is on Jolo, in retaliation for another bombing in the capital."

"What about Baya?" Mason asked.

The man hesitated. "Some of Abu Sayyaf may have moved to Pata Island," he said, lowering his voice a notch. "Baya may be with them. That is all I know."

"We can't move on him," Mason said. "Not until we know exactly where he is."

Torino stepped forward. "You were the one who said we had to gather intel," he said, nodding to the water. "The intel is out there."

"It's a civil war," Luna said. "You want us to walk right into the middle of it?"

"There is another small island," the local man said. "Twenty kilometers south of Pata. It would be a good place to go first if you want to watch and observe."

Mason recognized the island from the map. He thought about the idea, then finally nodded.

"I'll set a course that takes you out into the open water, away from most of the trouble," the man said. "You can circle around and approach from the southwest."

He went to work programming the GPS system on both boats while the rest of his men loaded the weapons and supplies. Mason noted how they kept glancing up at him without ever catching his eye, just like most of the men on the dock. But this felt different. It was the same way you'd look at a kamikaze pilot just before he took off from the flight deck.

Once they pushed off from the dock, it was finally just the four of them. A long morning of travel, and they weren't close to done yet. Torino piloted the fast boat, with Luna on board. Farhan piloted the hybrid, carrying Mason.

"I cannot believe we are going near Pata Island," Farhan said with a shiver in his voice. "It is a cursed place. More haunted than Jolo."

"I think that's the least of our problems right now," Mason said, watching the faster boat disappear ahead of them.

"There was a massacre there in 1981," Farhan said. "Before there was an Islamic State or Abu Sayyaf, it was the National Liberation Front, the Moros, who wanted to establish a separate Sulu state. The army invaded and lost over a hundred soldiers. So they bombed the island for two months straight. They killed over three thousand civilians. Men, women, children."

They rode in silence across the waves for another hour, until Mason could see something ahead of them. He pulled out a pair of binoculars and glassed the two boats. One was the cigarette boat with Torino and Luna. The other was a patrol boat, with "Maritim Malaysia" printed in block letters on its side.

"We circled around too far," Farhan said. "Do we turn around?"

"No. In this thing, they'll run us down in ten seconds."

Farhan stayed on course. A few minutes later, they were blasted by a bullhorn with words Mason couldn't understand. What he did understand was the assault rifle pointed at them from one of the patrol members.

"How's your Malaysian?" Mason asked Farhan.

"We're going to find out together, friend."

When Farhan pulled up alongside the patrol boat, two uniformed members of the Malaysian Maritime Enforcement Agency jumped on board. Mason kept his hands visible. He had no desire to die in the middle of a sea he'd never even heard of before this week.

Farhan took Mason's fake passport, added his own, and handed them to one of the officers. There was an animated conversation. Mason looked over at the other boat. Another officer was examining Torino's and Luna's passports.

Mason waited for ten minutes. The conversation grew less heated and was almost civil by the time the officers reboarded their boat and left.

"What did you tell them?" Mason said.

"We are treasure hunters," Farhan said, "searching for a wreck. They didn't want us anywhere close to Sulu, not with the *tembakan* going on. Which means fighting or gunfire. I told them we would go no further. Finish up within the hour and go back."

Mason looked over at Torino and gave him a nod. As soon as the patrol boat was out of sight, they continued directly toward the *tembakan*.

———

The sun was on its descent and shining directly in their eyes as they approached the islands. The farthest away was Jolo, the green slopes of its long-extinct volcano rising above the water. The smaller island of Pata was south of that. And even farther south was a small island called Kabingaan. On its southern coast, visually shielded from the other islands, was a natural cove.

The two boats anchored. The team waded ashore to find a half dozen shacks lined up along the beach. They were empty, with no signs of recent use. Farhan glanced up at the wall of palm trees that sheltered the cove and the beach, offering a slight relief from the relentless sunshine. Then he peered inside one of the empty shacks. "I do not like this place," he said.

Mason looked out to the open water. "I'm not crazy about it either."

"None of this feels right," Luna said. "Baya is too smart to come into the middle of a war zone."

"It was your intel that brought us here," Torino said.

"It wasn't *my* intel," she said. "You think I do this on my own?"

"Baya is arrogant," Torino said. "He believes he can go almost anywhere. And buy his way out of anything."

"He'll have his own boat, at least," Mason said. "Maybe a helicopter."

Torino nodded.

"I'm going to do some recon," Mason said.

"I'll go with you," Torino said. "Luna and Farhan will stay here."

"I'm going alone," Mason said.

"That's a bad idea."

Mason stepped up close and looked him in the eye. "I have operational control of this mission. And you're still compromised."

Torino had taken off the sling, but Mason knew that his arm was still not right. He could grab it and twist it if he needed to be more persuasive.

"It's just intel today," Mason said. "I won't move without you."

He waded out to the shore, climbed into the hybrid, drew up the anchor, then left the cove. Only when he was clear of the island and firmly in his seat did he open it up. The wind whipped his hair as he headed around to the north side of the island.

Pata Island was ten kilometers away. He saw it as soon he rounded the corner. Slowing down the boat, he set a crossing course one kilometer out, like a man walking past a wolves' den.

He picked up his binoculars and scanned the coast of the island as he went by. It was an unbroken wall of thick vegetation, until he spotted an opening and a gray concrete building. Mason took out his pad and made a note, then kept going until he was well north of the island. He idled in the open water and started to draw himself a map. Then he turned westward and crossed the north side of the island. He spotted another building, two stories high, with a rough road running in front of it. He paused at the northwest corner and drew in more details on his map.

As he was about to start his western cross, he heard another motor in the distance. He stayed in idle and listened carefully for the direction. He finally saw the boat rounding the far corner of the island and coming straight at him. It was moving too fast to avoid.

Mason picked up the Scorpion submachine gun and held it just below the level of the gunwale. When he saw the markings on the boat, he quickly put the gun in one of the long seat compartments. Then he stood with his hands in clear sight as the patrol boat approached him. This time it was the Philippine Coast Guard, the letters printed in English across the boat's side.

The boat approached, slowed down, and came abreast of Mason's starboard side. One Filipino officer grabbed Mason's boat with a long hook. Two other officers jumped aboard.

"I don't speak Filipino," Mason said, "but here is my passport."

"Sir, we all speak English," one of the officers said as he took Mason's passport and examined it. "Do you know where you are right now?"

*Stick with your cover*, Mason thought.

"I'm on a team of treasure hunters. We're searching for a wreck."

"You have no permission to be here," the officer said. "You are under arrest."

Mason scanned both boats and did a quick mental count of the officers. Four he could see, maybe another two or three on the other boat. Guns stowed under the seat. Money in his wallet, but he'd given most of it to the doorman to look after Belani.

He was officially fucked.

Everything froze for a beat. Then one of the men on the other boat called to the officer holding Mason's passport. It sounded urgent.

"Get out of here," the officer said, handing Mason back his passport. "Right now. Don't even slow down until you're back at your dock."

The officer jumped onto the other boat, even as it was already moving. He glanced back at Mason once more. "Now!"

Mason hit the throttle and headed south. He heard scattered gunshots in the distance, answered by other shots at a higher pitch.

*Enough intel for today. Time to get the fuck out of here.*

He scanned the western side of the island as he raced across the water, made the turn, and headed east, completing the circle around Pata. He sped through the ten kilometers back to the far coast of Kabingaan and pulled back on the motor as he got close.

The second boat was gone.

Mason stayed in an idle again, slowly drifting across the water as he took out his binoculars and scanned the shoreline.

"Where are you?" he said under his breath.

He finally moved the boat forward until he was close to the shore. Then he cut the motor, dropped the anchor, and took the Glock out of its compartment. Without the motor running, everything was silent except for the gentle lapping of the water against rocks and sand.

Mason jumped from the boat and waded to shore, the Glock already in his right hand. He went from one shack to another. They were all empty.

When he turned, he saw six men pointing assault rifles at his head.

———

The men were all uniformly short and lean, and all dressed in faded military camo. They all had bandannas wrapped around their heads. Two black, two green, one white, one bright red. They took Mason to the shore and waited as a boat came to pick them up. It was a fishing skiff with an outboard motor and an aluminum canopy. One of the men carried Mason's Glock, examining it with admiration.

It was a twenty-minute trip back to Pata Island. The boat was slow and loud, and it rode rough in the water. A cloud of oily smoke hung over the motor.

*Stay with your cover story. Even now. You're a treasure hunter. You have money. The Glock was just a reasonable precaution.*

*If they buy it, then they'll probably hold you for ransom. Meaning you're worth much more alive than dead.*

The boat pulled up to a ramshackle wooden dock on the south side of Pata Island. Mason was pulled onto the dock and then pushed along the sandy path that led into the woods.

They walked deep into the interior of the island until they reached a clearing. Three concrete buildings stood there. A water tower and a radio antenna rose above the tree line.

Mason scanned the area. No sign of his team. Where the fuck were they?

And then another fleeting thought that Mason could not keep out of his head: Had they abandoned him?

Two men pushed Mason behind one of the buildings. He fought off the urge to grab one by the arm and twist it until it broke, then ram his fist squarely into the nose of the other. As good as that would have felt, he knew that it would have blown his cover story and gotten him killed a half second later.

A rusted metal shed stood in a sunlit clearing. One man opened the door and directed him inside. He hesitated for a beat and then obeyed. The air inside felt like a blast furnace.

The door closed behind him. Mason heard the padlock being secured on the outside of the door. He sat down with his back against the metal wall, feeling the heat radiate into his body. He closed his eyes, slowed down his breathing, then his heart rate.

*You know this place. You've been here before. You're back in prison.*

*You made a whole new list of prison rules, stripped down to the basics. Now it's time to remember each one.*

*You exist from one moment to the next. You don't look ahead. You don't look back.*

*You survive.*

Two hours may have passed. It was hard to tell. Sweat dripped down his face in a steady stream. Finally, Mason heard the padlock being undone. The door opened and he blinked against the sudden harsh light.

A man stepped through the door. With the sun at his back, he was nothing but a silhouette. Until he came closer.

Mason stood up to face him. It was Hashim Baya, dressed in a clean white shirt, flowing orange pants, and sandals. With his neatly trimmed beard and serene eyes he looked like the world's deadliest mediation guru.

*You don't recognize me*, Mason thought, willing it into the other man's mind. *You only saw me in that van for a minute. You don't recognize me now.*

A second man came into the shed. He was one of the men who

had abducted Mason. Taller than the others, wearing a shirt weathered to a light shade of gray, and a red scarf wrapped around his head. He was holding an assault rifle—a version of the Pindad that seemed to be universal in this part of the world. This one had a rusted barrel and looked as if it needed a good cleaning. Unacceptable to any army sergeant anywhere. But Mason was reasonably sure it could still cut him in half if he made a wrong move.

"They brought you here all the way from America," Baya said. Calmly, like two men who happened to meet at a business conference. "They must think you're the best."

Mason didn't answer. Baya took came a step closer and actually smiled.

"It's good to see you again, Nick."

# 12

"That's not my name," Mason said, stepping closer. The guard leveled the barrel of his Pindad. Baya put out a hand for the guard to keep his finger off the trigger.

Baya shrugged. "It's not the name on your fake passport." He spoke perfect businessman's English, barely colored by any island accent.

"Why was I brought here?"

"If these men had any idea who you are," Baya said, "they'd demand a hundred million dollars from your organization not to behead you."

"I don't care about them," Mason said. "What do *you* want?"

"I want information."

"I don't have any."

"I doubt that."

"I just got off the plane a few days ago," Mason said. "Literally a few hours before the first time I saw you."

"The first time you tried to kill me."

"I was doing what they told me to do," Mason said. "Otherwise, they haven't told me shit about anything."

"I think you've probably figured out a few things on your own. But you can start by telling me where the others are right now."

"There's nobody else," Mason said. "I came here alone."

Baya shook his head slowly. "Don't do this, Nick. There were four of you. In two boats."

Mason didn't respond.

"He sent four people to kill me," Baya said. "And one of them was a woman. I should be insulted."

Mason stayed silent. But he clocked the key word: *he.*

It was a gamble, but what the hell: "So you know who sent me."

"Of course I do. And so do you."

"No," Mason said. "I don't know anything about him."

"But you've spoken to him."

Mason hesitated. "Yes. But only on a screen."

"You saw him on a screen," Bays said. "But where was he at the time?"

"I don't know."

"You didn't think to ask somebody?"

"I did. They didn't tell me."

Baya thought about it for a while. "I can't imagine you ever pictured yourself on this end of the world," he finally said. "How are you finding it?"

"Beats winter in Chicago."

Baya smiled. "You have no idea."

He took a bottle of water from his pocket. He opened the cap, held the bottle up and swirled the contents, as if examining a fine wine.

Nick looked at the water. Already he could feel an intense thirst building. It was the thirst of a man sitting on the bleachers at old Comiskey, for both ends of an August doubleheader.

"You need to stop acting like this is some kind of cheap American action movie," Baya said. "This is not *Mission Impossible.* You are not Rambo. The people who brought you here, this *team* of yours . . . Do you think they have the slightest interest in what happens to you?"

Mason couldn't help but flash back to those first hours off the plane, being rushed to the hotel and then standing on the roof as the helicopter hovered. One gun in his hand and no direct cover.

It was not a good question to ask him, and Baya clearly knew that.

"They are not going to rescue you," Baya said. "You're already a lost asset."

Mason didn't respond. But his mind was already rushing toward what would happen to Gina and Adriana if his "asset" status was really canceled.

"You know I'm right, Nick. So now you need to ask yourself, 'What is my next best move?' You seem like the kind of man who always keeps that question in his mind."

Mason stayed silent. But he was listening.

"I can help you," Baya said. "I can help you and I can help your family."

Mason's entire body tensed. *Your family.* There weren't two other words in the English language that would have had the same effect. "What are you talking about?"

"I know how your organization works, Nick. What other motivation would get you to fly to Indonesia? *Money?* I don't think that would do it for you."

Mason stared at him, waiting.

"You have a wife and a daughter."

Mason took a step forward again. The guard leveled the barrel of the Pindad at Mason's chest.

Baya put out one hand again. The guard stayed still but didn't lower the gun.

"I'm called the *terroriste*, the *'iirhabiun*, and yet I'm not the one threatening your wife and your child with death. Are you sure you're on the right side of this, Nick? Or how would they say in America, *Are you playing on the right team?*"

"My family has nothing to do with this," Mason said. "Any of this."

"You know that's not true," Baya said. "If you work for me, I will see that they are safe."

A dozen questions came into Mason's mind. He shut down every one.

*He's using the right words, but I can't trust it. Any of it. It's the ultimate game of Good Cop / Bad Cop, and I'm not stupid enough to fall for it.*

"What's your alternative, Nick? If they're not coming to save you, that means one of two things. Number one is, I let these men cut your head off. Have you ever seen it done? It's not quick and it's not clean.

Not the way these men do it. You'd think they'd be better at it by now. One swipe of a sword and . . ."

Baya mimicked a samurai taking a big downward swipe with his sword.

"They use an old, rusty saw," Baya went on. "I saw it once and I never need to see it again. But imagine what it would feel like, Nick, when the teeth of that saw touch the back of your neck and you realize that this is *really going to happen*."

Mason stared at him without blinking.

"Or we could just leave you in this shed," Baya said. "Do you know what happens to the human body when it's deprived of water for long enough? Every cell in your body begins to shrink. The water in your body is pulled into the bloodstream, in a desperate attempt to keep your organs alive. You become confused. You have delusions. Hallucinations. Your brain literally shrinks inside your skull, and the blood vessels start to rupture. Your kidneys fail. All of the poisons in your body are trapped inside you. It is worse than any beating you've ever had, Nick. Worse than any torture."

Baya swished the water that remained in the bottle, then turned it over and let the water pour out onto the concrete floor.

"Or maybe you'll experience both. When your body starts shutting down, you might even welcome the beheading."

He put the empty bottle in his pocket.

"If you will excuse me," Baya said, "it's getting a little hot in here."

The guard opened up the door and let in a bright flash of sunlight again. Baya turned and paused in the doorway. "I'll let you think about it," he said. "But your mind won't be clear for much longer."

The guard followed him out. Then the door slammed shut. Mason heard the latch of the padlock outside.

He closed his eyes and took a breath of the oven-hot air.

———

Sauvage sat in a hard plastic chair, staring at the large map on the wall as he waited for his flight to Cebu.

The American. His team. Whoever was backing them. They were already in the Philippines. They had weapons. They had intel.

Which brought up another question: How did an international police force, with 195 member countries and one man at the top of its most-wanted list, have less intel than whatever organization the American was working for?

Just how big was this organization, anyway?

He had a sudden, visceral urge to smoke a cigarette. Surely, there would be a duty-free shop somewhere on his journey where he could buy a carton of American cigarettes, if not his old favorite Gauloises.

Mireille had made him quit, all those years ago. And she would definitely not approve if he took them up again now.

With that thought, Sauvage felt the presence of the folded photograph in his billfold. He took the billfold out and opened it, held the photograph, the faces of his wife and his son pressed together.

He held the photograph in his hands for a full minute, without opening it. Today was not the day. Not yet.

He returned the photo to his billfold and continued to stare at the map and wait for his plane.

————

Mason sat with his back against the metal wall of the shed. The air he breathed was hot enough to be like a separate, living thing that inhabited his body. He closed his eyes against the dim light coming from under the door and swallowed.

He thought about the taste of a cold Goose Island, the feel of the bottle in his hand, sitting on the rickety front porch of the house on Ninety-Sixth Street. A White Sox game on the radio. Adriana riding her bike back and forth on the sidewalk.

*Where did that life go? How did I lose it?*

He didn't know how many hours he had been in the shed. All that time, and he hadn't had to get up and piss in the corner yet. Maybe he never would. As Baya had said, all the moisture in his body would be drawn into his bloodstream to protect his vital organs until, finally, his brain would start to shrink in his skull.

*Stop it,* he told himself. *Stop thinking about this and find a way out.*

He got up and ran his hands along the walls of the shed one more time, feeling the rough contours of the hot metal. One wall was slightly hotter. Did that mean it was facing east or west? They were too close to the equator for north or south to make a difference.

Did it even matter? Did knowing the fucking direction he was facing right now help him one goddamned little bit?

He tested the door, felt the resistance when he pushed. Two bolts on one side of the door told him where the outer latch must be. Did that make this the weak spot in the door, or the strong spot?

*Think. This shit matters. It might mean the difference between getting out of here and dying right here on this floor.*

He got down on his hands and knees and studied the lag bolts that connected the walls to the floor.

The concrete looked old. These bolts may not be sound anymore. Maybe the simple way out of this was just to lift this whole fucking thing in the air and slide out underneath.

He tried to get his fingers under the edge of the wall. He scraped his knuckles, licked them and tasted the salt and the blood.

He thought of lemonade. Pictured a big glass pitcher being made right in front of him. Lemons squeezed into the water. A cup of sugar dumped in and the ice rattling as it was stirred.

*One cup, please. I'll pay you anything.*

He sat back down and leaned against the wall. It burned his skin right through the shirt.

He lay down on the hard concrete in the center of the room, where the air might be a few degrees cooler. There were corrugated waves on the ceiling as he stared up at it in the dim light.

The waves. Lake Michigan. Sitting on a folding chair on North Avenue Beach, the downtown buildings rising behind him. The sun going down, making everything glow.

The water of Lake Michigan. The *fresh* water. Not salty. He could drink that entire lake right now.

No, go across the sand to Castaways. The sand is hot on your feet, but it's worth it. Sit on the deck and order a margarita.

*Hold the salt. Just give me the ice-cold lime juice, triple sec, and tequila. I'll shoot that right down, and keep 'em coming.*

*No, even better, remember the margarita that one time at the Cabana Club, at that hotel downtown. How'd they make that again? Grand Marnier, tequila, blackberries . . .*

*And cucumber! God damn, that's the most ridiculous thing I ever heard of, but I would kill for one of those right now. Every fucking guy out there right now, wherever the hell I am, this fucking island in the middle of fuck, I would mow them all down right now to have just one sip of that ridiculous blackberry and cucumber margarita.*

Mason sat up.

*I am not going to sit here in this oven and lose my fucking mind.*

He got to his feet, went to the door, and pounded on it.

———

The plane took off an hour and fifteen minutes late. When Sauvage landed at the Mactan-Cebu Airport, he prayed that his Interpol badge would help him avoid a long wait in customs. A half hour later, he had learned that he had missed the only flight to any city on the island of Mindanao. So now he was sitting in another hard plastic chair, waiting for the flight to Dumaguete, from where he'd have to catch the ferry to Dapitan.

Three words kept running through his mind:

*Infiltrate.*

*Locate.*

*Communicate.*

Meaning get close enough to Baya until you can locate his exact position. Then communicate that information back to Interpol. That was all he could do. That was his job, whether on the case or off.

He pulled out his phone, wondering if he should call Duval and imagining how that conversation would go if he did.

*Yes, I'm in the Philippines after all, Jacques. On my way to Zamboanga City. I'm going to find a boat somehow and get into the Sulu Sea, probably start with Jolo Island, where the Philippine military has been bombing the shit out of Abu Sayyaf. On the off chance I live through that, I'll see about finding Hashim Baya for you.*

He stopped. *And then what?*

*Infiltrate.*

*Locate.*

*Communicate.*

*And that's it. You're not going to make an international citizen's arrest. You're not going to convince him to give himself up.*

*You are not going to kill him.*

*Are you?*

Sauvage didn't know how to answer that. Not even to himself. All he knew was that everything he had done and every waking hour he had spent since burying his wife and only child was leading him to this plastic chair in this airport. There was literally nothing else he could imagine than being right here, right now, waiting for another flight and a ferry and then whatever else it took to get to this strange-sounding city. And then whatever came next.

———

Mason pounded on the door until he heard someone work a key into the padlock. He stepped away and pressed his back against the wall.

As the door opened, a brilliant rectangle of light was cast on the concrete floor. They'd be blind coming into the sudden darkness. It was his only advantage.

Mason saw the long barrel of the Pindad first. He grabbed it with his left hand and pulled it forward, trying to continue the man's momentum. Then he drove his right elbow into the man's face and twisted the gun to break the man's trigger finger. But now the man was holding on for one beat too long and the other men were already in the doorway before he could turn the Pindad and start mowing them down.

A rifle butt hit him square in the chest, knocking him back a step and taking his breath away. He rolled to his feet and put his shoulder into the man closest to him, driving him back into the metal wall and making the entire shed rattle with a sound like a gong.

The men were shouting all around him, foreign words that meant nothing to him, until finally he felt two different gun barrels pressed into his shoulder blades. One of the voices cut through all of the rest, louder and more commanding. Mason looked up and saw the tallest member of the group, the man who had come into the shed with Baya. He shouted again and gestured for the men to take their guns from Mason's back.

Mason came up onto one knee but one of the men grabbed the back of his neck and held him still until the tall man said a word, and a final rifle butt caught Mason in the ribs. He went down and stayed down as the door was slammed shut and the padlock relatched.

Mason stayed there for an eternity, coughing up what felt like the last drop of liquid from his body. Until he could finally take a breath and he rolled over onto his back, staring once again at the waves on the metal ceiling. Alone with the darkness, the pain radiating through his body, and always the unforgiving thirst.

———

Sauvage made his way through the Dumaguete Airport, a man traveling alone without luggage and feeling like a nameless ghost among the other people in the terminal. When he was out on the busy sidewalk, the heat of the long day still radiating from the concrete at his feet, he put up one hand and immediately caught the attention of three taxi drivers. They argued for a few seconds until Sauvage picked one of them and asked the man to take him to the passenger ferries.

Sauvage fended off a dozen questions along the way, pretending not to understand much English. When they got to the port, he paid the man in Indonesian rupiah, apologizing that he hadn't had the chance to change currency. He left the driver muttering to himself about the strange traveler with no luggage and no pesos.

Sauvage walked through the Dumaguete Seaport, which reminded him of a train or bus station, but here in a nation of islands, it was a network of ferries that did most of the transporting. He checked the map and the schedule and found the ferry to Dapitan, which was just across the narrow entrance to the Bohol Sea.

As he waited for another hour on yet another hard plastic seat, he took out his phone and checked for messages. If there had been any news on Baya, anything dramatic that had happened while Sauvage was traveling, Duval would have called to give him the news. He saw one voice mail from Duval and played it, but it was just his boss asking him where he was.

Sauvage joined a few dozen people shuffling onto the last ferry to Dapitan. The engine churned as it backed away from the port, and it negotiated its way through the other boat traffic until it was alone on the dark water of the Bohol Sea.

Sauvage scanned the other passengers. Mostly men, a few families. A way of life for them, traveling from one island to another. He remembered the great SuperFerry attack by Abu Sayyaf, back in 2004 when he was on the beat in Paris. Just a small item in the news that he barely noticed at the time. But he knew that it was the deadliest terror attack in this country's history, with over a hundred people killed. People just like the passengers he was looking at right now.

When the ferry arrived in Dapitan, Sauvage got off, walked out under the long blue awning to the street, and found a taxi driver who would take him all the way down the southern tip of the island, to the port in Zamboanga City.

They traveled down the rough two-lane road that ran along the shore. To the west, the sun was now going down over the Sulu Sea—a constant presence outside Sauvage's window. It was nearly dark by the time they got to the outskirts of Zamboanga City. The traffic picked up. Small trucks and vans, the ever-present motorcycles, and "jeepneys," the colorful half-jeep, half-minibus contraptions that were unique to these islands. A voice mail pinged on Sauvage's phone. Duval had called him while they were midway down, where there was no service. Sauvage listened to the message, once again asking him where the hell he was.

The heart of Zamboanga City was coming alive in the darkness. Sauvage saw scattered groups congregating in the narrow streets. Signs in English and Filipino promised cold beer and hot music. He felt the throbbing bass beat coming right up through the street and into his car seat.

"Take to me wherever I can find a boat for hire," Sauvage told the driver.

"A boat to go where, sir?"

"Out there," Sauvage said, pointing to the Sulu Sea.

"It is nighttime, sir."

"I'll arrange something for tomorrow."

"That is still not a good idea, sir. There is too much . . . *pakikidigma* out there."

"I'm sorry, what does that mean?"

"Trouble, sir. Shooting and bloodshed."

"I understand," Sauvage said. "Just let me off by the port."

A few minutes later, he was out of the taxi and standing on the edge of the darkening water, looking out at what some people called the last "pirate sea" in the South Pacific. It had been notorious enough in the 1970s when both the Moro National Liberation Front and the Moro Islamic Liberation Front battled the Philippine government for self-rule. Now it was Abu Sayyaf, injected with a new strain of Islamic extremism, who had taken over the cause with a degree of brutality and violence their insurgent fathers and grandfathers never could have imagined.

The official French Ministry for Foreign Affairs advisories used three degrees of warning for travelers: yellow for "Exercise a high degree of caution," orange for "Reconsider your need to travel," and red for "*Do not travel under any circumstances.*" This entire region of the Philippines, including the very ground that Sauvage was standing on at this moment, was marked red.

The sodium lights all around the dock area were burning now. To

Sauvage, this place didn't seem much different from any other Southeast Asian port, but then he noticed that he was the only person who looked as though he didn't belong here, and many of the men hanging around were doing a good job of watching him without being obvious about it.

At the end of the block, he saw the tall blue and white walls of the Coast Guard compound. He went to the gate that cut into the wall, and found a young uniformed guard standing watch. Sauvage showed his Interpol badge to the guard. It was obvious he had never seen one before, but he listened politely as Savuage asked to speak to whoever was in charge this evening.

The guard spoke a few Filipino words into his radio, then nodded for Sauvage to follow him. They walked through the well-appointed facility to the rear docking area, where a uniformed lieutenant was watching a maintenance crew service the engine of a sixteen-meter patrol boat.

Sauvage was still putting the words together in his head when he showed the lieutenant his badge. "I started my day in Jakarta," he finally said, deciding to lay it out straight. "I've followed four people to your city. I believe they're heading for Jolo or one of the other islands."

"What kind of people are you talking about?"

"One American man. Two others who are probably European, a man and a woman. And one man who I believe is probably Indonesian."

The lieutenant raised an eyebrow. "If this is true, it's a very bad idea for them. But wait . . . You said one American?"

"Yes."

"This crew stopped an American today," the lieutenant said, nodding toward the boat. "He said he was a treasure hunter."

"It was just him? Nobody else?"

"He was alone. My men were going to arrest him and bring him back, but then they were called away. They instructed him to leave the area immediately."

Sauvage thought about it. If this was his American, why would he be out on the water alone?

"Where was he?" Sauvage asked.

"In the open water between Jolo and Pata Island."

It had to be him.

"Could you take me out to the islands? Tomorrow morning?"

"That would not be allowed," the lieutenant said.

"Can you ask your commander in the morning?"

"I can ask him, and he will say the same thing."

Sauvage did some quick risk analysis in his head and decided to go ahead and say it. "What if Hashim Baya is out there somewhere?"

The lieutenant raised the same eyebrow again. "The Crocodile? On the Sulu Sea?"

"You know I don't have arrest powers," Sauvage said. "But Baya is Red Notice Number One right now, and if you happened to catch him while an Interpol officer was onboard to witness . . ."

He watched the lieutenant think it over. "Why don't you come back in the morning?" he said. "I will leave a note for the commander."

"Thank you. I will do that."

Sauvage shook the lieutenant's hand, and the guard returned him to the front gate. As soon as he was gone, one of the mechanics servicing the engine jumped down from the boat and followed.

———

The heat continued to press down on Mason's body. It was as real and tangible as any physical weight.

The light around the edges of the door had dimmed, then gone out completely, leaving him in darkness. The heat did not lessen. If anything, in the absence of light it became the only presence in the room, his only companion.

He thought about hot nights in Chicago, watching his daughter sleep, making love to his wife. And drinking, drinking, drinking—everything cold and good that he'd ever drunk.

He said good night to his wife and his daughter through parched lips, wondering if it would be the last time.

———

Sauvage found the first motel down the street from the Coast Guard compound, opened the window to let in a breeze off the water, then lay down on the bed still wearing his clothes. He listened to the noise of trucks and motorcycles passing by on the street.

He said the same thing he said every night before drifting off to sleep: "*Bonne nuit, Mireille, mon amour. Bonne nuit, Jean-Luc, mon grand garçon.*"

A few minutes later, there was a knock on his door.

# 13

The man standing at Sauvage's door was dressed in blue overalls with a great diagonal streak of motor grease like a sash across the chest. Sauvage's heart was pounding. He had already drifted off to sleep, hungry and exhausted in this noisy, alien city. No one knew he was here. Yet here was this rough character rapping on his door.

"I am sorry to disturb you," the man said. "I want to help you."

"How did you find me here? Did you follow me?"

"Yes, sir." He shifted uncomfortably. "I didn't know how else to talk to you."

"Why do you need to—"

"I was working at the Coast Guard station, and I heard your conversation with the lieutenant. About Hashim Baya."

The man paused to let that sink in.

"What about him?" Sauvage asked.

"May I come in, sir?"

Sauvage thought it over. It would be a foolish move, but then, after everything he had done in the past thirty-six hours, this wouldn't even make the top five.

He opened the door all the way. The man came in, scanned the room uncomfortably, then said, "You're a brave man for coming here."

"Why do you say that?"

"You don't understand," the man said, rubbing his hands together and looking at the window shade as if he expected someone to be standing on the other side, listening to every word. "If the Crocodile is on one of the islands, then you know the men who are loyal to him. They are *everywhere* in this city. And the commander will *never* let you go out on that boat. Not if you are going to interfere with the Crocodile's business. That has already been arranged for, if you follow what I am saying."

Sauvage nodded again. "I think I do."

"That's why I came here," the man said. "You need to hear these things."

"If what you say is true, then you're putting yourself in danger right now. Why would you do that?"

"Because they killed my brother. He took some German tourists out onto the sea in his boat. They captured the Germans to hold for ransom, but my brother wasn't worth keeping, so they cut his throat and threw him into the sea."

All of a sudden, they had something in common. Something more important than geography, age, race, class, or anything else.

"I'm sorry," he said.

"My other brother has the boat now. It is very fast. He will take you to the islands if you wish."

"When?"

"Tomorrow morning, as early as you can be at the dock."

"Do I need money?"

"I know he would appreciate some money for fuel. But helping you stop Baya and those . . ." The man hesitated to find the right word. "Those pirates would be payment enough. For both of us."

Sauvage agreed and thanked him, then showed him out the door. When the man was gone, he lay back down on the bed in his clothes. But he couldn't sleep.

———

Sauvage was up before the sun. A splash of water on his face, a bottle of Coca-Cola and a bag of chips from the vending machine, and he was down on the street, looking for an ATM. He took out as much local currency as his card would allow, then went to the dock.

He found the very farthest end of the dock, where he had been instructed to go, and found a single man standing there waiting for him. He nodded once but didn't otherwise introduce himself. The boat was a twenty-foot trawler, well past its prime, outfitted for fishing.

"Discreetly," the man said as he peered up and down the dock. He got into the boat and gestured for Sauvage to follow. "Discreetly."

There was a faded canvas canopy above the two front cabin seats. Sauvage sat in the seat next to the driver, and a few seconds later they were backing away from the dock.

Sauvage studied the man. He had a rough beard, making it hard to see the family resemblance to his brother. He kept his eyes on the water and the other vessels as he negotiated his way out to the open water. Only then did Sauvage relax. "I'm sorry about your brother," he said.

The man looked over at him with a tight grimace and nodded. "Thank you, sir."

Then he pushed the gas lever all the way forward, and the boat took off into the Sulu Sea, moving faster than Sauvage would have expected. The sun was just coming up on what would surely be another hot day, but with the early morning wind whipping against his face, Sauvage felt a chill.

It was only thirty minutes on the water until he saw a large island appearing to the west. He touched the driver's arm and gestured to it.

"Basilan," the driver yelled against the roar of the motor. He nodded to the south. Still up ahead.

Another hour passed. The sun was high enough off the horizon to heat the air, and any hint of a chill was gone. Sauvage felt the exhaustion catching up to him again.

*Wake the hell up*, he told himself. *You need to be sharp.*

*And remember the mission:*

*Infiltrate, which you're already doing.*

*Locate, which will happen any minute now.*

*Communicate.*

He checked his phone. Somehow, he still had just enough service for it to be usable.

Another large island appeared ahead of them. The driver nodded to Sauvage and then turned the boat to the east. Sauvage scanned the shoreline as they circled the island. A few beaches broke the thick tree line. Then he saw a dock and a group of buildings. As they went farther, another dock, more buildings.

The boat kept going.

"Isn't that Jolo?" he yelled.

The driver just nodded his head at another, smaller island ahead of them. Sauvage couldn't make any sense of it, but then as they rounded the smaller island he saw something he didn't expect: a yacht.

Forty meters long. Gleaming white in the morning sunlight. Long and thin and clearly built for both speed and luxury. It was anchored a quarter mile out from the smaller island.

Every mistake Sauvage had made in the past two days ran through his mind in quick succession. Coming all this way on his own, telling a group of strangers who he was looking for . . . Right up to trusting a man who would follow him to his motel room, listening to his story about a brother's death on the Sulu Sea and not examining the one tiny nagging doubt it had left in him: What were the odds they recovered the body out here? And if they didn't, how would they know his throat had been cut?

And now with the sudden appearance of the yacht . . . How many men in this part of the world would own something like this?

Sauvage slipped his cell phone out of his pocket, aimed it at the yacht, and took a photo. He glanced back and forth between the phone and the driver as he quickly composed a text message to Duval. But when he looked down, the phone was knocked from his hand and went skittering across the deck.

As Sauvage grabbed at the wheel, the boat veered hard to the right, heading straight toward the yacht. The driver struggled to control the wheel, his face just inches away, until he took out a cheap knock-off revolver and stuck the barrel in Sauvage's ribs.

"Discreetly," the driver said as he calmly steered away from the near collision. Now they were close enough to the yacht for Sauvage to see a man standing high above them on the foredeck. He was wearing a green shirt, just like the scores of men Baya had sent into Singapore. This one was holding a gleaming Pindad assault rifle, and he gave them a barely perceptible nod as they passed by.

Another two men, dressed in faded clothes and wearing bandannas and both bearing older versions of the same Pindad, were waiting for them on an old wooden dock looking so rotted it was a wonder it supported their weight. The driver cut the engine and let the boat drift to shore.

Sauvage took out his wallet.

"Too late for that," the driver said. "We are already here. And I will be paid well enough today, thank you."

But Sauvage wasn't going for bribe money. Instead, he quickly pulled out the folded photograph of his wife and daughter, then palmed it as he put his billfold back in his pocket. He waited for the driver to look up at one of the two men on the dock catching the boat's bow before he took his chance to tuck the photograph into the waistband of his pants.

Whatever was about to happen next, he'd be damned if he let anyone take Mireille and Jean-Luc from him.

———

Mason opened his eyes.

A thin line of light burned around the edges of the door. His throat was on fire. It was hard to swallow. His clothes were caked with the salt of dried sweat.

He sat up, feeling the room spin until a clang at the door jarred everything into place. Then he heard a key scrape into the padlock, the latch open, and the bottom of the door screech against the concrete. Mason tried to get to his feet.

The sunlight blinded him. Figures moved in the light—aliens from another world, wavering and shapeshifting.

One of the figures was suddenly close to him. A man on his hands and knees, the stranger's face inches away from Mason's. Then something swung through the hot air and hit the man in the back of the head. He went facedown against the concrete.

The door slammed shut again. The lock was relatched. The man next to Mason stayed where he was and did not move.

There were two of them in hell now.

———

Some time ticked by. The line of light around the door grew brighter, and the heat in the air pressed down with more force against Mason's skin. But nothing burned hotter than his thirst.

The second man did not move until finally he made a low, grinding moan. He pushed himself up from the concrete, stayed halfway up for a long time, then finally rocked himself back to a sitting position. He shook his head as if trying to clear his vision. When his eyes were focused, he stared across the room at Mason.

"It's you," he said, wiping blood and spit from his mouth.

Mason didn't bother responding.

"Where are we?" the man asked. He had a pronounced French accent, each syllable spoken evenly.

Mason shrugged. "Hell."

The man nodded. "How long have you been here?"

"Forever."

"I work for Interpol," he said. "My name is Martin Sauvage." He pronounced his first name like a Canadian hockey player. Mar-*ten*. With the *n* sound dissolving in his mouth before he could finish it.

"Did you follow me here?" Mason asked.

"Yes. You and your team."

"Bad idea."

Mason repositioned his back against the hot metal wall, leaning into it with the opposite shoulder.

"You know this is not about you," Sauvage said. "I want Baya."

Mason didn't respond.

"Is he here?"

Mason nodded once. Sauvage settled his back against the opposite wall of the shed. He wiped more blood from his mouth and then rubbed the back of his head where he'd been hit.

"Don't tell me you came here alone," Mason said. "Because that would the stupidest fucking thing I've ever heard."

Sauvage considered this for a moment. Then he said, "I came alone."

———

More time passed. Both men sat across from each other with their eyes closed.

The silence was broken by the lock being undone and the door being pulled open abruptly. The tall guard poked his head in first, verifying that there would be no ambush this time. Then he brought in a wooden folding chair and set it up in the middle of the room. Once this was done, he stood waiting by the door until a conversation outside was concluded and Hashim Baya came into the room. He was wearing a fresh, clean version of the same outfit he'd had yesterday: loose-fitting pants and sandals, with a tailored white shirt made from the lightest fabric. Perfect for a large man in a very hot climate.

Baya pulled the chair back a few feet so that he could sit and regard both men at once.

Sauvage was already rolling forward, as if to get to his feet. The guard leveled his Pindad at Sauvage's chest until he sat back down.

"Mr. Mason," Baya said, "I trust you have introduced yourself to Monsieur Sauvage?"

"We didn't get that far," Mason said.

"Nick Mason," Baya said, speaking to Sauvage. "From Chicago. He came here to kill me."

Then Baya took out Sauvage's Interpol badge from his own pocket and examined it. "And you came all the way from France to do what? Capture me? Bring me to justice?"

Sauvage stared at him.

"You do this because they have told you I am a criminal? Because they put my name on a Red Notice and then wound you up like an obedient robot and set you on my trail? You got closer than most, I will grant you that."

Sauvage kept silent.

"All those men outside," Baya said. "Are they criminals too? Because they wish to have their own country again? Determine their own destiny? The Sultanate of Sulu, their birthright, which has been here for centuries, and yet even now they are invaded, colonized, enslaved?"

He paused to study both men.

"Tell me that these men are the criminals," Baya went on. "Just because they resist. Tell me that I'm a criminal for listening to them. For understanding them. For supporting them. Tell me that this man right here . . ." Baya pointed at Mason. "Tell me he's a criminal because they forced him to come here against his will. Because I interfere with the smooth flow of their poison and their dirty money, and they've told this man they will kill his family if he doesn't do everything they order him to do."

That got Mason's attention. He didn't like hearing the circumstances of his life discussed so casually. And once again he had to wonder just how this man knew so much about the organization. And about himself.

"Tell me that Mr. Mason's ancestors were criminals," Bays said, "because they stood up to King George and demanded freedom. Tell me that *your* ancestors were criminals, Monsieur Sauvage, because they stormed the Bastille and dragged King Louis and his wife out of their castle and strapped them to the guillotine."

Baya took out a white handkerchief and wiped the back of his neck.

"Tell me," Baya said. "Tell me who the criminals are. And who gets to decide."

Sauvage kept staring at him for one more beat, then finally spoke. "You are the criminal," he said. "And God decides."

Baya's head snapped back in surprise. "God does."

"Yes."

"Which God are you talking about now?"

"The God who watches innocent women and children being blown up by the bombs you pay for."

Baya nodded his head slowly. "Do you know the history of this island?" he asked. "And what happened here? The day that three thousand people were killed by the Philippine Army? Not soldiers. Civilians. Men, women, children. So many children. Right here, Monsieur Sauvage. On this island, where we are talking right now."

Baya looked back and forth between Mason and Sauvage, then turned his head to glance at the guard.

"Remind us when this happened," he said to the guard. "What year was it?"

The guard remained silent, but he gripped his Pindad tightly.

"Not from some long-ago era, was it? Not a page in a history book? It was something that happened in your *father's lifetime. In my* lifetime, because I'm a little older than all of you. It was one generation ago."

The guard nodded, squeezing the gun.

"So now these men fight," Baya said. "Just like their fathers fought. If I help them, it is because I have chosen my side in this fight, because I believe in their cause. In return, they honor me with their trust."

He looked hard at Mason.

"Which is why the two of you are still alive right now. By tomorrow, I won't be able to stop them from making a video of you, Mr. Mason, so they can send it to the people you work for."

Then over at Sauvage.

"And you, Monsieur Agent of the International Police, I think they know that nobody would ever negotiate a ransom for you. Not officially. So unless you have some kind of back channel, I hope you are not too attached to your head."

Baya stood up. He folded up his handkerchief and put it back in his pocket.

"You should *both* think about what you have to offer me right now," he said. "Because I am your last hope."

The guard opened the door. Both men left and shut the door behind them. Mason looked over and could barely make out Sauvage's face in the darkness.

"They'll be able to track my cell phone signal," Sauvage said. "It was on until I got to this island."

"You told me you came alone," Mason said. "So how long will it take for them to decide you're in trouble and start looking for you?"

"They'll probably start thinking that way tomorrow."

"After they've already cut your head off."

"You got any ideas," Sauvage said, "I'm listening."

Mason shook his head and went back to silence. Until finally Sauvage broke it again: "That story Baya told us about the three thousand civilians. He left out the part about the MNLF massacring a hundred Philippine soldiers. The bombing was in retaliation, which doesn't make it right, but—"

"Just shut the fuck up," Mason said. The thirst was sapping his strength now. And it physically hurt him to talk, but he couldn't help himself. "You think I want to hear a fucking history lesson right now?"

"Half a story is a lie. I just want you to know."

"I've been in this shed for two days," Mason said. "You don't need to give me a sales pitch on what an evil piece of shit this guy is."

"We shouldn't be fighting right now," Sauvage said. "We should be working together."

"Working together for what? So you can arrest me as soon as we get out of here? I'll kill you first. You understand that, right? Hell, I'd kill you for a cold beer right now."

"My boss says I'm not even supposed to be looking for you," Sauvage said. "Besides, I'm Interpol so I can't arrest *anyone*. Not unless you're planning a vacation in France."

Mason banged the back of his head once against the metal wall. "No backup, no comms. He fucking walks right into a terrorist camp. And I thought *American* cops were dumb."

A beat of silence, Sauvage staring across at Mason. He said, "You are right, but I have my own reasons."

"What you were saying about innocent women and children," Mason said. "I take it that's personal."

"Yes."

"When did it happen?"

"In 2015. The Paris bombings."

Mason nodded. He didn't need to hear more.

"At least I got to see him," Sauvage said. "One time. Face-to-face. I did my best to get to him."

Another silence. Sauvage dropped his head and Mason could see him trying to swallow. "They need to give us water," he said. "We're going to die of thirst before we die of anything else."

Mason just looked at him.

*You have no idea what real thirst feels like, my stupid cop friend.*

———

Gunfire.

The faraway sound snapped Mason awake. He had slipped into a dull, sick half-sleep, dreaming about the sensation of cold water against his skin and in his throat. The interior of the shed was in complete darkness now. Sauvage's voice cut through from the other side of the room: "Military?"

"Probably not," Mason struggled to say, barely recognizing his own voice. "Not at night."

Mason struggled to his feet, sliding his back up the metal wall. His head was pounding, his eyes going in and out of focus. He tried to orient himself, remembering the brief moments before they put him in this shed. He had the impression that they were close to a shoreline, maybe a hundred yards. But as the gunfire got louder, he realized it was coming from the opposite direction, from the heart of the island's interior.

A diversion? A simple strategy, but probably the best available. Come in loud from the long side, leave the short side open.

He listened carefully, caught a rapid-fire sequence that had to be a machine gun. Maybe one of the Scorpions.

Voices outside, speaking commands Mason didn't understand. But he recognized the urgency. Then the sound of the lock being unlatched.

"Get down," Mason told Sauvage. "Play dead."

"What?"

"Just do it."

Quick calculations in his head. *If I'm dead, they lose my value and they probably just shoot the cop because who the fuck cares. But if the cop is dead and I'm still alive...*

*For one second, they won't know what to do.*

That would be his one chance.

As Mason pushed himself from the wall, he felt the room spinning. More noises outside. The voices louder. The lock being worked, pulled at, a key inserted wrong, dropped on the ground. Yelling. Recriminations. The sound of a man being pushed away, the impact of his body against the outside of the door.

Sauvage was on the concrete floor now, facedown. Mason stood over him. As he bent forward, he felt his whole body about to topple over. He put a hand down, pushed hard on Sauvage's back, and heard a sharp breath come out of him.

*Stay quiet, you dumb cop.*

He braced himself, made a wider stance with his feet, brought his spinning head up slowly until his body was upright. For a moment, he felt disoriented and weightless, as if he were floating in the void of outer space, until the door screeched open and he was suddenly back inside a dark shed on a nameless island on the edge of the Sulu Sea—a man too far from home and going mad with thirst. A flash of light assaulted his eyes. He couldn't see. Couldn't focus. The blurred faces of two men. Two gun barrels pointed at him. A single bright shining light exploding inside his dried-up brain as one of the men pointed his gun barrel at him and yelled, "We go now! We go now!"

"Help him," Mason said, swallowing hard against the desert of his throat and forcing the words out. "You have to help him. I think he's dead."

A single second as the two men looked at each other, stretching into another second before the nearer man stepped forward. Mason didn't move. He stayed standing above Sauvage, one foot on each side of him.

"Move away," the man said, and then he gave Mason exactly what he wanted. He extended the gun at Mason to push him away, not barrel first but holding it out horizontally, like a hockey player throwing a cross-check with his stick.

*Now.*

Mason didn't try to hit the man in the face or take the gun away from him—mistakes he had made the last time. Instead, he simply turned the gun toward the second man, relying on the first man's lack of trigger discipline.

The shots came out in a three-round burst. Two of them went right through the thin metal wall, but the third hit the other man in the throat. He fell back in shock and dropped the rifle.

The first man was yelling now and trying to pull the rifle back. Mason pulled in the opposite direction, then twisted it as he let it shoot back and the stock hit the man right in the chin. Mason followed that with the heel of his hand to crush the man's nose and then swung the Pindad around to put a three-round burst in his head.

"Get down!" Sauvage yelled, and he pulled Mason down to the floor before he could even think about reacting. Another Pindad was being fired from outside the shed, and the rounds came right through the walls. One of them hit the other man, who had already taken one in the throat, and he went all the way down.

When the Pindad fired from outside the shed had exhausted its thirty-round magazine, the sound gave way to a heavy silence. Mason rolled over across the concrete and fired out the door. It was pure darkness, his eyes not yet readjusted, but he heard the final cry of the man standing outside, and then the sound of his body hitting the ground.

Mason scrambled to his feet, fueled by his last reserves of adrenaline. He came through ready to fire, then didn't stop moving until he had crossed the clearing and was standing with his back against the trunk of a great palm tree. Only now did he make out the dim rays of moonlight filtering down through the thick trees. He looked back at the shed and saw Sauvage emerge a moment later, holding the other man's Pindad. A sudden volley of gunfire once again broke the silence, shredding leaves and sending Sauvage to the dirt. Mason returned fire, aiming for a narrow gap in the foliage.

Sauvage crab-walked his way over close to Mason and stood behind a nearby tree. "The dock is this way," he said, nodding to the southeast. "I saw some boats when they brought me in."

They heard more gunfire in the distance, more intensive than any Pindad could produce. Definitely the Scorpions.

*Where's the shore-side help?* Mason asked himself. Surely, the plan couldn't rely on him escaping on his own.

"Let's go," Mason said. "Move."

He pushed his way through the thick foliage. With the moon obscured, it became an exercise in blind combat with each branch and hanging leaf. Staying quiet was impossible. He kept pushing through, feeling the sting of the thorns tearing at his arms and face. Sauvage was right behind him.

They both fell forward when they came to a ravine. Mason picked himself up and took a breath. He was kneeling in filthy brackish water and felt an overwhelming desire to bend down and drink it. But then he heard more gunfire in the distance and knew he had to keep moving. He spotted moonlight ahead. A break in the trees. He climbed up the bank of the ravine and peered over the edge.

There was a rough path of washed-out tree roots and stones leading down to the edge of the sea. A small fishing boat with a tattered canopy was secured with a single rope tied to a tree branch on shore. It wasn't much, but the engine looked big enough to take a man to safety.

"Your ride," Mason said, his voice virtually gone now, his throat all but closed. "Go to one of the bigger islands. Call for help."

"We'll both go," Sauvage said. "You can't stay here."

"I've got help coming," Mason said. "If I miss them, I'll put them in danger."

Even as he said it, Mason wondered how he had suddenly turned into such a team player after being abandoned on this island for two days. If it were just Torino and Farhan who might get killed or captured, with no Luna involved, would he feel the same way?

"That's insane," Sauvage said. "You have to come with me."

"You can't arrest me, remember?"

"I'm not arresting you, Mason. I'm trying to save your life. Get in the boat and we'll both go look for the rest of your team."

"They'd kill you, soon as they found out who you work for," Mason said. "I wouldn't be able to stop them."

Sauvage was still hesitating. Mason pointed the Pindad at the cop's chest. "Get the fuck out of here," he said. "Right now."

Sauvage held up his own Pindad. "I could have killed you already. I know a few agents who would have."

The two men stayed frozen in place for a long beat, until finally Sauvage lowered his weapon. "Don't blame me if they catch you," he said. "But if you do get out, make sure your team knows that Baya's boat is out there. With at least one shooter onboard."

"What . . . How do you know it's Baya's boat?"

"I saw it on the way in. A Millennium superyacht, with a man in a green shirt standing guard."

Mason nodded. Then he gave Sauvage a hard push that nearly sent him tumbling down the path. When Sauvage regained his balance, he glanced back at Mason one time, then turned and went down toward the water.

Mason waited to see if Sauvage got gunned down by anyone hiding at the shore. But he made his way onto the boat, started it with a sudden loud roar, and took off into the heart of the sea.

There was more gunfire in the distance, followed by yelling, then screaming, then what sounded like a series of urgent commands. It sounded too close, and Mason was already regretting his decision to send Sauvage off on his own.

*Since when do you care what happens to a cop?*

Mason shook his head clear, then kept working his way through the trees and brush, keeping the shore in sight. He was pushing his way through a dense patch when he happened to glance toward the water. It was a single glint of moonlight off a piece of metal trim, or he would have missed it completely. He couldn't tell what kind of boat it was, or if it was friendly or foe, but there it was, grounded at the shore, mostly hidden by overhanging mangrove branches. He paused and waited, listening carefully. Then he decided to move closer. As soon as he took one step, he sensed the presence behind him. He held his breath.

A hushed voice. "Mason!"

Luna.

Mason turned. A flashlight clicked on once, just for a second. Twenty feet behind him, slightly to the left.

"I'm here," Mason said back.

"I see you," she said. "I almost shot you."

Luna emerged into a patch of moonlight. She was dressed completely in the same coal black as her hair. She had a Glock in each hand, a penlight held in her mouth like a cigar, and a set of night-vision goggles over her eyes.

She flipped up the goggles, took out her satellite phone from a pocket, and hit a few keys. Only then did she finally look at him closely. He had a hundred bloody scratches all over his face and arms.

"What the hell . . ."

"Water," Mason said. "Anything. Now."

"I couldn't find you at the compound," she said, tossing him a pint bottle. "I was working my way back to the boat."

*Giving up on me*, Mason thought. *And getting the hell out of here.*

He didn't speak again until he drained the bottle. It felt so good, like pouring life itself into his body. The thirst in his throat was extinguished, but his head was still spinning. He needed more. Gallons and gallons more. "What the hell happened, anyway? When I came back from Jolo, you were gone."

"Abu Sayyaf found us," she said. "If you had taken the faster boat, we never would have gotten away in the hybrid."

"Yeah, you're welcome. But why the fuck didn't you come after me until tonight?"

"Come after you *where*? We didn't know where they took you. Do you know how many little islands there are around here? You're lucky we found you at all."

There was another burst of gunfire from the other side of the island.

"I messaged them that we're on the move," she said. "They're working their way back to the other boat. We need to go meet them."

They climbed down through the thick to where the boat was hidden under overhanging branches. It was the hybrid, capable of running quietly when needed. And right now it was what they needed. Luna got behind the wheel, and Mason pushed the boat away from the shore. He took a moment to catch his breath before pulling himself in.

"You okay?" Luna asked him.

"Just tell me you have more water in this boat."

Luna nodded toward a cooler. It was full of water bottles. Mason grabbed one and poured it down his throat. Like the first, it was the most delicious pint of lukewarm water he had ever tasted.

When the bottle was empty, he threw it on the deck, opened another, and forced himself to go slower. He could practically feel the water coursing through his body, reviving him and finally starting to clear his head.

"We'll dump this boat when we get to the fast one," Luna said, "and get the hell out of here."

"Did you see a yacht on your way here?"

"I saw *something* in the distance, but—"

"Baya has a boat around here somewhere."

"How do you know that?"

*Because my friend the Interpol cop told me.*

"Never mind how," he said. "Can you find it again?"

"Yes," she said. "Probably. But what about—"

"Do you want to go find Baya and finish this right now? Or do you want him to pull up anchor and leave?"

She nodded, and without another word she put the boat in gear and took them out to find Baya's yacht.

# 14

Mason and Luna stayed a quarter mile away from the island, circling it slowly. The hybrid, running purely on electric power now, was eerily quiet. Mason sat with a Glock 17 in one hand, a bottle of water in the other.

They kept one eye on the shore, watching for Abu Sayyaf or any other version of trouble. They kept the other eye out for Baya's Millennium yacht.

"I sent Torino another message," Luna said as she slipped her sat phone back into her wet suit pocket. "I told him to hang back while we make a try for this."

Mason looked over at her. The only light was a faint glow from the boat's instrument panel. "What did he say to that?"

"I didn't wait for an answer," she said as she stared straight ahead, watching the dark water in front of them.

Finally, they came around a bulge in the island's perimeter and saw faint lights in the distance. Luna slowed the boat to a dead idle. They drifted in near silence.

"It's not moving," she said.

"Looks like the right length."

"We can't get too close."

"No kidding."

She glanced over at him and asked him the question of the night: "How good a swimmer are you?"

The true answer to that was complicated. Growing up on the South Side, Mason had had plenty of chances to swim. Not just in pools around the South Side but also in Lake Michigan. But when other kids were learning how to do a flip turn, Mason was learning how to open a locked car door without breaking the window. When other teenagers had summer jobs as lifeguards, Mason was delivering twenty vehicles a week to local chop shops.

"I won't drown," he said.

Luna put the boat back in gear and pointed it toward another good hiding place—a small natural cove with overhanging foliage. Mason grabbed a large branch and looped a rope around it.

"Wet suits in here." She opened up a locker beneath a rear seat and pulled out a black wet suit.

"I don't need one," Mason said. "I just spent two fucking days in an oven. Being cold sounds okay right now."

"Don't be an idiot. It's a quarter mile in open water." Then she took off her pants and shirt. She stood in the faint moonlight, shaking out her wet suit, wearing nothing but a thong.

Mason thought he'd left all physical desires on the other side of the world, on top of being dehydrated half to death, but the sight of her lean and muscular body stopped him. Then he shook it off and went into the locker and pulled out a man's wet suit. He stripped down to his underwear and worked the snug neoprene over his body. He'd never worn one before.

When they were both dressed, she gave him a holster to put over his suit and then handed him one of the Glock 17s.

"You can fire this thing underwater if you need to."

He nodded as he strapped the gun into the holster. "I know."

The final gear was a pair of flippers for each of them. By the time Mason went over the side, Luna was already ten yards ahead of him, swimming with smooth, efficient strokes. She stopped to tread water as she looked back at him.

The salt water stung every cut and abrasion on Mason's body, but as soon as he started kicking with the flippers, he could feel himself propelled quickly through the water.

*Hell of a triathlon. Two days of near-lethal dehydration, a quarter-mile swim in the open sea, then an assassination.*

Luna paused for a moment and let him catch up to her. "Think you can swim a little quieter? The boat would have made less noise."

"Just go," Mason said.

She turned and swam. Mason kept moving behind her, trying to smooth out his stroke. The lights on the yacht ahead were burning brighter and brighter. They were getting close.

Luna gave him a nod, then dived under and swam below the surface. Mason knew he had to do the same. They were too close now to go any farther on the surface. As he ducked under the water, everything went dark and quiet. He propelled himself, swimming frog style, willing himself to take one more stroke, one more, one more. *You can't surface yet. They'll see you and put a dozen rounds through you right here in the water.*

When he could hold his breath not a second longer, he finally came up for air. Gasping louder than he wanted, he looked up and saw a man standing on the top deck. He was dressed in the Baya-brand green shirt, holding an assault rifle and, fortunately, facing in the opposite direction.

Until he suddenly turned.

Mason went down again, back into the dark and quiet depth. He stayed down and didn't even try to move for twenty seconds. Then finally, he frog-kicked toward the boat. When he came up again, he was so close to the hull, his head bumped it. Luna was a few feet away.

They both kept still, waiting and listening. Then they moved to the back of the boat. Like many yachts, this one had a low afterdeck for access to secondary craft, for Jet Skis, for swimming, for whatever a rich yacht owner felt like doing. Mason lifted himself out of the water, just high enough to see another green-suited bodyguard sitting in a chair, maybe ten feet away. There was a soft glow from a series of lights running on the underside of each gunwale, and a wall of smoked glass led into the rest of the lower deck. Mason caught a glimpse of an assault rifle across the man's chest. Then a quick flash on the man's face. His eyes were closed.

*I wonder if Baya knows one of his guards is asleep on the job*, Mason thought. He came back down and held up one finger to Luna, then closed his eyes and tilted his head against an open hand.

She nodded back. This was a break that made their next step a little easier, but they still didn't know how many other guards were on the boat, aside from the one man at the very top. Just the two of them would be manageable, especially if one of them was asleep. Three or more, and this would quickly turn into a suicide mission.

Again.

But Mason didn't have time to see it that way. For him, it was just one more moment that demanded a surrender to the beta state of complete awareness. *Mission mode.* Everything happening in one eternal *now*, flowing into the next, until the objective was complete and Mason could become human again.

They both slipped off their flippers and put them on the deck, then pulled themselves up, this time high enough to survey the entire afterdeck. A half dozen empty deck chairs. The sleeping guard with the assault rifle on his chest. Luna nodded again and they both pulled themselves up onto the deck, moving as quietly as they could. The air carried a light chill.

Then the man's eyes opened.

For one instant, Mason and the guard looked at each other. In the next instant, Mason was taking the Glock out of its holster, cursing himself for not having the weapon already drawn—a mistake born of pure fatigue. In the next instant, the man was fumbling with his assault rifle.

Then there was a sudden sound like a bird in flight, and Mason saw the hilt of a knife protruding from the center of the guard's chest. The expression on the man's face was something beyond shock and alarm. He looked over at Luna, frozen in her follow-through.

As he pitched forward, Mason quickly moved to catch him. A scream was forming in his throat. Mason pulled the knife from the man's chest and, in the same motion, drew it across his throat.

Mason held on to the man, one hand held tight across his mouth as the blood poured from his neck. There was a sound from above them. Mason pulled the man toward the glass door of the cabin, beneath the roof half-covering the afterdeck.

Mason and Luna held their breath as the guard above them looked down at the section of the deck he could see. Mason waited for the upper guard to spot the spreading pool of blood, surely made visible by the gunwale lights. But the guard said something in whatever language he shared with the other guard—by the irritation in his voice, probably asking him if he had fallen asleep again.

The voice went quiet. Then footsteps came down an outer staircase. Mason listened hard to gauge the exact rate and direction. He stood up and went to the starboard side of the deck as Luna tried to peer through the smoky glass wall, into the rest of the cabin.

A dozen different events all happened within the next few seconds. As soon as the upper guard put his foot on deck, he was shocked by the sight of a man in a black wet suit, swinging a fist into his face.

Mason put his weight into the punch but felt one bare foot lose purchase on the slick blood all over the deck. The blow glanced off the guard's cheek, but Mason's momentum took his body weight into the man's chest. As he tried to swing his Pindad around, Mason brought up the Glock with his free hand and put the barrel of the gun into the man's gut. He fired two times—precisely the thing he didn't want to do, because now everyone else on the boat, or anywhere within a nautical mile of it, knew that the boat had been invaded.

Luna caught the slightest glimpse of movement on the other side of the smoky glass. She went down just before it was shattered by a blast of at least a dozen automatic rounds.

Mason went down on the opposite side of the deck, waiting for another blast. He looked over at Luna. She was covered with pebbles of glass but unhurt.

Mason couldn't see anything in the darkness of the inner cabin. Whoever had the assault rifle was holding every advantage, and every ticking second made the situation worse. Baya could already be on the radio, calling for reinforcements.

Mason caught Luna's eye. He gestured for her to keep her head down. Then he kicked one of the deck chairs. As soon as it slid across the deck, another blast tore it to pieces. Mason slid two feet and opened up with the Glock, firing every round he had, trying to form a pattern that might give him one hit.

The gun clicked empty and he rolled back. His ears were ringing. He waited.

Then he kicked another chair and it was instantly torn apart by the next volley.

Luna came up this time, but she was too close.

"No!" Mason yelled, but she wasn't listening to him now. She got up to one knee with the first guard's Pindad and opened it up. It was on full auto, not the standard three-shot burst, so it was a nonstop deafening storm as she sprayed the interior of the cabin. Mason waited for the return shots to come, to turn this woman into a bloody rag doll, but she fired and fired until all thirty rounds were spent.

When she was done shooting, she stayed exactly where she was. Mason watched her, the shots still roaring in his ears.

Nothing moved.

She looked over at him, then finally stood up. Mason pulled himself to his feet, careful to avoid the pebbles of glass. Without a word, they both advanced into the interior of the cabin. Luna drew her Glock. Not that it mattered anymore, because either she had already killed whoever was inside or she hadn't. And if she hadn't, then both she and Mason were already destined to die in the next few seconds.

They walked into the main cabin room. Leather furniture, torn by bullet holes. A splintered teak table. Most of the large television screen had been shot off the wall, with just a few black shards remaining. All but one of the pot lights over their head were also destroyed, so only the faintest light was cast down on the scene.

Two men lay dead on the floor, open eyes staring up at nothing. One wore the standard green shirt. The other was clearly the captain of the ship, with a once-white suit that was now turning pink from all the blood. Both men had been carrying Pindads, and now the rifles lay on the deck, each man's trigger finger still in place.

There was a door on either side of the television. The first was unlocked. A small but well-appointed bathroom. Empty.

They went to the other door. It was locked.

Luna stood back to shoot at the lock. Mason put out a hand to stop her and gave the door a kick, just over the latch. Without shoes it hurt like hell, but the door swung open. Luna stepped inside, found a light switch, and turned it on.

It was a bedroom, with a king-size bed, a dresser, and a separate door into another empty bathroom.

"Baya's not here," Mason said.

Luna nodded. Mason saw that her eyes were focused on the closet door.

"Okay, time to leave," Luna said loudly as they both inched closer to the door. They stopped in front of it for a beat; then Luna threw the door open.

Inside was a woman, huddled on the floor beneath a rack of clothes. Her head was turned down, away from them, her lace head covering pulled over her face as if that would be enough to make her invisible. She was holding a cell phone. Luna reached down, grabbed the phone, and checked the number she was calling.

"Who is this?" she said into the phone. No response. She ended the call and threw the phone on the bed.

"Get up," she said to the woman.

The woman didn't move. Luna pushed off the lace covering, grabbed her by her long black hair, then pulled her out of the closet. She let out a short cry of pain as she came to her feet, but otherwise she remained silent.

She was wearing an abaya dress, jade green with an elaborate pattern of gold and white. Maybe forty years old, trim and attractive. When she finally looked up, Mason saw piercing dark eyes. She stood up straight, as if finally drawing on a source of strength in that exact moment—more than enough to face the invaders. "He is not here," she said.

Luna stepped closer to her. Their hair was the same shade of black, but the woman's was straight and neat and Luna's feral curls still glittered with pebbles of shattered glass. "Are you lying to us? There's not some secret hiding place on this boat?"

The woman looked her in the eye. "If my husband were on this boat," she said, "do you think he would hide like a coward and leave me here alone?"

Luna nodded. "Then where is he?"

She didn't answer.

Luna put the barrel of the Glock against her temple. "Where is he?"

The woman closed her eyes and took a sharp breath. "He is on the island, meeting with the leaders."

Luna looked over at Mason. He nodded. It checked out.

The woman's eyes were still closed. She was faintly trembling.

"We can wait for him," Luna said as she lowered the weapon from the woman's head. "He's probably already on his way out here."

"He'll have an army," Mason said. "We won't have a shot at him."

"Will he come with his men?" Luna asked Baya's wife. "Or will he just send the army and stay behind?"

"He will come," she said, finally opening her eyes. "And you will both be killed."

"We don't have surprise on our side anymore," Mason said. "Nowhere to hide, minimal cover, no exit. You really want to bet on the one-percent chance we get a shot at him before we both die?"

Luna shook her head in disgust. "Fine. You're right."

"Let's get out of here," Mason said. And then to Baya's wife, he said, "Tell your husband we're coming for him. And next time—"

"She won't have the chance," Luna said. Then she raised the Glock and shot Baya's wife in the head.

# 15

The gunshot in close quarters was beyond deafening. Baya's wife collapsed to the floor like a marionette with its strings suddenly cut.

"Why did you do that?" Mason's own words sounded as if they came from somewhere far away.

Luna holstered her Glock and walked to the door, brushing past Mason. "Let's go."

Mason took one last look at the body of Baya's wife. Yet more blood spreading and staining the floor of this boat. Then he turned and left the room, negotiating the bloody wreckage of the main cabin until he was back on the afterdeck. In the distance was the unmistakable sound of boat motors screaming at full throttle.

Luna was already putting on her flippers. Mason quickly sat down and did the same, then jumped into the water after her. She swam back in the direction of the cove where their boat was hidden, moving smoothly through the water with powerful strokes. Mason struggled to keep up with her. He could feel his last reserves of adrenaline starting to wane.

The noise of motors grew in volume. He lifted his head for one stroke to listen, put it back down again, and tried to move even faster. *Smooth*, he told himself. *Long and smooth in the water. You're a fucking dolphin.*

When he finally got to the boat, Luna was climbing in. As Mason stood up in the waist-deep shallows, he glanced back and saw other lights out on the water, approaching the yacht.

"What do we do?" Luna asked him. "Hide out here? Run on the water? Or go inland on foot?"

A bright spotlight was now being played across the water around the yacht. Mason looked up at the tree branches above his head and the meager cover they gave the boat from this vantage point. On land, someone would have to work hard to find them, but from the water they'd be an easy target. If they went inland instead . . . *No*, he thought, giving the island a quick scan. *Not enough hiding places. Not if they spot the boat and know we're here. They'll be able to take their time at that point, spread out and hunt us down.*

That left one option.

"Let's go," he said.

He untied the boat and pushed it out into the water, then climbed aboard. Luna pressed a button, and the electric motor purred to life. So much quieter than the gas motor, but from inside the boat it sounded like a loudspeaker broadcasting their presence. "As soon as we're clear," Mason said, "go like hell."

Luna kept the boat close to shore, moving at electric speed with no lights until they had rounded a bend and were out of direct sight. Then she switched to gas power and opened it up. Mason grabbed another bottle of water and downed it. Then another. He looked back and saw nothing behind them but the dark shadow of the island and the night-time horizon of open water.

"I'm keeping the lights off," she said. "If we hit something, we're fucked."

Mason nodded. They might be fucked no matter what they did.

He glanced back one more time and saw a light emerging from the outer edge of the island. The light rode high on the water. "They're coming," he said. "I think it's the yacht."

"That thing is too fast," Luna said. "They'll pick up on our wake. Or if they have marine radar."

Another group of islands appeared ahead—dark forms taking vague shape and growing in size as the boat approached them.

"We can buy some time here," Mason said, nodding to the islands.

"If we land on any of them, they'll see the boat."

"We're going to have to do something," Mason said. "Get close here, then go around."

Luna took a quick glance over her shoulder as she rounded the island, her hair whipped into a frenzy by the wind. "We'll never outrun them. We're going to have to fight."

"There's two of us," Mason said. "We've got two Glocks and one is empty."

"Then reload!"

Mason shook his head and checked behind them again. The light had disappeared behind them, but he knew that it would reappear in the next few moments.

"We've got one shot," Mason said. "Leave the throttle open."

"What are you talking about? Are you crazy?"

"Probably," he said. Then he grabbed her and threw her over the side.

He took one more second to readjust the steering wheel, then jumped in after her. The boat churned past him, heading toward an opening between two more small islands. He spotted her a few yards away and swam toward her. She was treading water in the darkness, with just enough moonlight for him to make out her face. They both watched the boat, a hundred yards away, then two hundred. It was starting to drift to the right.

"Come on, sneak through, you son of a bitch," Mason said, like a football fan leaning into a field goal try.

The motor drifted into the shallow water near the island and churned in the sand for one sickening moment, but then it kicked left and regained its bearings, heading out into the open sea.

A moment later, they heard the sound of another motor, and the superyacht roared into view. Forty meters long and moving way faster than anything that size should be able to.

"Down!" Mason said, and they both ducked their heads under the water. As they stayed below the surface, suspended in the utter darkness, Mason could feel the great twin motors even from forty yards away, like a hollow churning in his gut.

He finally came back to the surface when he could hold his breath no longer. Luna came up a few seconds later. They were alone, without a boat, just off the shore of a nameless tiny island in the Sulu Sea.

"You still have your sat phone?" he asked.

She nodded. Then she started kicking toward shore. Mason followed her. When he was close enough to shore, he stood up on the sand, rocks, and rotting tree limbs, then made his way carefully until he was standing on dry ground. In the dead middle of night, after everything he'd been through, the air felt cold against his dripping hair and the exposed skin of his face, neck, and feet. He started to shiver. Ironic, so soon after nearly dying of heat stroke.

Luna took out the sat phone and punched in a message. How the hell Torino and Farhan were going to find them in exactly this place, Mason didn't know. Would they have to wait until daylight?

"I did my best to describe where we are," Luna said. It was hard to make out her face in the thin moonlight. "We need to find shelter. I'm starting to shiver. And you are too."

Before he could answer, she walked away, down the edge of the waterline until it was obstructed by a great tree half-fallen into the water. Mason went in the other direction, peering into the darkness until he came upon a narrow passage leading into the island's interior. He followed it several yards until it stopped at a rough wooden lean-to— nothing more than a few broken-up wooden boxes and some driftwood propped together to form a crude triangle. It was either someone's secret hideaway or maybe the home of someone who had no other possessions, someone who was now long gone.

At the mouth of the lean-to was a small firepit lined with stones. There were old ashes inside, pebbled with chunks of charred wood. Mason knew that starting a fire would send a visible plume of smoke into the air. *Pretty fucking stupid, but goddamn that would feel good right now.*

He started to shiver again, and this time the deprivation in his body made him feel light-headed. He leaned over and caught himself with his hands on his knees.

Luna appeared behind him. "What's wrong?"

Mason shook his head. "Nothing."

He felt a warm hand pressed against his neck.

"Leave me alone," he said as he turned away. "I'm fine."

"You're losing body heat. We both are."

She led him inside the lean-to. His bare feet felt the bed of leaves and, below that, something like an old towel or cloth. The air smelled like damp earth.

Mason felt his wet suit being unzipped and then pulled down. He tried to push her away, but his hands found nothing to grab on to. Instead, he pitched forward with the momentum and went down onto his knees and elbows. When he rolled over, she was above him, unzipping her own wet suit.

It was too dark to see anything but the contours of what happened next, but he felt every inch of it with his naked skin as she covered him. Her wet hair brushed against his cheeks as he held on to her, his body clinging to the warmth despite everything else that raged inside his head.

"Get the fuck off me," he said. But she held on tight until his body warmed. And then began to respond to hers. It was something he could not control. How many years had it been since the last time he touched his wife this way? Then, even after getting out of prison, the times with Lauren before he sent her away for her own safety. Then with Diana until Cole killed her for betraying him. Just the idea of touching another woman this way again was like an almost forgotten memory, like something Mason had put away forever—something left on the other side of the world with the rest of his old life.

Then he flashed on the image of Luna calmly putting the gun to the head of Baya's wife and pulling the trigger. As if it meant nothing to her at all. He was about to throw her off him, but she bent his arms back and stayed on top of him, straddling his waist. The heat kept building. It was as irresistible as it was inevitable, after all of the adrenaline and desperation they had both lived through tonight.

"Why did you kill her?" he asked. "She was no threat to us."

"Shut up," she said as slid down just to enough to work herself against him. "Just shut the fuck up."

His hands slid down from her shoulders to her hips. She was still just a dark form against the faintest moonlight, but she rode on top of him until she finally curled forward with her head against his as a great shudder took hold of her body. She put her mouth against his and he felt her warm breath mixing with his own.

"*Laisse-moi faire*," she said. "*Laisse-moi faire*." Mason didn't understand the words, but he understood the feeling behind them. She needed something and she had waited too long to have it. But what he gave back to her wasn't sex; it wasn't even *fucking*. It was nothing intimate at all, but rather a purely physical release, a distilled anger that reverberated between them after all of the death and terror they'd shared and knew they would share again.

When they were done, they lay wrapped together, still sharing their warmth. Mason wiped the sweat from his forehead.

"Haven't you seen enough by now?" he said.

"Enough what?"

"Enough fucking blood for one lifetime."

She took a long time to answer. "You're letting yourself *feel* it," she finally said. "It's going to destroy you."

"How can I not feel it? I'm still human. And so are you."

"Yes, we are human, the most savage animal on earth. We will never be anything more than that."

Mason didn't know how to answer that.

"You kill people," she went on. "Just like me. That's what we do. It's what we *are* now. You can't keep holding on to this impossible idea you have, that you're some kind of honorable assassin. There is no such thing. It gets in your way and it's probably going to get you killed. Maybe *both* of us killed."

"How did you even get here, anyway?"

"Why does that matter?"

"Because I want to know," he said. "I never had a choice."

"Don't even try to say that to me," she said. "There's *always* a choice."

"And what was yours?"

"What, you want my life story?"

"Yes," he said. "As long as we're here, I want your fucking life story."

"I grew up in Romania," she said. "My mother met a rich man in Bucharest, and he fell in love with her and brought her back to Monaco. But then she found out that he made all his money as a con man, and he asked her to act as bait for the scams he ran on high rollers at the casinos. Lots of Saudis with oil money. Some Russians. He didn't *force* her to do this. As I say, it was a choice and she made it. She kept doing it even after I was born. But then they picked the wrong mark, and she was killed."

She stopped for a moment, as if maybe, finally, something was breaking through the wall of stone she had built around her emotions.

"I was fifteen years old," she went on. "My stepfather didn't want me around, so he threw me out on the streets. I looked old enough to make my own money then. Old enough but also young enough to be valuable to a certain kind of man. I had learned things from my mother. I did whatever I had to. Until I finally found the wrong mark, just like my mother had. You do it long enough and your luck will always run out."

She paused again. Mason stayed silent. There were frogs outside that they could hear now, night insects. The lapping of the waves. Those were the only sounds on this abandoned island.

"I killed this man in a hotel room. I didn't try to escape. I didn't do anything. I didn't *feel* anything. I just sat there and watched his blood spreading on the carpet. And then I called the front desk and told them to send the police. A few minutes later, a man opened the door with a key. But he wasn't a detective. It was Torino. He told me I could either come with him or I could wait for the police and spend the rest of my life in a prison cell. Which even in a place like Monaco was the same size as a cell anywhere else in the world. So I chose to go with him."

"He trained you," Mason said.

"That's what he would say. But I think I trained him just as much."

"He thinks you're his property too. I can see it every time he looks at you."

"He can think what he wants."

"He's dangerous now," Mason said. "Having his command taken away from him—he can't handle it."

"If we have to kill him, we will." Again, saying it with no emotion, like an item on a to-do list. Mason couldn't help wondering, even as she was still lying on top of him, if killing him would ever go onto that list as easily.

"Tell me the truth," he said. "You've got to be so fucking tired of this."

"I don't think about it."

"You don't think about getting out?"

"Getting out and doing what instead?"

"Anything," Mason said. "Fucking *anything* but killing people. How long do you think you can keep doing this?"

"I don't look ahead. I learned that a long time ago. I deal with today. I deal with right now."

*Zen master with a gun*, Mason thought. *Great.* But then it hit him that what she was saying sounded exactly like the rules he had made for himself a long time ago. Rules that had kept him alive on the street, and then later in prison.

She still had one leg across his, and her hair smelled like something totally foreign and exotic, but it was mixed with sex and his own sweat. Whether he wanted it or not, he could feel the heat building between them again.

In the next moment, from somewhere out on the open water, they both heard the faraway sound of a boat motor. Luna was about to get up when Mason grabbed her by the arm. "Just tell me," he said. "If I see a way out, will you help me? I need to know."

She looked down at him. There was finally enough ambient light to see her face clearly. "You will never find a way out," she said. "But if you can do the impossible . . ."

He waited for more. But then she pushed herself away from him, picked up her wet suit, and took it outside. Mason grabbed his and followed her. When they were both zipped up again, they stood on the edge of the water, listening carefully. The motor was a higher pitch. Not Baya's. As the volume grew, Luna took out her flashlight.

"Think it's them?" she asked.

"One way to find out."

"If it's not, we're dead."

"That's how we find out," Mason said.

Luna turned on her flashlight, flicking it on and off three times short and then one long. The boat slowed. A light onboard repeated the three short, one long pattern.

The boat turned and came to the shoreline. Luna climbed over the gunwale, Mason after her. Farhan helped them both up and gave them towels. Torino was at the wheel. He looked at Luna once, then stared at Mason. Mason stared back.

"Let's go!" Luna said. "I think I hear Baya's boat."

"You went after him on your own," Torino said.

"Yes," Mason said. "He wasn't on his boat."

"So it was the wrong plan," Torino said.

"*Let's go!*" Luna yelled.

Torino put the boat in gear, still staring at Mason. Then he finally turned and pushed the throttle forward.

Mason sat down hard on the seat, surprised at the sudden jolt. Farhan sat across from him and handed him a bottle of water. "I am so glad to see you, my friend."

Mason nodded, then looked over at Luna, then at Torino's back as he drove the boat.

———

Instead of going back to Zamboanga City, Torino took the boat south, all the way to Malaysia and the port city of Sandakan.

When they got to the Sandakan airport, Mason stood alone on the tarmac, still barefoot and wearing his wet suit, watching the dawn sky over the palm trees and going over everything that had happened in the past forty-eight hours.

He wondered whether that cop made it out alive. Whether he would ever see him again.

His gut told him yes.

Farhan came up from behind, carrying a large paper bag. "I found some clothes for you," he said. "Some shoes too. You can change once we get on the plane."

Mason took the bag and checked inside. Cheap jeans and a gray T-shirt, some rattan shoes that were a couple of sizes too big. But it beat a wet suit.

"Thanks," Mason said.

"When you were taken, Torino and Miss Luna fought over what to do next. Torino wanted to leave you. I feel bad for saying that, but I think you should know it."

"Big surprise," Mason said. "He's not my biggest fan."

"Miss Luna insisted that we stay in Zamboanga City. She talked to others in the organization, gathered more intel, even went out on her own the night before last to do recon. When she came back, Torino told her she was being a fool and risking her life for nothing."

Mason nodded. He had wondered whether he would eventually have to kill the man. That didn't seem to be a question anymore.

"She finally spotted some of Abu Sayyaf's men on that little island where they were keeping you," Farhan said. "Do you know how many islands just like that are out there?"

Mason nodded again.

"I don't think she could have convinced him to wait another day," Farhan said. Then he turned toward Torino and Luna, both standing in silence a hundred feet away. "But please don't tell him I told you any of this."

"Why *are* you telling me?" Mason said.

Farhan looked surprised. "Because you are my friend. And because you promised to take me to America with you."

Mason was about to shut that idea down for good. But then he had a thought: *This guy is giving me important information. If he ends up helping me get out of here, I'll personally buy him a seat next to me on the flight home to Chicago.*

A small private jet landed on the tarmac and taxied to the hangar. Mason recognized it as the same jet that had flown them to Zamboanga City. They all boarded, and everyone remained silent as the plane took off. Torino sat next to Luna and finally whispered a few words to her, but she ignored him and stared out her window.

A few minutes after that, the video screen came to life.

It was the boss. "Full report," he said. He looked tired, agitated.

"We failed to reach the target," Torino said.

"I was talking to Mr. Mason," the boss said. "He had operational control."

Mason didn't say anything.

"Mr. Mason, your report."

Another beat of silence, until Mason spoke: "You have a leak."

The boss absorbed this. "How do you know?"

"Because Baya knew everything," Mason said. "He knew my name. He knew we were coming and that there would be four of us. In fact, he seemed to know a hell of a lot about your organization."

"So you spoke to him personally."

"Yes. He wanted more information from me."

"Be more specific," the boss said. "Exactly what did he want to know from you?"

"He wanted to know how to find you."

*The same thing I want to know myself.*

The boss's eyes went wide for one half of a second. It was the first time Mason had ever seen something break his composure. "What did you tell him?" the boss asked.

"I didn't tell him anything," Mason said. "What would I have said?"

"You should have killed him there and then, Mr. Mason. This was your chance."

"I was in no position to do that."

"I don't want to hear it. You failed. And you know what the price will be."

Mason stood up and went closer to the screen, as if he could reach right through and put his hands around the man's neck. He was already picturing a van pulling up outside a house in Colorado, a team of men getting out and going inside. He tried to stop the movie in his head right there. Because any scene that came after would be something beyond his worst nightmares.

*Breathe*, he told himself. *Keep talking. Keep your cool. It's your only chance.*

"Listen," he said, keeping his voice even. "This mission was blown because of a leak in your chain of command. You can't hold me accountable for that. You can't hold *my family* accountable."

"We've already had this conversation," the boss said. "More than once. I've given you every opportunity to—"

"I can't save you if I'm dead," Mason said.

"I hardly need *saving*, Mr. Mason."

"He's the most dangerous man in the world," Mason said. "And the only thing he wanted from me was information on finding *you*. Which means he's coming after you. And that makes me your best friend in the world."

"After all of these failures," the boss said, "why should I have any confidence that you can still get to him?"

Luna stood up and approached the screen. "Because we know where he'll be," she said. "Within the next twenty-four hours. We have a location, and we'll be there waiting for him."

"If you have intel," the boss said, "then now is the time to share it."

"Did you not hear what Mason said about the leak? We need to go alone. With no other support. Until we all know where the leak is, it's the only way."

The boss thought it over.

"It costs you nothing to give us another twenty-four hours," Luna said. "We will be there and we will kill him."

"Twenty-four hours," the boss said. And then the screen went blank.

Mason looked at her and thought, *I'm the one who spent two days in Baya's compound. What does she know that I don't?*

"Tell me where we're going," Torino said, "and what else we'll need."

"*We* aren't going anywhere," Luna said. "Mason and I are going alone."

# 16

Agent Sauvage sat in the terminal, waiting for the flight that would take him from Zamboanga City back to Jakarta. In the past twenty-four hours, he had been taken captive by Abu Sayyaf, locked in a shed with an American assassin, and then finally visited by the one man most responsible for the death of his wife and son.

*Baya. I faced him.*

Sauvage replayed every word said, every subtle shift in body language. The encounter had done nothing to lessen his obsession with bringing the man to some form of justice, even after the brutal escape, after stealing that boat and making a run back to Zamboanga City, running out of gas and drifting in the middle of the Sulu Sea, hearing the motor and wondering if Baya or Abu Sayyaf had caught up to him again and the sound would be the last thing he ever heard, the relief when he saw it was a Philippine patrol boat, then the dread that he would have to explain why he didn't have his Interpol badge. And how the whole story would surely get back to Duval within two minutes. Now, sitting here in this airport, wearing every mile of the past day on his face and feeling more tired than he'd ever felt in his life . . .

He still wasn't ready to give up.

He would catch some sleep on the plane. Then he'd try to get to Mason's apartment and see if he could catch up with him again.

It was his only hope of staying on the trail.

Just as the plane was about to board, his phone rang. *Duval. I'm not ready for this yet.* But when he checked the screen, he didn't recognize the number. It was coming from America.

"Who is this?" he asked.

"This is Agent Payne from the FBI. I hope it's not too late to call. I know you're in France."

"No," Sauvage said. "It's early. My office is in Jakarta now."

"Jakarta . . . Okay, that's not what I was expecting. But I wanted to get back to you on this photograph you sent me. I ran it through our database and I have a name."

"Nick Mason."

"Wait," the agent said after a pause. "If you know his name, why did you—"

"I didn't know it when I sent the image. I'm sorry if I wasted your time. But as long as I have you, what else can you tell me about him?"

"It's actually a whole story, but I can tell you that Mason was five years into a twenty-five-to-life at Terre Haute when he met a major player named Darius Cole there. Apparently, some strings were pulled to get him released."

"That's a hell of a set of strings."

"You could say that. Cole got himself sprung about a year later. But then he showed up dead in his town house, and Mason disappeared. He's still a person of interest in the case, along with half a dozen other cases, and we'd *really* like to talk to him. But now I'm guessing you're going to tell me we won't find him anywhere near Chicago."

"I don't think Jakarta qualifies, no."

"How the hell did he get there? We have no record of him traveling out of the country."

"You just told me he got himself out of a twenty-five-to-life," Sauvage said. "I don't think a fake passport is that big a swing."

"You're right," Payne said. "But here's what I'm thinking. See, we don't have an extradition treaty with Indonesia, so I can't ask you to detain him for us. Is there any chance he'll travel to Singapore? Malaysia? The Philippines?"

On any other day, Sauvage would have laughed. "I'll keep an eye on him," he said. Then he thanked the man and ended the call.

————

The plane carrying Mason and the rest of the team landed at the smaller Halim Perdanakusuma Airport and taxied to the private terminal. When they were off the plane, Mason caught up to Luna and pulled her aside. It was his first chance to talk to her alone since her announcement on the plane.

"You gonna tell me what the plan is?" he asked. "How do you know where Baya is going to be?"

"He grew up in the Aceh province, on the island of Sumatra. So did his wife."

Mason waited for more.

"Aceh is the only province in the country that practices Sharia law."

*Sounds like a fun place*, Mason thought. "I still don't get it."

"That's where she'll be buried," Luna said, "with her head pointing toward Mecca, after they wash her body and wrap her in white linen."

"Let me guess," Mason said. "Within twenty-four hours."

"That's the custom, yes."

Mason weighed this in his mind. "Is that why you killed her? You were thinking ahead?"

She shrugged. "It was in my mind. But I might have killed her anyway."

He let that one go. "So how do we get there?"

"There's a commercial flight at twelve fifteen out of the main airport. We can't use any organization resources if there's a leak. Don't tell anyone else what we're doing."

Mason nodded. As he looked over her shoulder, he caught sight of Torino. He was standing twenty yards away with his arms folded across his chest, staring at both of them.

————

When Sauvage deplaned at the Soekarno-Hatta Airport, he had a few minutes to gather his thoughts as he walked through the secure area of the terminal. After clearing the security checkpoint, he hadn't made it ten steps through the bustling crowd when his path was blocked by his boss, Jacques Duval. "We're going to the office," Duval said. "Right now."

"Any chance I could stop by my place first? Change my clothes?"

*And maybe slip out and go see if Mason is at his apartment . . .*

"No," Duval said. That was the last word he said for the next thirty minutes as he made his way through the morning traffic. When they were in the Interpol office, they stood next to each other in the elevator, walked down the hall, and sat on opposite sides of Duval's desk. Even then Duval stayed silent, until he finally pulled out a pad of paper and clicked open a pen.

"Debrief," Duval said. "Start at the beginning. Everything you've done."

Sauvage took a moment to compose his thoughts, then gave his boss the entire story. After seeing Nick Mason twice, how he worked through the security feed at the airport, spotting the gap and using that to find the fake passport. Then using tax records to find the company on the passport, finding Mason going into the office building and trailing him around town for several days, to his apartment, where he was apparently watching over a young girl from the *kampung*, then following Mason to the Philippines and getting himself captured by Abu Sayyaf, meeting Mason there and learning his name. Finally coming face-to-face with Baya. Then the escape, and the phone call to Duval in the middle of the night from the Interpol chief in Manila, asking him if he had lost an agent in the middle of the Sulu Sea. By this point in the story, Duval had stopped writing and his eyes were closed.

There was another long silence until Sauvage couldn't take it anymore. "Jacques," he said. "I'm sorry."

He got himself ready for an explosion. An all-out assault for putting at risk not just himself but also the reputation and the core mission of

Interpol in Southeast Asia. But Duval went in another direction: "No, *I'm* sorry," he said. "This is my fault."

Sauvage shook his head once, thinking he hadn't heard right. "How is any of this your fault? I'm the one who—"

"Who went looking for Baya, I know. On your own. With no support. No communication. It's the most irresponsible action I've ever seen. By a policeman, by an Interpol agent. By anyone, anywhere."

"I'm still waiting for the part where any of this is your fault. Because you didn't realize I was such a fuckup? Why don't you just stop playing around with me and—"

Duval leaned forward over his desk. "Martin," he said, his voice softening, "it's my fault because I didn't understand how desperately you wanted to get this guy. That *nothing* would stand in your way."

"But that's why you brought me here. That's the exact reason."

"No, I brought you here because you're a great cop and I wanted somebody I could rely on. If I'm being honest, I wanted a familiar face. Somebody from *home.* Don't you understand? It was selfish of me. I wasn't thinking about what this would do to you. I never should have brought you here."

"I wanted to come here. You know that. Even if you hadn't asked me, I would have found a way to get here."

"I can't blame you for that," Duval said. "I probably would have done the same thing myself. But it was my job *not* to let it happen. It's too close for you. Too personal."

"Jacques, come on. What else was I supposed to do? Stay in Paris? And do what?"

"Grieve for your wife and your son," Duval said. "Heal yourself. That's what you should have been doing."

"You can't send me back, if that's what you're about to say."

"Martin, you know I'm right. This place has been eating you alive ever since you got here. And when I took you off the case, I should have known you wouldn't be able to leave it alone. I shouldn't have let you stay here another day."

"I can't leave yet, Jacques. Please."

"We'll catch Baya. I promise you. And you'll be the first person I call when we do. Now, go to your apartment and pack your things, Martin. You're flying home tomorrow morning."

———

On his way to his apartment, Mason stopped in one of the myriad cheap electronics stores, picked up a burner phone, and texted Luna the number. His old phone was still in Baya's pocket, and he probably needed a new one for this next mission, anyway. Until the leak was found, he needed to be extra careful.

Of course, if he was betting on who the leak was, he already knew where his money would go.

When Mason got up to his apartment, his first sight was Belani sitting at the table with the doorman's wife, doing math lessons. When she looked up at him, her normal shy smile was quickly replaced by something else. Something like fear. But then as she got up and came to him, he realized that she was just alarmed by the scrapes on his face from the island brush, not to mention how flat-out exhausted he must look. The fear was on his behalf, not her own.

As he sat down on the balcony, she came out to him with a glass of ice water. After everything he had just been through, it was as if a part of him that had been switched off suddenly powered back to life. They still didn't have many words they could say to each other, but she brought out his laptop and waited for him to open it and check Adriana's Instagram feed. A soccer game. Some more new clothes. Apparently, Brad had an unlimited budget for blue jeans. It hurt Mason to see it, hurt him more than Abu Sayyaf guards hitting him in the ribs with their rifle butts. But he needed it too. He needed to see these images from his daughter's life to remind himself why he was here and why he kept going.

Belani leaned over to see the photos. She got excited when she saw the shot of Adriana with the soccer ball. "*Sepakbola!*" she said, which Mason assumed had to mean "foot" and "ball."

"*Sepakbola,*" he said back to her.

Mason put a hand on her head as he stood up. The room spun for a moment, but he quickly recovered. He still wasn't 100 percent, but nobody bothered to ask him if he needed some time off before going after Baya again.

He went into the bedroom, changed out of his cheap clothes and shoes, and splashed some water on his face. On his way out, he handed the doorman another wad of money and thanked him. Then he stepped into the street to catch a cab to the airport.

————

Sauvage felt numb as he cleaned out his desk. The window behind him looked down on the busy traffic, the capital city cranking up for another day of heat and chaos. But the noise of over ten million people didn't penetrate the thick glass, and already Sauvage felt separated from the city he felt he was finally getting to know.

As he went through his personal files, he emptied the contents of each folder into the plastic tub that would be sent on to the confidential bin, where it would be shredded and then burned. But when he pulled out his folder on Hashim Baya, he hesitated. It was overflowing and as thick as a suitcase, and it represented the one mission that had brought him to this part of the world in the first place—the one mission that had driven him every single day since he got here.

He held the folder in both hands. Everything his life had become was right here in one bulging stack of papers.

And he couldn't let go. Instead, he put the folder into the gym bag and covered it with the extra set of clothing he kept in his bottom drawer. Then he shook a dozen hands on his way to the elevator and left the building for the last time. When he got to his car, he started it, put it in gear, and headed in the wrong direction.

Going after Baya on his own was the worst protocol violation of his entire career. Nothing else even came close.

*Until now.*

*Because if Nick Mason made it out alive and is back in Jakarta . . .*

When Sauvage got close to Mason's apartment building, he had his answer. Mason was not only alive, but heading out the front door of his building and getting into a cab.

———

Luna rode the elevator to the fifty-second floor of Gama Tower, stepped out, and walked through the glass doors of Pacific Logistics International. The receptionist looked up for one half a beat and then back down at her computer screen. Luna continued down the hall, keyed in the security code on the unmarked door, and stepped through.

She was in fresh clothes: black jeans and a black blouse. If she was pretending to be something—a hotel worker, a waitress, a prostitute— then she would dress the part. But if she simply wanted to disappear into the background, she always went with all black. Today, she even had a black lace head covering folded in her back pocket. She planned to put it on when she landed in Aceh, not because she gave a damn about the local customs but because it was one more way to avoid a stranger's lingering eye.

Luna didn't see any of the support personnel as she walked down the hallway. She paused for a moment, wondering why the place was so quiet. She looked into one room, then another. Nobody.

*What the hell?* she thought, but now wasn't the time to worry about it. She had one last batch of intel to gather in just a few minutes.

When she got to her control room, she sat down and powered up three different computer screens. She studied a map of Aceh first. On the northern tip of the island of Sumatra, it was the only province in Indonesia allowed to govern itself according to Sharia law. If you were caught drinking alcohol, or gambling, or consorting with a member of the opposite sex who was not a spouse or family member, you could be caned in the public square. If you were gay or trans, the punishment got a lot worse.

Aceh would have gone on being its own little world in a country that most of the world ignored, but then in 2004 a major earthquake in the Indian Ocean sent a massive tsunami through Aceh, killing 170,000 people and leaving another half million homeless. Boats docked offshore were driven several blocks inland, crashing through downtown buildings. This was Hashim Baya's hometown, suddenly the deadliest city on earth. But he was reportedly in Europe that day. Otherwise, his career financing terrorists might have ended, and Luna and the organization wouldn't still be trying to track him down almost two decades later.

She started compiling a list of locations throughout the city where a burial service might be held for Baya's wife, beginning with the Baiturrahman Grand Mosque. Then she did a worldwide news search to see if anyone else even knew that the woman was dead. She didn't come up with anything.

*He knows that we know, so he'll be careful. But he won't let his caution keep him away.*

Luna continued to collect all of the information she could find, working with the clear-eyed resolve of an assassin. There was no time for remorse. The fact that she was the one who had killed Baya's wife was just a detail.

As she downloaded the intel to her phone with double encryption, she glanced at her watch. She would need to leave for the airport soon. Mason would meet her there, and then they would go on a commercial flight to Sumatra. No support from the organization. They would be freelancers working completely off the grid.

Luna hesitated for a moment, looking at the open doorway. Then she started searching through her databases for any information she could find on *the boss*. There was no name to work with. She didn't have a location, not even a country. It amazed her, now that Mason had her thinking this way, just how little she knew about the man who held the ultimate power over her life.

She brought up the one incidental recording she could find from one of his video calls. The face appeared on her screen: mid-fifties. Close-cut dark hair, a hint of gray on the side. The model of "dead serious."

He was western European, or at least mostly so. Luna thought she saw something Slavic about his lean face. But then, someone else probably would have seen another ethnicity altogether. Maybe even part Asian.

*Why am I doing this? What would I do with this information even if I knew exactly who this man is and where to find him?*

She never let herself imagine life outside the organization.

Would she want it, even if it were possible?

A voice broke through her reverie: "What are you doing?"

Luna turned to see Torino standing in the doorway. She hit the Escape button on her keyboard, which was set up to instantly kill all open screens.

"You can talk to me," he said, one eye on the darkened screens. "It's just us. Everyone else is gone, and the office will be wiped by the end of the day."

"Wiped?"

"Like it never existed. If there's a leak, this location is compromised."

"What a pain in the ass." She stood up and put her phone in her hip pocket.

"Where are you going?" he asked.

"The airport."

"To go where?"

"I don't have time to give you the details," she said. "I need to go."

"You're afraid I'll try to stop you? Or try to warn Mason?"

"Warn him about what? He knows what this mission is."

"Does he, though?"

Torino hadn't moved from the doorway, with one shoulder leaning against the frame.

"What are you talking about?"

"You're the leak," he said. "You've made sure that every mission has failed so far. But this time, you're not going to tip off Baya. You're going to kill him and you're going to make sure Mason dies too. If I gave a damn, I'd feel sorry for him."

She went up to him and looked him in the eye. "Why would I do that?"

"For the same reason anyone betrays a team. Or a country. Or a family. Because they put their own ambitions above everyone else."

"I don't have time for this." She tried to push past him, but he held firm.

"You already made sure that my command was taken away," he said. "I'll never be trusted again. So now when you and Mason take out Baya and Mason doesn't come back . . ."

"Torino," she said, taking a beat to compose herself. "If this is about you and me . . ."

"You got what you wanted from me. I understand now, that's all it ever was between us."

"You're acting like a child." She tried to push past him again. This time, Torino grabbed her wrist. A tenth of a second later, his eyes were watering from the pain as Luna grabbed his triceps muscle in the exact place where he had been shot.

"Don't make me do this to you," she said. "Just let me go and wish me luck."

He nodded in surrender, his eyes closed. She let go of his arm.

"*Buona fortuna*," he said, but as she turned to go, she felt something press against her lower back, followed immediately by fifty thousand volts of electric current that shut down her entire body.

———

Mason worked his way through the busy Soekarno-Hatta Airport, the first time he'd been back here in the big airport since that first day stepping off the plane from Chicago with a counterfeit passport and no idea what he was about to face. The time since had been measured by days on the calendar, but already he felt as if he owned a new skin and a new pair of eyes. And for the first time since coming here, he finally felt that he had found the one ally he could trust, and the one chance to finally fulfill his mission.

He knew that it didn't mean a plane ticket home yet. Or forgiveness of his obligations to the organization. Or even permanent safety for his family. But for now, it would be an immediate threat lifted. And a chance to buy a little more time to find his way out.

When he came to the gate for the flight to Banda Aceh, he looked for Luna. She wasn't here. The plane was boarding in twenty minutes.

Mason took out his new phone and keyed in Luna's number. It rang through with no answer.

He called Farhan and got through immediately. "Yes, friend," Farhan said.

"Do you know where Luna is?"

"No, I do not."

"Are you at the office?"

"No, sir. The office is being cleaned out. By the end of the day, there will be no trace."

This didn't surprise Mason. Not any more than the vintage Mustang that Darius Cole had turned into scrap metal after his first job. But it didn't help him, either.

"She may be held up in traffic," Farhan said. "You know how bad it can be."

*If she was just stuck in traffic, she'd still answer her fucking phone.*

"What else can I do?" Farhan asked.

"I don't know. I'll call you if I need you."

He ended the call. Then he called Luna one more time. No answer.

Fifteen minutes until boarding. Luna had all of the intel. Without her, Mason would have no idea where to go, what to do. No gun, no plan, no fucking chance.

"Taking a vacation?"

The voice came from behind him. Mason glanced around to see Agent Sauvage.

"You made it out," Mason said.

"So did you. I'm glad."

"You followed me. Again."

Sauvage nodded.

"I should have left you on that island."

"You wouldn't have escaped without me."

"If you're saying I owe you—"

"I'm not," Sauvage said. "But you realize that we're back in Indonesia now."

"You still can't arrest me."

"You're right. But this is my assigned country. Meaning I can go grab any one of these cops and have them do it for me."

"You're not going to do that."

"Why not?"

"Because if I don't get on this plane, I don't get to Baya. And if I don't get to Baya, he keeps on giving people money to blow people up."

"I'll get to him," Sauvage said. "Eventually. The right way."

Mason looked him in the eye. "The right way? Are you fucking kidding me right now?"

Sauvage stared back at him.

"You're not going to stop me," Mason said. "You're going to stand there and watch me walk through this gate. And the reason you're going to do that is because this thing with Baya is personal for you. I got that much from what you said on the island. So you're going to ignore every bullshit cop code you ever knew and you're going to let me go solve both of our problems."

Sauvage thought about it for a beat. Then he nodded to the gate and asked, "You're going to do this by yourself?"

Mason didn't answer.

"What I said about getting a cop to arrest you," Sauvage said, "that was a bluff. I don't have a badge anymore. My boss took it away and he's sending me home. So I'm not a cop again until I land in Paris."

"Why are you telling me this?"

"Because you're right. I need you to find Baya. But I think you need me too."

"No. I don't."

"My boss never wanted me to find you," Sauvage said. "And now I think I understand why. He knew I would stop thinking like a cop if it meant getting to Baya."

"Cops never stop thinking like cops."

"And killers never stop thinking like killers."

Mason shook his head and let that one go.

Sauvage lifted his briefcase. "As much as you think you know about

Baya, I promise you I know more. Every piece of his life. His history, his habits, his connections. It's all in here."

"No," Mason said. "No fucking way."

"I already bought a ticket," Sauvage said. "As soon as I saw you come in here, I checked the board and I knew where you were going. Baya was born there. His parents were born there. His wife was born there. What's happening in Aceh?"

"You are not getting on this plane."

"What are you going to do, Mason? This is a commercial flight, not your private jet. Which is interesting, by the way. It means something has changed. But we can talk about it on the plane."

Mason turned his back to him and dialed Luna's number one more time.

"You know I'm right," Sauvage said. "Whatever you're about to do, you can't do it without me."

# 17

The plane was two-thirds full, with enough empty seats for Mason and Sauvage to sit together in a back row and keep an open row in front of them. Mason scanned the other passengers. All Indonesians, but with a subtle difference: Every woman on the way to Aceh was wearing some sort of covering on her head.

"How do you know he'll be in Aceh?" Sauvage asked Mason. "This will be the first time in two years."

"He'll be attending a funeral."

Sauvage processed this. He was about to ask for the identity of the deceased, but the look on Mason's face gave him the answer.

"Twenty-four hours to bury her," Sauvage said, and stared out the window. A minute later, he added: "This man will be out of his mind. He was devoted to her."

Mason shrugged. "I won't blame him for feeling that way."

"He'll have dozens of his men at the funeral. Maybe hundreds."

"The green shirts," Mason said. "But that will make it easier to find him."

"But not to get close to him."

Mason thought about it, then asked, "Why *green* shirts, anyway?"

"Green is an important color in Islam," Sauvage said. "It represents paradise. The Aceh flag is green. So are the Saudi flag and the Pakistani flag."

Mason nodded again, then lowered his voice. "You understand what I need to do today. I'm not letting you come along so you can put handcuffs on him."

"I didn't bring handcuffs," Sauvage said. Then he went back to staring out the window.

———

Three hours later, the plane landed at the Sultan Iskandar Muda International Airport. Mason pulled out his cell phone and called Luna again. Still no answer.

*What the fuck am I supposed to do now?*

He called again, with the same result, after they had made their way through the airport and were standing on the busy street. Everything about this city looked and felt different to him. Many more of the buildings were white and clean. There were young deciduous trees mixed in with the palms. Men and women were dressed modestly, with head coverings on the women and more muted colors on everyone. It was such a contrast from the chaos and bright colors of Jakarta, but the one thing that stayed constant was the intense heat, the low clouds, and the heavy air that always felt like one minute away from rainfall.

"First and second priority," Mason said to Sauvage, "weapons and transportation."

Sauvage put out a hand to hail a taxi. A little Mitsubishi pulled over and they stuffed themselves in the back.

"*Tolong ke pasar,*" Sauvage said to the driver, working through the words slowly. "*Perlengkapan . . . Petualangan.*"

"I asked him to take us to the market," he said to Mason. "Somewhere we can buy outdoor supplies."

"Like what, tennis rackets?"

"Nobody's going to sell you a gun here," Sauvage said. "A knife, maybe."

"For fuck's sake," Mason said under his breath. He pulled out his phone again and dialed Luna one more time. "I'm going to have a penknife in my pocket and still no fucking idea where this guy is."

"We should rent motorcycles," Sauvage said as the taxi pulled into traffic. "Easiest way to get around."

"We'll be more exposed," Mason said. "But you're right."

He looked out the window as the taxi took them into the heart of the city. Almost two decades after the tsunami, there was still active construction going on everywhere. Large cranes putting up buildings, more young trees dwarfed by tall billboards. Few English words that Mason could understand, almost everything in Indonesian and, occasionally, Arabic. He did a double take when he saw a large fishing boat sitting on top of a two-story building. Left there as a reminder of the tsunami.

The taxi dropped them off at an open-air market with dozens of stalls selling food, clothing, souvenirs—everything except guns. Sauvage handed the driver a wad of rupiah as they got out.

They worked their way down the stalls until they found a souvenir stand selling gleaming knives with L-shaped wooden handles. "This is a *rencong*," Sauvage said. "Part of the national martial art."

Mason tested the blade. It was sharp, but the whole thing felt too light to him. He pictured the blade separating from the handle on first contact. "This is a toy," he said. "Can we find something better?"

They worked their way down another row until they got to the end and found a table stacked with serious knives. As soon as Mason slid the eight-inch blade out of its sheath and weighed the solid handle in his hand, he knew he was in business.

"How much?" he asked, but the vendor glanced over Mason's shoulder and then suddenly cast his eyes downward. Mason turned to see a pair of men in black, loose-fitting clothing, with the Aceh flag on the left shoulder.

"*Wilayatul hisbah*," Sauvage whispered. "The religious police."

"You're fucking kidding me," Mason said. "Are we going to have a problem?"

The policemen locked eyes with Mason for a long beat, then kept walking down the row.

"If we were women trying to buy blue jeans, we'd have a problem," Sauvage said.

*But the foreign man buying a deadly weapon—that's okay*, Mason thought. He shook his head, put the knife back in its sheath, and gave the vendor some money. The vendor looked confused.

"We're not haggling," Mason said. "Take the full amount and deal with it. In fact, make it two."

He grabbed another knife, just as solid with a slightly shorter blade, and handed the vendor more money. Then he handed the second *rencong* to Sauvage, who hesitated before slipping the sheath through his belt.

As they walked away, Sauvage asked Mason if he'd ever killed a man with a knife before.

Mason flashed back to the first time: the bathroom at the strip club, the target standing in front of a sink, looking up but not registering the threat until it was too late. Two puncture wounds to the lungs, then the blade drawn across the throat. Mason holding the man, breathing his last breath with him, the two men staring at each other's face in the mirror. Until the man slid to the floor in a spreading pond of blood and it was only Mason looking at himself.

"None of your fucking business," Mason said. "Now, let's go find Baya."

———

When she opened her eyes, the first thing Luna saw was the blade.

She blinked, cleared her vision, and shook her head. She recognized the knife. It was Torino's precious antique Latama stiletto, made in Italy in the 1930s, taken by an American soldier during the war, and later stolen and brought back to its rightful country by Torino's grandfather. She had heard the story behind the knife but didn't pay much attention at the time. Now the blade was a lot more interesting to her because Torino was holding it casually in his right hand. In his left hand was the stun gun he had taken out of her desk and applied to her lower back.

He was sitting across from her, watching her intently. There was a spot of blood high on one sleeve, where Luna had opened up his bullet wound. But when she tried to move, she realized she couldn't. Her wrists and ankles were taped to the chair.

"What are you doing?" she asked him.

"I'm waiting."

"For what?"

"For your confession."

"What time is it?" she asked. "You're going to ruin the mission."

"Just stop, Luna."

"Torino!" she said, her voice rising. "Don't be a fool! Let me go!"

"Make all the noise you want," he said, weighing the knife in his right hand. "We're all alone, remember?"

———

Mason and Sauvage exchanged phone numbers so they could keep in touch if they got separated. Then they rented motorcycles and rode through the heart of Banda Aceh, the capital city, with the heat from the pavement radiating all around them. They parked next to the Baiturrahman Grand Mosque, which was like a city of its own—seven towers surrounded by white marble-tiled grounds and fountains. Mason took a few steps onto the marble and heard someone yell at him. He turned to see one of the locals, dressed in a white robe, pointing to Mason's shoes. Mason took them off and left them at the edge of the grounds with hundreds of other pairs.

"The funeral mass will be simple," Sauvage said as they walked through the devout visitors and the few casual sightseers. "Most of the prayers are silent. The body will be wrapped in white, and it'll be taken directly to the cemetery and buried without a coffin. Facing Mecca, of course."

"I don't need to know any of this," Mason said. "Just help me find the funeral."

"He will not be left alone today," Sauvage said. "Not for one minute. Mourners, friends—they will be all around him. Not to mention his usual bodyguards."

Mason stopped for a minute. With the clean white marble stretching out in every direction, the minarets towering over him, a different culture he knew nothing about, in a city he didn't even know existed.

Could he do this? Could he disrupt a sacred funeral service and kill the grieving widower?

An image came to him: a black van, parked outside a house in Colorado. Gina inside, in the kitchen, Adriana sitting at the table, doing her homework.

*Yes, I can*, he answered. *I can and I will, if that's the only way to keep the doors shut on that black van.*

And with that thought quickly came another:

There were no steps in this plan for after he took out Baya. No escape route.

Mason was not going to survive this day. He would never get back to Chicago. Never see Gina or Adriana again. But if he did the job, he had to believe that the terms would be honored and his family would be left alone.

It was his only hope.

But even as Mason was realizing this, he glanced to his right and spotted a green shirt. "Over there," he said as he clocked the man walking on the opposite side of a large fountain. Mason quickly circled around, losing sight of the man, catching one more glimpse, then losing him again. When he finally got to the other side, the man was gone.

"I just saw another one," Sauvage said when he caught up. "Over here."

The two men went off in a new direction, following the second green shirt. But once again the wearer was gone when they got there.

It was like Singapore all over again, only this time they were on Baya's home turf.

"What happens next?" Mason asked Sauvage. "What if they've already had the service?"

"We could try to find the burial ground, but that part will go quickly. Traditionally, there'll be an evening meal afterward. With close friends and family."

"There," Mason said, pointing to a spot behind him.

Sauvage turned to see a third green shirt. Mason was already in motion, heading back the way they had entered the grounds.

"That car," Mason said, nodding to a black sedan. The green shirt got into the passenger's seat. Another green shirt was behind the wheel.

Was Baya in the backseat?

They both scrambled to find their shoes and put them on, then got on their motorcycles. The black sedan stood out from all of the other vehicles—the much smaller cars, the *becak* for hire, which were essentially motorized rickshaws, plus the undersize urban buses and the throngs of motorcycles. Mason had been on busy streets before. He had driven a stolen Cadillac down Michigan Avenue during rush hour when he was sixteen years old. Had weaved a beater Chevy Nova through the girders beneath the elevated tracks on Wells Street, just like Jake and Elwood in *The Blues Brothers*, when his wife was about to give birth to their daughter. Had raced Darius Cole's vintage Camaro down the back alleys of Canaryville, trying to shake a Dodge Hellcat driven by an SIS detective. But he'd never ridden a smoking, wobbling two-stroke motorcycle down streets like this before, threading the needle between other vehicles, ignoring the honking and shouts all around him, even pushing his way through the pedestrian traffic at every lawless intersection.

The sedan was still a full block ahead of him. When he checked behind him, he didn't see Sauvage.

Mason was beyond tired at this point, beyond hungry, still suffering from the same thirst that had never left him since those hours in the hot shed. The sun was going down at its usual early hour now, not even six p.m. and already every minute growing dimmer, and Mason was chasing green-suited ghosts, but there was nothing else he could do now, with no support, no intel, no plan at all except pure *movement* fueled by desperation and a merciless ticking clock.

If he could catch up to the car, he could try to stop it.

*And then get mowed down by the men in the green shirts, surely both of them with guns and no hesitation to use them even on a busy street.*

A river cut through the center of town, and now the black car was working its way across one of the few bridges. Mason had to fight even harder to keep up in the bottlenecked traffic as every car, every motorcycle, every *becak* squeezed in tight all around him, fighting for every unclaimed square foot of street.

The street came to a Y on the other side of the bridge. Mason stopped and looked in both possible directions.

*Fuck me. Which way?*

He checked behind him and caught a glimpse of Sauvage on the bridge.

*Hell with it*, he thought, and took off to the right.

A block later, he saw the black sedan ahead of him. Traffic thinned out enough for him to settle back and make sure he wasn't spotted. He followed for what felt like another mile, through the strange darkening streets, until the sedan finally pulled into the driveway of a hotel.

It was the Hermes Palace, the nicest hotel Mason had seen in this city by a long shot. He stayed on the street, partially concealed by the lighted fountain, and he watched carefully as the two doors opened and the two green shirts got out. He waited for one of them to open the back door. At the sight of Baya, Mason was ready to move.

But the back door never opened.

Mason took out his phone, called Sauvage, and told him to come to the Hermes Palace. A few minutes later, Sauvage arrived on his bike. "Was he in that car?" he asked.

Mason shook his head.

"Then what next? He could be anywhere right now."

Mason nodded to the hotel entrance. Sauvage turned to see the same thing Mason was seeing: a dozen green shirts all milling around outside the front door.

"They're waiting for him," Mason said as he took out his phone again and tried Luna's number one more time. "Wherever Baya is right now, I think this is where he's going to end up."

————

Luna stayed silent. She watched the blade as Torino tapped it against the arm of his chair. He was close to her, his own chair pulled up so that his knees were touching hers. The tapping of the blade was something that would be an irritation under any other circumstances. Now it felt like a small mental torture. A prelude for whatever came next.

She flexed her wrists. They were tightly taped against her own chair. Her arms were starting to lose their circulation and go numb.

"I can sit here all day," Torino said.

Luna didn't answer. She flexed her ankles. They weren't taped quite as tightly as her wrists. She pressed one foot against the floor. Then the other. If she tried, she might be able to put some force into this. She could rock the chair and then maybe support her own weight.

*Then what? You manage to rock forward and now you're on your feet, hunched over because you're still taped to this chair.*

She studied Torino's face. His cold eyes. The angle of his neck.

By coming so close, he made himself vulnerable. *How to make him pay for this mistake?*

She started to put it together, creating a film reel in her head and then watching it happen in imaginary slow motion, frame by frame. *Rock back just enough, then come forward with enough momentum to swing your own weight and the weight of the chair past the tipping point.*

The next move had to happen without hesitation. He would be over the surprise by then and would already be moving forward to knock her backward.

The essential question in any martial art: *How do I use that move against him?*

She couldn't turn from it. Couldn't redirect it. But she could meet the force directly, use his momentum to hit something soft with something hard.

She played the reel in her head again. From the beginning, every step.

And then her phone rang.

"Give it up, Mason," Torino said, turning his head toward the cell phone on the desk.

*Now.*

Luna rocked back a few inches, felt the helpless sense of vertigo as she was about to go too far. But then she recovered and swung all of her weight forward.

All the way to her feet.

———

Across the street from the hotel was a row of shops: a teahouse, a food market, a hair salon, and a small clothing store. Single-story structures with no vantage points. Up the street, to the north, a bank. To the south, another hotel, much less luxurious. Three stars instead of five, but it was tall enough and the rooms on one side overlooked the entrance to the Hermes Palace.

Mason and Sauvage went inside and checked in. Sauvage asked in his broken Indonesian to see a map of the hotel. They picked a top-floor room on the north side and paid cash.

When they got to the room, Mason went to the window and opened it. A screen, no safety glass. He pulled the single chair over, and as he sat down to wait he flashed back on his first hours in Jakarta, being taken right to the huge Sultan Hotel complex, going to the roof and waiting for Baya to land in his helicopter.

This wasn't Jakarta. It was Baya's hometown. Did that mean he wouldn't have to sneak in from the rooftop?

"I can call the police now," Sauvage said. "He's going to be *right there*, in that hotel. They can surround the place."

"How many cops in this city . . ." Mason said, "in *this* city, would go into that hotel and arrest Hashim Baya?"

"Then, Detachment Eighty-Eight. The Owls. He doesn't own them."

"Maybe not all of them." Mason closed his eyes and took a beat to measure his next words: "But it doesn't matter. Because having the special ops take him down doesn't do me any good. Unless you can *guarantee* me they'll put a bullet in his fucking head. *And* do it in the next couple of hours."

Sauvage didn't try to answer.

"If you want to help," Mason said, "tell me how I can get in that hotel. What's my cover?"

"He's probably bought out every room. There's nobody in there but his own men."

"Flowers," Mason said. "A huge bouquet, to be delivered personally."

"No. That's not the tradition here."

"Fuck."

He looked back down at the front entrance next door. The sky was getting darker, but like any five-star hotel, the Hermes Palace was lit up like Las Vegas.

"If I had a sniper rifle, I'd probably have a shot from here," Mason said, closing one eye and focusing on the few yards between where a vehicle would stop and the front door.

He knew he was dreaming. Even if he had a rifle like that and had taken the time to dial it in, for him the shot would be a ten-percenter.

*Eddie, you'd be able to put it right in the man's earhole. Why do you have to be on the other side of the world?*

Mason closed his eyes again. *Mission mode*, he told himself. *Right now*.

"We need food," Sauvage said. "And something with caffeine. I'll be right back."

"If you're going out, I need you to pick up one more thing."

"What's that?"

Mason nodded to the men still standing outside the Hermes Palace's front door. "A green shirt. As close as you can get to one of those."

———

Luna ducked just in time to drive the crown of her head into Torino's nose. She felt and heard the cartilage give way and knew that Torino's tear ducts and nasal blood vessels would all open up immediately. She felt the chair turning as she came through the impact, so she threw her weight and committed to it so she wouldn't go down face-first. Instead, she landed hard on her right shoulder and then rolled onto her back.

Torino was also on his back, blinking against the involuntary tears. "*Puttana!*" he said, Italian for *whore*. He felt for the stiletto, but by now

Luna had already rocked herself back again, using every muscle of her core to bring her knees toward her face. The legs of the chair came along for the ride as she gathered the weight and prepared to drive it downward. In that fraction of a second, she flashed on everything that had happened between them. Torino coming to her in that hotel room after she had killed a man for the first time, taking her away before the police arrived. Everything he had taught her in the years that followed. The few moments when the closeness between them had inevitably pulled them into something else completely, even if there was always a part of herself that she held back in reserve—an instinct of sheer survival that would never fail her. All of it, every day working together for the organization, such a nightmare of a life but for the fact that she could never imagine something better for herself, which was why she adjusted and adapted and did whatever was necessary and now this was just one last thing she had no choice but to do as she brought the chair leg down across Torino's neck. The coup de grâce, meaning literally "blow of mercy," as the merciless force crushed the trachea with a horrible wet snapping noise and fractured the cricoid cartilage and collapsed his vertebral arteries.

Torina had taught her this. And now as he put both hands to his throat, he tried to roll over, his eyes wide and no words forming in his mouth. Luna lay back, her head hurting where she had hit him, and her shoulder throbbing where she had landed hard on the floor. She didn't look at Torino again, but she heard him try to get up and then go down for the last time.

As she caught her breath, she knew that she had just moved from one challenge to another, because now she was lying on the floor, wrists and ankles still heavily taped to a chair, in an abandoned soundproof office.

———

Sauvage crossed the dark street, avoiding the lighted streetlamps. He found food and bottles of Coke at the market. Then he went into the clothing store next to the hair salon. There was a large assortment of men's and women's clothing crammed into a small space, but he found a *baju koko* shirt that didn't have the exact styling and trim, but it was the right shade of green and probably just big enough to fit Mason.

As he went to the register, he saw a random assortment of cheap plastic toys, including a gun. It was made to look like a semiautomatic, too small and crude in its details. If you knew your way around guns, it wouldn't fool you for one second.

*But what the hell, who knows?*

Sauvage put the toy gun in his belt, on the opposite side from the knife. When he got back up to the room, Mason was still watching the front entrance to the Hermes Palace.

"No change?" Sauvage asked.

Mason shook his head.

"You need to eat something."

Mason didn't move.

"Eat something, damn it." He handed him a plastic bowl of *bubur ayam*: rice, chicken, and vegetables. Then a fork and a bottle of Coke.

Mason started eating without taking his eyes off the Hermes Palace. He wasn't even thinking about it, but his body obviously needed it, because it was gone in less than a minute. He took a long swig of Coke and put the bottle down.

"All of his men are here," Sauvage said. "He *must* be nearby."

"It may not matter," Mason said. "I'm running out of time."

"You can't let the clock push you into a suicide mission."

Mason glanced over at him for just a second, but it was enough for Sauvage to see it in his face: He had already accepted the idea that he wasn't going to get out of this alive.

In the next moment, Mason's face was lit up by a flash of light from the street below. It was the headlights from another black sedan as it pulled into the driveway. Both men watched carefully as the rear doors were opened. Two people got out. An older man, dressed in a black suit. And a woman. It was hard to guess her age, because her face was covered by a black veil, but she walked slowly.

Another sedan pulled in right behind the first. Mason kept watching. Two more men. Black suits. But neither was Baya.

Finally, a third sedan. Two more men got out. They were partially obstructed this time by one of the pillars holding up the canopy. The first man . . . No, not Baya, but there was a resemblance.

The second man . . .

"I didn't get a good enough look at him," Mason said. "But the rest—they've got to be Baya's family."

Having his family in the room changed the equation. *How can I use that vulnerability to my advantage?*

Mason surveyed the building one more time, trying to pick out any new details he might have missed. With no map of the building, no blueprints, not even a quick visual recon of the interior, he was operating almost entirely in the dark.

He'd be a fool to walk in the front door. There was one side door that he could see—probably locked and accessible only with a room key. Surely there was a service entrance in back. That would be his entry point. Stay off the elevator, unless there was a service elevator. Then try to find one green shirt standing somewhere on his own and disarm him, assuming that he was carrying under the loose shirt. Assuming that they *all* were carrying under their shirts. Take the gun and keep moving.

Finding and infiltrating the room would be the hardest step, should he get that far. There were no external balconies on the building, so no way to come through the window unless he rappelled down from the roof, and only if he could break through the glass cleanly. Possible but not ideal.

"So what's the plan?" Sauvage asked.

"The plan is improvise," Mason said as he took the green shirt from him. "And get lucky."

# 18

Luna surveyed the room. Torino's body lay between her and the door, and the door was closed. She didn't think she'd be able to stand tall enough to reach the knob, even if she could get close to it.

Her phone was on the desk, but again, she didn't see how she could get one hand high enough reach it.

Could she reach it with her mouth? Pull it down onto the floor?

But no, it was too far away from the edge, unless she could somehow get her entire body onto the top of the desk.

She closed her eyes and clenched both fists, feeling the tight bonds. *Stay cool . . . Stay cool . . . You're a fucking iceberg, baby.* She opened her eyes and rocked herself over until she could get to her knees.

She wasn't sure she could even get back up to a sitting position.

*Get your ass off this floor, you stupid cow. If you don't get up, they won't find you for a fucking week.*

She looked over at Torino's body and felt a sudden urge to kick his lifeless face.

*The knife.*

It wasn't on the floor next to him, at least not on the near side. She craned her neck to see over to the other side.

It must be . . .

*Under him.*

She replayed the way he had pushed off the floor, holding himself up for a few seconds before collapsing.

She rolled back onto her side and started working her way over, a centimeter at a time, until one foot was close to his body. Then she coiled her body as much as she could, releasing and pushing off with her sore shoulder, trying to exert some kind of force against his chest.

The body didn't move.

She tried again. If the body moved, it was impossible to tell. But she didn't know what else to do.

"*Pizda mă-tii!*" she yelled, going all the way back to her original Romanian as she kept ramming the body over and over again.

An eternity later, sweating and exhausted, she finally glimpsed the shiny black handle of the knife.

———

"I'm going to the back of the hotel," Mason said. He had his cell phone on speaker setting, with Sauvage on the other end of the open line. The *rencong* knife was tucked into his belt and covered by the loose-fitting shirt.

As Mason took a long loop around the Hermes Palace, staying in the shadows, Sauvage stood across the street, listening to Mason's progress on his cell phone, watching for police cars, or more backup for Baya's men, or anything else that might be useful information. It was all that Mason had asked of him so far.

"I have to tell you something," Mason said. "You probably already know this, but I need you to hear it." He stopped at the back fence, where a line of tall trees sheltered the pool area from the street that ran behind the hotel.

"Go ahead."

"If I don't take out Baya . . ." Mason said, pausing to find the right words. "Then my wife and my daughter will both be killed. It's not a maybe. It's going to happen."

"Where are they?"

"They're in Colorado. You can't go there and protect them. And there's nobody you can call."

"So what are you asking me to do?"

"I'm not asking anything," Mason said. "I'm just giving you the reality. One of two things is going to happen. Either Baya dies tonight, or my family dies tomorrow."

Sauvage reached into his pocket and pulled out his most valuable possession: the folded photograph, by now water-stained and even more battered after everything it had been through.

"Are you there?" Mason asked.

"I'm right here," he said. "I understand what you're telling me."

In the silence that followed, Sauvage made a decision. For the first time since November 2015, as he stood on a dark street in the most foreign corner of a foreign country, he finally unfolded the photograph to see the faces of his wife and son.

*Mireille. His Mimi.*

*His Jean-Luc.*

His whole life in one image. It had been taken at Euro Disney, the only time they ever went. Not knowing what to expect and having a perfect day. *Like every day*, Sauvage realized now that he looked back at that time of his life. Perfect like every single day, if only he had known to appreciate it then.

He studied the two faces in the dim light. He had always wondered if seeing this photograph would knock him over like a punch to the gut. But the effect was somehow more subtle and yet stronger at the same time: a combination of bittersweet gratitude and a dull ache in his heart.

*I understand what's driving you, Mason. If I could go back and save them, I would do anything.*

*Anything.*

He folded the photograph together and put it back in his pocket. He wiped his face, watched the hotel, and waited to hear something else on the open phone line.

A few hundred yards away, Mason was following the fence line until it came to a tall locked gate with a sign that read *Hanya personel yang*

*berwenang.* Mason pulled himself up to look over the top of the gate and
saw a loading dock with one truck, apparently empty. He eased himself
over the top of the gate and landed softly on the pavement.

"Loading dock," he said softly into his phone. "I'm going to try
the door."

Mason pulled on the door and it opened just as someone was coming
out. A member of the kitchen staff, dressed in white. Annoyed at the
intrusion, he started to say something to Mason, but then he registered
the green shirt and cut himself off. Mason kept his head down, waved
the man away with one hand, and kept moving.

He pushed his way past several more kitchen staff members, through
a set of double doors, and found himself in a dining room. There were
no guests, just two more staff members wiping down empty tables. They
both glanced at Mason and went back to their jobs.

"No green shirts yet," Mason said into his phone.

"Two out front right now," Sauvage said. He tried to peer through
the front door into the lobby. "Several more in the lobby. Can't tell you
exactly how many."

Mason slid up to the edge of the dining room entrance and looked
out into the lobby. There were at least six green shirts he could see. He
glanced up and saw the underside of a long internal balcony that ran
the length of the lobby, with staircases leading up from either side. At
least two more green shirts were standing on the balcony.

Mason ducked back into the dining room. The men wiping the
tables continued to ignore him.

A sudden flash of green, and Mason put his back to the wall. One
of Baya's men came into the dining room and yelled something at the
cleaners. They took their rags and hurried into the kitchen.

Baya's man stood there scanning the room, but he hadn't turned
yet. He was maybe ten feet away. Mason reached out toward the door,
then in one move pushed it shut and drove himself forward. With the
door closed, it was just the two of them. Mason caught him as he was
whirling around, put one arm around the man's neck, and with the other
hand drew the blade from his belt.

The man fell backward with the knife held against his neck. He hadn't even drawn his gun yet.

"Your gun," Mason said. "Take it out. Slowly."

"Sir," the man said. "I have no gun."

"The hell you don't. Take it out."

Mason reached around with his free hand and felt along the man's waistline.

"I have no gun," the man said again. "But the others do. As you can see."

Mason froze for a beat. Then he looked up and saw two green shirts standing at the entrance to the kitchen. They were both holding semi-automatics. The lobby door that Mason had closed was pushed in a second later and two more green shirts came in with two more guns.

A fifth man came in. He carried the air of a squad leader as he came close and stood over Mason.

"Stand up," he said. "You are coming with us."

———

Outside the hotel, Sauvage heard every word on the other end of the line.

*You are coming with us* was the last of it, followed by a few indistinct sounds—a cell phone being handled roughly, then silence.

Sauvage moved closer, standing just behind the hotel sign to peer into the lobby windows. He saw several green shirts moving around and felt helpless to do anything about whatever was happening to Mason. *Do I rush in there? And then what? Wave my little plastic gun in the air? Announce that everyone in the hotel is under arrest by the man who didn't have arrest powers even when he still had his badge?*

One of the black sedans came around from the back lot and stopped by the front door. Sauvage couldn't see everything that was happening, but it looked as though Mason was being put in the back seat with two green shirts, and two more green shirts were getting in front. Sauvage went back to his motorcycle to follow the vehicle. But then another black sedan appeared on the street and turned into the driveway.

Then another and another. Sauvage counted eight vehicles in total, some of them with family members sitting in the back seats. When the last car left the hotel, Sauvage pulled out onto the street and followed.

The caravan headed west, making its way through the heart of the city, past the hospital and several mosques and the convention center. The traffic thinned as the caravan reached the outskirts of the city. There was only one road now, leading through the dark trees and the small towns of Lampisang and then Lho-nga. Sauvage could smell the sea before the road turned at the coastline, and now the Indian Ocean was on his right as he traveled south along the shoreline. He kept his headlight off. There was enough light from the moon, and the caravan lit its own trail like a long, glowing snake on the road ahead.

When they passed through the town of Meudhen, Sauvage started to worry about the gas left in his motorcycle. How much farther were they going?

It was a full hour on the road when the caravan rounded a large bay and Sauvage, his hands numb now from riding on the rough road, knew that he would have to stop for fuel soon. When they came to the town of Calang, Sauvage remembered something important about it: It was a town completely obliterated by the 2004 tsunami, with thousands of its residents never seen again. Now there were a handful of rebuilt businesses on either side of the street, but the town's history felt like a bad omen.

Why were they all coming here, so far from the capital?

A few minutes later, he started to understand the answer. A secondary road turned off to the Calang Airstrip, but a barricade was blocking it, with a sign that indicated the airport was closed. The sign was old enough to have been there since the tsunami.

Sauvage rode on farther until he came to a place where he could stop the motorcycle and hide it in some thick brush. Then he started walking, pushing his way through the foliage until he could see the abandoned airport. It had a fence around the perimeter, untended and pushed over in places. A single dark building sat next to the runway. Nearby, a large tent had been set up. A long string of lanterns hung from the tent's edges, and in the midst of this dark abandoned airport they gave the whole scene a surreal glow.

Sauvage watched the sedans parking by the tent, the occupants getting out and milling around in the light. So many green shirts, with a dozen other men and women wearing black.

A single car sat near the runway itself, apart from the others.

*Mason must be in that car.*

Sauvage watched and waited. Until finally, a speck of light appeared in the sky. It came from over the Indian Ocean and grew in size until the lights separated and Sauvage made out the dark shape.

An airplane.

In the next few seconds, two long strings of light appeared on either side of the runway. But they weren't electric runway lights. Instead, there were a dozen green shirts stationed on either side of the runway, each man about twenty yards away from the next, and each tending a large metal bowl from which a bright fire emitted its light.

The airplane banked, circled, and then descended toward the runway, guided by the burning lights. It was a Learjet big enough for eight to ten passengers. It rolled in over the abandoned runway surface, hitting a few bumps, until it finally came to a stop. The engine turned off, and all was silent.

Then the doors on the single car all opened at once, and in the light from the fires Sauvage saw Mason being led to the plane.

————

Mason sat in silence. Over an hour had passed. They had taken his phone and his knife.

There were four other men in the car, two in the front and one on either side of him. They were young, with wiry strength and battle-scarred faces, and for the first time Mason understood who these men really were. They weren't anonymous cult zombies. They were young men who had grown up on the streets, with hard lives and no one offering them anything better. In Chicago, they'd be wearing gang colors. Here on the other side of the world, it was a green shirt.

As they were driving, Mason had become vaguely aware of water outside the right-hand windows, and a string of headlights behind them. When the car finally stopped, the driver got out to move aside a barricade. Then the car proceeded down a rough road, through an open gate and along the interior of a fence line. The car stopped and they waited.

Mason would have one chance. When he saw Baya, there would be exactly one single moment when he could find a way to kill him, if he acted fast enough and with total commitment. Mason would be dead two seconds after Baya, but that was already the price of admission.

*One chance, and you better be ready, because when it passes it will not come again.*

When the driver turned off his headlights, Mason saw a long string of firelight, with another line running parallel. Between them was a strip of pavement. A runway?

A few minutes later, a plane landed. A small Learjet, about the same size as the jet Mason had flown on with the rest of the team. The plane ran over some rough spots in the pavement, then came to a stop just a few yards from the car.

All four car doors were opened at once and Mason was pulled out. The jet's door came down, and he was pushed up the steps, with the driver right behind him. Mason blinked in the sudden bright light. When he turned into the interior of the plane, he quickly took stock. There were three men in the cabin. Two green shirts, and Hashim Baya, sitting at a table in the rear.

Mason glanced behind him. Only the driver had followed him. Nobody else. There were three green shirts now, instead of four. Not counting the pilot and copilot, who Mason didn't perceive as an immediate threat. The math had just improved.

"Mason," Baya said.

As Mason studied him more carefully, he saw a man who had aged several years in the past twenty-four hours. His eyes were red, his cheeks drained of color.

"I wanted to see the man who killed my Maryam," Baya said.

"I hate to tell you," Mason said, "but a man didn't kill her."

Baya took a moment to process that. "But you were there. You could have stopped it. You could have said there is no reason to do this."

"Maybe. Probably not. Does it matter?"

"I want to take your family from you," Baya said, "so that you know this feeling."

*Says the man who buys bombs for the terrorists.*

"But I can't do that," Baya went on. "Because the man you work for will beat me to it."

Mason stared at him.

"So I will take something else from you instead," Baya said. "The young girl you have living with you in Jakarta—she will be sold to a sex dealer in Pattaya. By tomorrow, some fat Australian will pay extra to break her in and they will tell her that you sent her there."

Mason took a step forward. Both green shirts flanking Baya pointed their guns at his head.

"You can think about that in the last hours of your life," Baya said. "Maryam's family is here to grieve with me. But before we do that, I'm going to watch her three brothers beat you to death with their own hands."

———

Sauvage studied the scene carefully. *What are my odds here?* he asked himself. *Dozens of armed green shirts. One of me, holding a knife and a toy gun.*

He had surprise on his side. That was it.

And the darkness. He also had the darkness.

He pushed his way through the last barrier of palm fronds and looked down the fence line. He spotted the gap and moved quickly to step through. Now he was on the airport grounds. Maybe forty yards to the runway. Fifty yards to the first man tending the fire lines. Which meant he had spent the past few minutes in the vicinity of a bright light. He had divided the world into light and utter darkness, and he would stay blind to the dark for the next several minutes, until he got his night vision back.

Sauvage continued forward, staying low to the ground, hoping that his dark clothing kept him hidden long enough. With the plane on the ground, already he could see the men leaving their fire bowls and starting to walk toward the plane. But the man closest to him had the farthest distance to walk.

Forty yards. Thirty. Twenty. Ten. The man sensed the movement behind him and was about to turn. But Sauvage was already on top of him, covering his mouth with one hand while he pressed the plastic toy gun to his temple.

"*Bergerak dan mati*," Sauvage said, meaning roughly *Move and die.* For one second, the man acted like a regular human being and not a man who had sworn his life to his leader. It was all the time Sauvage needed to slip the man's gun from his belt. He looked down the line. No one had noticed what was happening yet. Sauvage took his hand from the man's mouth, just long enough to transfer the gun to his dominant hand and then strike the man in that magical spot just below the ear. The sudden blow to his vagus nerve turned off the current to his brain and he went down. Not for long, but long enough not to be a problem during the next ninety seconds.

The men on the opposite side of the runway were crossing over to join the others as they all moved toward the plane's right-hand door. Sauvage went against the grain, crossing to the empty side and moving down the runway, again hoping to stay hidden from the other eyes that hadn't yet regained their night vision. When he was close to the plane, he ducked down and came nearer, using the stairs to obstruct most of the direct sight lines. Within a minute, he had reached the far side of the plane.

The easy part over, the next step was about to get seriously *vache*— the all-purpose French term for anything hard, horrible, or bloody.

Sauvage took one last moment to check the gun he was holding. Baya had equipped his men with the P1 9mm, a Pindad-made version of the Browning Hi-Power. He checked that a round was chambered. Then he crossed himself, something he hadn't done in thirty years. He came out from the underside of the jet and jumped onto the stairway. He was a black-clad ghost who appeared and then disappeared just as quickly, taking the steps two at a time.

He grabbed the first green shirt he saw by the back of his collar and pointed the gun into the cabin. A tenth of a second later, he had narrowed his focus to Hashim Baya, sitting behind a table in the back.

"Move and Baya dies!" Sauvage yelled.

Another green shirt, on the left side of the plane, fired his gun and hit the man shielding Sauvage. Mason went for the man on the right, striking the gun hand and then twisting the gun away from his trigger finger. As soon as he had the gun in his own hand, he swung it around and placed it against Baya's head.

"You heard the man," Mason said, addressing the two other green shirts who were still alive, as well as the pilot and copilot, who were just now opening the cockpit door to see what the hell was going on. "If you move, he dies."

"Everyone stay calm," Baya said, smooth and level. "I don't care what happens to me anymore. And these men can't go anywhere."

"You're wrong," Sauvage said. He turned to the pilot and copilot and said, "Close that door and get this plane back in the air."

# 19

Several dozen men in green shirts, plus another dozen family members, could all be heard shouting, some even pounding on the outside of the jet until the engine's whine grew loud enough to drown them out. A minute later, the jet was lumbering back down the rough runway, rolling with no other light than the moon, and then it took off into the sky.

Mason collected the guns from the two remaining green shirts on the plane and told them both to sit down. Sauvage took the gun from the dead body on the cabin floor.

"Where are we going?" Baya asked. He hadn't moved from his place behind the table, and his voice was still dead calm.

"I hear Bali's nice this time of year," Sauvage said.

"I don't think we have enough fuel," Baya said.

"Then anywhere," Sauvage said. "An airport that's actually open and functional would be good."

"You think you're going to arrest me?"

Sauvage exchanged a look with Mason.

"I know I won't be getting off this plane alive," Baya said. "Not if Mr. Mason is involved."

Mason had to fight the urge to shoot him right then. Better to be back on the ground first, because only an idiot fires a gun inside a plane while it's in the air.

But Baya was right about not getting off this plane alive.

"I suspected that the organization and Interpol were working to-gether," Baya said. "But I never thought it would be so cozy. *The enemy of my enemy is my friend*—isn't that how it goes? You both want the same thing badly enough that a cop would accept a hired assassin as a partner."

"I'm not a cop right now," Sauvage said. "I'm just a father."

He took out the photograph of his wife and son and put it on the table in front of Baya. "What do you see?"

Baya glanced down at the photograph with indifference. "I see two Europeans who wake up every day not knowing how much horror and misery their privileged lives have caused for the rest of the world."

Sauvage took the photograph back. "Maybe we all could learn a few things," he said. "But they'll never get the chance, because your bombs killed them."

Baya gave him a thin smile as he nodded and said, "I'll take their extermination as a small comfort in my last hours."

His words hung in the air as the plane continued its ascent. For all of Baya's smooth talk, the expensive clothes, the jet, the yacht—every-thing that had created the illusion of a sophisticated man—now that facade had been dropped, as it always must in the end, and the true, burning core of this man was exposed.

Sauvage stared down at him for a beat, then raised the gun and lev-eled the barrel at a point between Baya's eyes.

"Easy," Mason said. "Let's get on the ground."

"No, you'd better go ahead and shoot me now," Baya said, staring back at Sauvage with the same thin smile on his face. "While you still can."

Sauvage lowered the weapon, looked over at Mason, then back to Baya. "What are you talking about?"

"You made a mistake," Baya said. "With nothing else to lose, why wouldn't I take both of you with me?"

If either of the two green shirts understood what Baya was saying, they did a masterful job of keeping their faces set in stone. Mason got up and went to the cockpit door, stepping over the dead body. He pounded his fist on it. There was no response.

A beat later, the floor suddenly tilted sharply and Mason was thrown into the right-hand seats. As he glanced back, he saw the two green shirts fighting their way to their feet. Sauvage had gone down to his knees.

The plane leveled again, just long enough for Mason to get to the cockpit door. "Are you really going to kill yourselves in this plane?" he shouted. "For this madman, you're going to end your own lives?"

The plane tilted back in the opposite direction, and Mason was thrown from his feet again. Sauvage was on top of the two green shirts, and one of them was clawing at his face. He still had the gun in his hand and he swung the butt of the gun at the man's head.

Before Mason could reach the cockpit again, the door swung open. The pilot and copilot came spilling out. Mason was half right: One of them obviously didn't want to die. But which one?

One of the men had his hands around the other's throat, pounding his head against the floor. Within a second, Mason realized that the man wanting to live wouldn't waste time trying to incapacitate the other—he'd be back in the cockpit, trying to regain control. Mason wrapped an arm around the man on top, exerting all of his force against the man's neck and pulling him away from the other. He hoped to God he was right.

Immediately, the other man rolled to his feet and staggered back to the cockpit. But by now the plane had tilted back hard the other way, and as Mason looked out the window he saw the dark shadow of the ground—much too close.

The plane tilted once more as the man in the cockpit grabbed the yoke and tried to level it. Mason was thrown toward the back of the plane, losing his breath as he slammed into another body. When he struggled to get back up, he found Sauvage's free hand and tried to pull him from the floor.

But in the next second everything else was obliterated—everything but the sheer impact and the shockwaves that rippled through the plane's metal shell as it hit the ground and then a long sickening moment as everything turned sideways and seemed to hang there forever and then another jolt and the sounds of trees snapping and metal grinding and more windows breaking.

And then nothing.

For a long time, nothing but silence.

Silence and darkness.

———

Luna rocked the chair back and forth until she was finally close enough to touch the knife with her fingers. It brought her face close to Torino's in a final intimacy.

She fumbled with the knife handle for a minute, her fingers numb and almost useless—until she found a grip and could turn the blade upward, toward the tape on her wrists. She worked the sharp tip against the edge of the tape, then finally felt it slice through, maybe a quarter inch. She worked the blade higher to cut another quarter inch.

She took a break to catch her breath, commanding herself to stay patient. Then, trying not to look directly into Torino's lifeless eyes, she went back to work.

An hour later, or two, or three, or whatever time had become for her, she felt blood streaming down her wrist from where she had nicked herself. Her hand was so slick with it, she dropped the knife and had to spend several precious minutes working her way around to pick it up again.

*After all this, you're going to bleed to death right here on the floor.*

She carefully worked the tip of the knife against the tape, feeling the blade working its way into her skin again, but she didn't care anymore because it felt so close to being loose. One more quarter inch of tape cut, and then she clenched her fist and let out a scream as she felt it moving. And then suddenly, her hand was free.

She grabbed the knife and quickly cut through the tape on her other hand. Then one ankle, followed by the other. She got to her feet and kicked the chair away, stared down at Torino, and held her wrist against her shirt, trying to stop the flow of blood.

She found the roll of duct tape on the desk and wrapped it around her wrist three times, covering the wound. She bit at the tape and ripped it and smoothed the edge down.

When she picked up her phone, she saw a dozen different notifications. Eight calls from Mason and four from Farhan. She called Mason back first. It rang several times and then went to the anonymous voice mail.

Their twenty-four hours were almost up, she realized as she checked the time. She rocked Torino's body with a kick. *Even dead, you found a way to fuck all of us.*

———

Mason opened his eyes to a faint light. He turned his head to locate it. Moonlight shining through the broken windows on one side of the plane. His ears were ringing.

Mason pushed himself up, grunting with the effort. The first thing he saw was a dead man in a green shirt, slumped over one of the seats with an unnatural bend in his neck. The second thing he saw was another dead green shirt, this one with his head through the window.

Mason's neck screamed with pain as he turned to see the rear of the plane. Sauvage was on his feet, taking one slow step after another, moving toward Baya, who was still strapped in his seat behind the table. He looked shaken but alert.

"Sauvage," Mason said, but the man did not answer him. He had drawn the *rencong* knife from his belt.

"Sauvage," Mason said again. He tried to pull himself to his feet.

A movement—Baya reaching into a leather bag on the seat next to him. His hand reappeared holding a gleaming silver semiautomatic.

"Sauvage!" Mason grabbed a seat back and pulled himself up, his head reeling. He was only twenty feet away, but it felt like something playing out on a movie screen, with no way for him to stop it.

The look of pure hatred as Baya leveled the gun at Sauvage's body mass—an expression that looked almost like ecstasy in the last instant before he pulled the trigger. The sudden, deafening sound crashed from one side of the plane to another as the impact hit Sauvage square in the chest, but he did not go down. He took another step forward as Baya pulled the trigger again. Another explosion of sound, another impact in

Sauvage's chest, but now he was falling forward and the knife was still held tight in his right hand.

As Sauvage's body came crashing down on the table, the weight of his fall drove the blade into Baya's neck, just below his Adam's apple. Mason was finally on his feet now, and he stepped forward in time to catch Sauvage's body as it slid from the table. There were two entry wounds in his chest, and he was about to take his last breath as he looked up at Mason's face.

Mason laid Sauvage's body down on the floor of the airplane. Baya was clutching at the knife in his throat with both hands, making a dull rasping noise as the blood poured out of him.

The silver semiautomatic was on the table. Baya took one hand away from the knife and grasped for it. But Mason snatched it away before he could reach it.

Without another thought—no reflection, no emotion, no feeling of either triumph or remorse—he stuck the gun in Baya's face and pulled the trigger.

Mason dropped the gun onto the table. He spotted the travel bag next to Baya's body, reached into it, and took the man's cell phone. Then he reached down to check Sauvage's pulse, knowing that it was a futile gesture.

Before he stood up, he saw the half-crumpled photograph of Sauvage's wife and son. He picked it up and smoothed it out as well as he could, looking at the two faces. He was about to place it in Sauvage's hand, but then he thought it would probably get lost when they dragged his body out of the plane. Even in his pocket, it would be taken when they stripped the clothes from his body.

*I'll keep this for you*, he said silently. *I'll remember them.*

When Mason got to the front of the plane, he saw that the copilot was alive. He was still sitting with the yoke in his hands. His eyes were closed and he was taking deep, deliberate breaths, one after the other.

Mason put one hand on the man's shoulder. He squeezed one time and then left him there as he unlocked the plane door and pushed it open.

The stairs went down only halfway and then stopped. Mason climbed down on the steps and then dropped to the ground. This was too much motion for his head, and he bent over and threw up. Then he went to the road and started walking south. The plane had landed on the road and slid off into the trees.

Mason dialed Luna's number on Baya's cell phone as he walked.

"Mason," she said when she picked up. "Where are you?"

"I don't know," he said, looking up and down the road. "In Aceh, south of the city. On the coast."

"Baya . . ."

"Is dead. But you have to listen to me. This is very important."

"What is it?"

"Go to my apartment. There's a young girl there. She's in danger."

———

An hour later, Mason was at the small airport in Kuala Pesisir, south of Calang. He had gotten himself off the road when the emergency vehicles came by, then hitched a ride on the back of an empty cattle truck. He didn't want to go back to Banda Aceh, not with some of Baya's men still there and possibly looking for him. So now he was sitting under the glaring fluorescent lights of this single terminal on the shore of the Indian Ocean, waiting for the organization's jet to come pick him up and take him back to Jakarta.

When the phone rang, he answered it immediately. It was Luna.

"There was a woman in your apartment," she said. "She was unconscious in the bathroom, but she's still alive."

"The doorman's wife," Mason said. "But what about—"

"She's gone, Mason. The girl is gone."

# 20

It was early morning in Jakarta when Mason finally rushed off the plane and into the private terminal. Luna was there waiting for him, and they went right out to the street where she had left the car waiting.

"Where's Farhan?" Mason asked.

"He's out looking for the girl. He said he knows a few places that I wouldn't."

"There's a neighborhood a few blocks away from the office," Mason said. "That's where she lived. And that's where . . ."

He stopped dead.

"What is it?" she asked.

"How many people knew I was keeping the girl at my apartment?"

She shook her head, keeping her eyes on the road. "You know the answer to that better than I do. What were you doing with this girl, anyway?"

"It's a long story," he said, "and Farhan knows it better than anyone."

Mason picked up the cell phone and called Farhan's number. There was no answer. A sick sense of dread was building in his gut.

"What is it?" Luna asked.

"Baya knew all about her. He said he was going to send her to some place called Pattaya."

"That's in Thailand. It's a sex trade center. As bad as Bangkok, or maybe worse."

*She's nine fucking years old*, Mason thought. *If you were part of this, Farhan, you are a walking dead man.*

"Come on," he said, "let's get to the office and I'll show you where to go next."

They worked their way through the early morning traffic, Mason cursing every slowdown. As they got closer, they made a turn and Mason saw the Gama Tower in the middle distance. Before the car had come to a stop again, he threw open the door and got out.

"Hey!" Luna yelled after him. "How am I supposed to find you?"

But Mason was already off, running down the sidewalk, dodging pedestrians, crossing streets and ignoring the honking horns. As he neared the tower, he had to stop to orient himself.

He had found it the night he tried to buy her freedom. He could find it again.

He ran through the streets, trying to remember every possible landmark. It had been daytime when Farhan first took him to the *preman*, the man who effectively owned Belani, who rented her the spot on the street to sell the sunglasses and then sold her time to the rich family as a domestic slave. Maybe the *preman* was involved in taking her from his apartment or maybe he wasn't, but if she was being sent to Thailand, he'd know how it would happen and where Mason needed to look to find her.

*We made this turn, just before this bridge. Then we turned again.*

He came to a stop.

*Fuck me. Think. Remember.*

He saw a shop with a line of secondhand bicycles lined up in front. Mason went down the street and paused at the next intersection.

*Two more turns. Maybe three.*

He took one turn, convinced himself it was the wrong way, came back and turned the other way. Came back again and went straight.

There had been no name on the front. Just a shack with a metal roof and a broken-down fence on three sides . . .

*Painted yellow.*

He went down one block, then another, was about to turn around again, when he saw a flash of yellow down another street.

*That's it.*

He ran down to the door and pushed it open. The same rough wooden bar was there, held up by the same shipping crates turned on their sides. The same big, bald bartender was behind the bar, serving four morning drinkers.

"Where is he?" Mason said.

The bartender came around from behind the bar, moving slowly. His right leg was wrapped tightly with gray cloth. The same knee Mason had kicked out when the man came at him with the cricket bat.

Mason went up to him and stood six inches from his face. "Where is your fucking boss?"

"No boss here," the man said.

"Where did he go?"

"He is doing sex on your mother."

Mason looked away for a moment. Then he grabbed the man and slammed his head down on the bar. The wood broke and sent a half dozen drinks flying.

"Where is he?" Mason asked again, bending down to grab the man by both ears.

"I do not know!" the man said, his mouth filling with blood. "He is gone!"

Mason let go of the man's ears and went to the office door. He pushed it open and saw the small desk wedged into the room where he had tried to bargain for Belani's freedom.

"Where is he?" Mason asked the rest of the room. "Somebody tell me where he is. I have money."

Four faces looked back at him. Nobody said a word.

Mason was about to step away from the doorway when he stopped dead. He smelled the air. Stale beer, human sweat, raw sewage from somewhere outside the bar.

And Old Spice.

Farhan had been here.

Mason scanned the bar until he saw another door. He tried it and it was locked, so he took one step backward, kicked it down, and walked into a dark storage room. Old kegs, cardboard boxes, empty bottles. The smell of Old Spice was stronger.

There was one more door at the back wall. Mason kicked it open and almost fell out of the building. The back was propped up precariously on wooden stilts, overlooking a fetid stream with barely moving water that reeked of human waste. And directly below the door was Farhan.

Mason jumped down next to him. He put his hand on Farhan's neck. He was alive.

"Mr. Mason," Farhan said as he opened one eye. The other was swollen shut.

"What happened?"

"He took her away. I tried to stop him."

"Where did he go?"

"Penjaringan," Farhan said. "On the *Anjing Kuning*."

"What does that mean?"

"The port is Penjaringan," Farhan said. "The boat is called the *Anjing Kuning*, the Yellow Dog, like the name of the bar."

"Can you move?" Mason tried to help lift him from the bank of the stream, but Farhan let out a yell of pain as soon as Mason touched him.

"Stay here," Mason said. "I'll send help."

He reached up and grabbed the doorframe, then pulled himself back into the building. When he was back inside the barroom, he was faced by five men, including the bartender, who was now back on his feet.

"Everybody get the fuck out of my way," Mason said. As he took a step, the bartender reached out a huge hand to stop him. Mason took the hand and bent back the middle finger, breaking it and sending a lightning bolt of intense pain right up the man's arm. Another man swung at him. Mason ducked the blow, grabbed the man's belt, and swung him like a human battering ram into the face of the third man. He hit the fourth man in the throat and send him to the floor gagging. The fifth man backed away and ran out the door.

When Mason was outside, he stopped a teenager on a motorcycle and asked him for the street name. Then he called Luna and told her where to find Farhan. He gave the teenager the last wad of money in his pocket, asked him to go keep Farhan company until help arrived, then asked to borrow his motorcycle. A minute later, Mason was heading down the street on the bike, with a vague general idea of where to find the port called Penjaringan. He worked his way north through the ever-increasing traffic as the morning rush hour kicked in. He drove through intersections and up on sidewalks, until he finally saw the water of Jakarta Bay ahead of him.

When he was at the port, he asked one man where the *Anjing Kuning* was docked, then another man, then another man, until he finally got the right answer. It was a typically busy morning at the harbor, the two main docks running far out into the bay on both sides with cranes and warehouses and men loading and unloading cargo ships. A narrow causeway for vehicles led out through the middle of the harbor, with smaller vessels tied up on one side. That was where the *Anjing Kuning* had its slip, and the causeway created a natural bottleneck for Mason to catch the *preman* if he was still here.

He was halfway down the causeway when he saw the small truck coming toward him. The driver's face flashed in the morning sun for one brief moment, but it was all Mason needed. He slowed down on the motorcycle and then hopped off just in time to send it underneath the truck's front tires. The truck skidded several yards, scraping the bike along the rough pavement until it finally came to a stop.

Mason ripped open the door and pulled the *preman* from his seat. He hit him in the face three times and sent him to the pavement. Then he turned him over and hit him again.

"Where is she?" he demanded.

"She is gone," the *preman* said, spitting blood.

Mason dragged him to the edge of the causeway and dropped him into the shallow water. He jumped down and pushed the man's head under, held it there as the man thrashed at the water with both hands. Mason pulled him back up for one second, then put him back under.

He pulled him up again. The *preman* was coughing blood and seawater and scratching at Mason's arm with his fingernails.

Mason put him back under a third time, then finally brought him up and put his face close to his.

"Show me where the boat is, and if you say it's gone I swear to God I will drown you right here."

"There," the man sputtered, pointing to a fifty-foot trawler in the bay. It was a hundred yards out. "The boat is there."

"If she's not on that boat," Mason said, "I promise you I will find you and I will kill you."

"She is on the boat," the *preman* said. "Please."

Mason let him go, jumped back onto the causeway, and ran down toward the end of the dock. There were a dozen different boats in the bay, and he struggled to keep his eye on the *Anjing Kuning* as he ran.

He saw a man putting a cover on a twenty-foot speedboat, jumped onto the open bow, and told him to start it up. The man didn't speak much English, and Mason clearly scared the hell out of him, so Mason pushed the man over into the passenger seat, started the boat up himself, and slammed it into reverse. The man looked as if he was about to jump out, but Mason put a hand on his shoulder. "Stay here," he said. "You're safe. I need you."

Mason slammed it into forward gear and gunned it, avoiding the larger vessels in the harbor, coming so close to one that the speedboat's owner covered his face with his hands.

"Where the fuck did you go?" Mason said as he pushed the boat at top speed, scanning one boat after another—until he finally spotted the *Anjing Kuning.*

He put the boat on a course to intercept the larger cargo boat, crossing in front of its bow, then turning to come back across again. He could see the pilot waving at him frantically and screaming words that he couldn't hear. Finally, the boat slowed in the water and Mason pulled up beside it.

"Take it," Mason said to the speedboat's owner, just before the two vessels bumped together. Mason stood up on the gunwale and reached for the other boat's rail. For two seconds, he was hanging by one hand over the water, until he pulled himself up and landed on the deck.

The captain and the only other crew member approached Mason, eyeing him as if he must be some kind of maniac or criminal or both.

Mason pushed past them and opened the door to the hold. All he saw were stacked boxes of cigarettes.

"Where is she?" Mason yelled, grabbing the captain by his shirt.

The captain shook his head as if he didn't understand, but the crew member pointed to the forward cabin. "We do not want trouble," he said. "They are in there."

Mason didn't have time to process why he would say *they*, but it all made sense when he threw open the door to the forward cabin and saw five young women huddled together on a long wooden bench. He searched their faces, all of them much older than Belani, until finally they broke apart and revealed the child they had been shielding with their bodies.

Mason went down on one knee, and Belani rushed into his arms. After everything he had been through in the past three days—from one end of the country to the other on airplanes and motorcycles and boats, through the running and the death and all of the trauma he had endured—he could finally breathe again as he held on to her, saying, "It's over. It's over. I found you."

She didn't understand the words, but that didn't matter to either of them as she kept holding on to him as tight as she could.

# 21

As Mason took Belani off the boat, the five young women who had been aboard with her quickly disappeared, escaping back into Jakarta, into whatever lives had almost been taken from them. The *preman's* truck was still on the causeway, its front wheels still jammed by the wreckage of the motorcycle, but the *preman* himself was gone. Mason made a mental note to find the owner of the motorcycle and buy him a new one.

He called Luna and she came by in the car to pick them up. "Farhan's at the hospital," she said. "I'll check on him later."

She caught Mason's eye in the rearview mirror. He was sitting in the back seat with Belani, who was still holding on to him with obviously no plans to let go. Luna looked away and shook her head as if to say, *This is something I did not sign up for.*

When they were all back at Mason's apartment, the doorman and his wife were waiting for them. The doorman was visibly shaken by everything that had happened to his wife, but he was just as relieved to see Belani's face as he was to see his wife on her feet again already. As Mason noted the bandage on her forehead, it occurred to him that Baya's men would have had to kill her to keep her away.

But they hadn't.

If the organization had taken Belani, they would have killed the doorman's wife and anyone else who got in the way. He didn't know what that said about each side of this. Not that it mattered anymore.

While the doorman's wife made Belani a bowl of *soto*, Mason pulled Luna aside. "I need to see my daughter," he said. "Right now. The way you did before, at the office."

"There is no office anymore," Luna said. "But let me see your laptop."

She sat down and signed in to her database, worked her way through the various panels and commands, then stood up and handed the laptop to Mason. On the screen was the same view of the kitchen in Colorado. Gina was wrapping up a sandwich on the bartop. Probably making tomorrow's lunch for Brad. Adriana was sitting on one of the stools, drinking a glass of milk.

*They're twelve hours behind*, Mason thought. *Adriana's going to bed soon.*

Mason stared at the scene, watching the girl he fell in love with on the South Side of Chicago. And the other girl he fell in love with the minute she was born.

"I want to call them," Mason said.

"You can do that now," Luna said. "You've earned that right. You completed your mission."

Mason looked at her, wondering why she was saying this as if it were her decision to make. He didn't press it. Instead, he took the laptop into the bedroom and then pulled the phone from his pocket. He still had Baya's phone. If someone was really tracing this call, it was going to be a hell of a surprise for them.

Mason dialed the number, feeling more nerves now than when he'd been sure he would die on the airplane with Baya. He watched the video as he listened to the phone ring ten thousand miles away. There was a slight delay in the feed, so it took a few extra seconds for him to see Gina reach for her cell phone.

"Hello?" she said.

"Gina, it's Nick."

A long pause. Nick watched her as she looked over at Adriana, then left the room. "Where are you?" she asked.

"A long way away."

"Someone from the FBI came here and asked me a lot of questions. Have I heard from you, do I know where you are or what you're doing."

"What did you tell them?"

"I told them I didn't know anything. Which is the truth."

"Keep telling them that if they come back."

"Nick, why are you calling me?"

He hesitated. There were so many things he wanted to say to her, he didn't even know where to start. "How's Adriana doing?"

"She's doing fine. It took a while for her to adjust, but . . . I mean, she's doing just fine."

"Can I talk to her?"

It was Gina's turn to hesitate. "She's at a sleepover tonight. I'm sorry."

Mason took the phone away from his ear. He kept watching the screen. Adriana was still sitting at the kitchen bar top, waiting for her mother to finish her phone call in the other room so she could go to bed.

"Nick, are you there?"

"I'm here," he said. "Just give her a kiss for me, okay? Tell her I miss her."

"I'll do that."

"Please," he said. "Tell her that."

"I will. I promise."

"Okay," he said. "I'll let you go now. Please take care of yourself. And Adriana."

"I will, Nick."

She ended the call. He kept watching the screen as she came back into the room. Adriana looked up at her, but Nick could tell that she was doing her best to act like the phone call was about a PTA fundraiser or something. She got down from the school and followed her mother out of the room. As he kept watching the empty kitchen, he wondered if Gina would really deliver his message.

———

"What happened to your arm?" Mason asked. He had just checked on Belani, sleeping in the guest room, and came out to see Luna cutting off the duct tape and applying a fresh bandage.

"Torino and I had a disagreement," she said, not looking up from what she was doing. "He thought I was the leak. And now he's dead."

She said this as if it were a matter of only passing interest.

"I thought *he* was the leak," Mason said. "And then I thought it must be Farhan."

She shook her head.

"Whoever it was," he said, "they told Baya about Belani."

"Yeah, about this girl," she said as she finished taping up her wrist. "You think picking up kids off the street is a good idea?"

"Didn't you live on the streets once?"

"What about it?"

"I know helping her doesn't make up for all of the things I've done, but—"

"One thing has nothing to do with the other," she said. "It doesn't work that way."

Mason went over to the window and looked out at the city. He stayed there for a long time, going over everything that had happened. And everything Baya had said to him. Everything Sauvage had said too.

Finally, he turned and saw Luna about to leave the apartment.

"Before you go," he said, "I need you to help me find somebody."

———

The lights were off when Jacques Duval stepped into his house that evening. This surprised him. He usually left a light on. Maybe a bulb burned out.

Or maybe Nick Mason was sitting in a chair in the living room, waiting for him with a Glock in his lap.

"Nice place you have here," Mason said when Duval clicked on the light.

Duval did an admirable job of not jumping out of his skin.

"You must be Mason," Duval said. "Why am I not surprised?"

"Have a seat," Mason said. "I want to ask you a few questions."

Duval put down his briefcase and sat on the sofa. He took a quick glance behind him, in the direction of the kitchen.

"The gun in your cabinet's not loaded anymore," Mason said. "I didn't think you Interpol guys were allowed to carry, anyway."

Duval looked down at his feet.

"Baya told me that the people I work for are in bed with Interpol. I didn't think about it much at the time. But now it makes sense. And then I remembered something your man Sauvage told me. He said you told him not to bother trying to find me. What kind of a cop says something like that?"

Duval kept looking at his feet.

"Unless you were afraid of what would happen if I led him to Baya. Your little double-agent scam would be over. How much was Baya paying you, anyway?"

Duval began to shake his head slowly.

"I was with Sauvage when he died," Mason said. "We were working together. Your worst fucking nightmare come true."

Mason took out Baya's cell phone and paged through the recent call history. A few seconds later, Duval's phone rang. Duval didn't bother answering it.

"Just in case I needed confirmation," Mason said. "You told Baya everything he needed to know. To stay one step ahead of us. *And* the police. *And* to nearly get a nine-year-old girl shipped off to Thailand."

"I didn't know that would happen."

"You told him about the girl I was protecting. What the hell did you *think* would happen?"

"Just stop," Duval said. "If you're going to kill me, go ahead and do it."

"Who was your contact on my side?" Mason asked. "How high up the ladder?"

Duval looked up at him.

"It was the boss himself, wasn't it. I'm impressed. What can you tell me about him?"

"You work for him. Why would I know anything you don't?"

"Humor me," Mason said. "Tell me what you know. Where is he located? Do you have his phone number?"

Duval gave him a half smile and shook his head. "You of all people should know what would happen if I gave you any information."

"Worse than what I could do to you right now?"

"Yes, actually. Much worse. You can shoot me in the head and I'll be dead. If Zander kills me, he'll keep going until everyone I've ever loved is dead too. My kids back in France. My new grandson. It'll be the last thought that goes through my mind, knowing that everyone else will be paying the same price."

"Zander," Mason said.

Duval muttered a string of words to himself in French.

"His name is Zander," Mason said. "Now we're getting somewhere."

"I don't know anything else," Duval said. "I swear to you. He always calls me. The number's not traceable. I have no idea where he's calling from."

Mason nodded. "Okay. I believe you."

Duval dropped his head again, rubbed his hands together, took a long breath, then finally spoke with an unsteady voice:

"Are you going to kill me now?"

# EPILOGUE

On another hot morning in the second-biggest city in the world, Mason walked down a narrow street near the river, between makeshift stalls selling tea and street food and clothing. He held Belani's small hand in his.

Farhan had been busy ever since getting out of the hospital. He had called Mason that morning, and in exchange for what he had achieved, Mason promised him that if he ever did find his way back to America, he would not only take Farhan with him but would personally escort him to a Sunday doubleheader and buy him as many pierogis as he could eat.

There was a woman ahead of them, with three young children. When she turned to face them, Belani let out a scream and started running. "Mama!" she cried—the same word in Indonesian as in English.

The woman went down to her knees in the dirt and gathered up her lost child. The other children all jumped into the pile.

Mason stood and watched the scene, until finally the woman bade him come close. She stood up and hugged his neck.

When he was free, he turned to leave. He knew he'd be back to check on them, to give her money every month and to make sure all of the kids were safe and going to school, but this felt like a time they needed to spend together as a family.

But Belani would not let him go. She grabbed on to his hand again and pulled him into one of the tea shops. The whole family sat down at a table and started talking to each other at once. Mason caught the owner's eye and gave a twirling motion with one finger. *Bring whatever they want.*

Mason's phone rang. When he stood up to answer it, Belani looked up at him in alarm until he gestured that he wasn't leaving, just stepping out onto the street for a moment.

"Where are you?" Mason said to Luna.

"I'm in Bodrum, Turkey," she said. "Zander got on a boat here yesterday. I think I've narrowed it down to either Malta or Tunisia."

"You need to be careful."

"I know that," she said. "If he finds out we're this close . . ."

"I'll stay here until he calls again. He needs to believe we're waiting for the next assignment. Then I can try to join you."

"I have to go," she said, and the call ended.

Mason stood there for a moment and looked up at the afternoon storm clouds building over his head. Another day in Jakarta, even as he heard a rumbling that could have been thunder but sounded more like a bomb exploding in the distance. Like a reminder that even though Baya was gone, another man or another group or another nation would always be there to take his place. And to deliver a new installment of terror on the people who never deserve it.

As the rain started to fall, it felt like yet another reminder that some things can last a lifetime without ever changing. And that Mason would have to keep circling the world and spilling more blood, maybe even his own, if he ever hoped to be free.

# ACKNOWLEDGMENTS

This book would not have been possible without Shane Salerno, who helped bring Nick Mason to life (and changed my life at the same time). Thanks also to Ryan Coleman and to everyone who's been with me from the beginning: Bill Keller and Frank Hayes, Maggie Griffin, Jan Long, and Nick Childs.

And as always, to my wife Julia, my son Nicholas, and my daughter Antonia. You are and always will be the three miracles in my life.